Praise for Jack Cady

"An exceptional writer."

—Joyce Carol Oates

"[Jack Cady is] a lasting voice in modern American literature."
—*Atlanta Constitution*

"Jack Cady's knack for golden sentences is an alchemy any other writer has to admire."

—Ivan Doig

"Jack Cady is above all, a writer of great, unmistakable integrity and profound feeling. He never fakes it or coasts, and behind every one of his sentences is an emotional freight that bends it both outward, toward the reader, and inward, back to the source."

—Peter Straub

"A writer whose words reverberate with human insight."
—*Publishers Weekly*

"His structural control and the laconic richness of his style establish Cady in the front ranks of contemporary writers."
—*Library Journal*

"When Cady settles into yarn-spinning, his stories have the humor and comfortable mastery of Faulkner or Steinbeck."
—*National Review*

THE CADY COLLECTION

Fathoms

Collected Writings, Volume 2

Jack Cady

FAIRWOOD PRESS
Bonney Lake, WA

Fairwood Press
21528 104th Street Court East
Bonney Lake, WA 98391
www.fairwoodpress.com

Series Cover Design by Jennifer Tough
Cover Design by Darin Bradley
Book Design by Aaron Leis
Collection Editorial Direction by Mark Teppo

ISBN: 978-1-933846-89-7
First Fairwood Press Edition: August 2019
Printed in the United States of America

Original publication information about the respective stories is located
on page 214.

Contents

... hooked me, and carried me through the story quickly. I heard Jack speaking in my ear (I *still* hear Jack speaking in my ear) as I read, and I knew I had something special.

I also knew I had a fight on my hands. Ed Ferman was an East Coast man of a particularly Thurberish type, the kind who seemed frightened by any idea of wide open spaces. And here was the quintessential tale of wide open spaces, a story about back roads and ghosts, a purely American tale, but an American tale of an America that Ed had never experienced and never wanted to experience.

He read it and remained unmoved. He told me to bounce the novella. I refused. We held that impasse for months.

Finally, I called Jack and explained the situation. I knew I could wear Ed down eventually, but it would take time.

Jack laughed. He was in no hurry. I was. I felt embarrassed by the situation. Here I was, the editor of the magazine, and my publisher had decided to thwart me on one of the best stories I had ever read.

I warned Jack that my gambit might not pay off. He shrugged. He had all the time in the world, he said.

I only wish that were true.

It took more than 18 months for me to wear Ed Ferman down. In that 18 months, other novellas I had purchased over Ed's protests were nominated for awards. He decided maybe I had an eye for these things.

"The Night We Buried Road Dog" appeared in the January 1993 issue of *The Magazine of Fantasy & Science Fiction* as the cover story, illustrated by the marvelous Kent Bash, an artist known for his automobile art as well as his science fiction art.

The novella hit the field like a bomb, and suddenly, Jack Cady became a "new" writer—at least inside the tiny sf genre. Everyone wanted his work. "The Night We Buried Road Dog" became one of the quintessential F&SF stories, one of the stories mentioned in tandem with other genre-defining stories from the magazine, like Daniel Keyes' "Flowers For Algernon" and Stephen King's Dark Tower tales.

"The Night We Buried Road Dog" received nominations for every major award in the science fiction and fantasy field. The novella won four of them, including the Nebula and the Stoker.

It also made two year's best collections and since then, has been reprinted several times.

But "The Night We Buried Road Dog" isn't the sum total of Jack's work. I published a few more of his stories before I retired from editing (the first time) in 1997. He continued to publish stories in *F&SF*, as well as other magazines and anthologies.

Each story has that distinct voice, warm and inviting, yet commanding and confessional at the same time.

Jack Cady's voice.

The man is gone. I'll never share a bad convention meal with him again or a good restaurant meal when the convention is over. We'll never discuss our love of the sea again, or talk about why we love literature.

But his voice remains. His stories remain.

Jack Cady is one of literature's greatest treasures. If you've never read his work before, you're in for a real treat.

If you have read his fiction, then you know.

Settle in. Relax. And listen as Jack Cady beguiles you with stories that seem deceptively simple, and always go straight to the heart.

—Kristine Kathryn Rusch
Lincoln City, Oregon
September, 2015

Fathoms

The Night We Buried Road Dog

BROTHER JESSE BURIED HIS '47 HUDSON BACK IN '61 AND THE ROADS got just that much more lonesome. Highway 2 across north Montana still wailed with engines as reservation cars blew past; and it lay like a tunnel of darkness before headlights of big rigs. Tandems pounded, and the smart crack of downshifts rapped across grassland as trucks swept past the bars at every crossroad. The state put up metal crosses to mark the sites of fatal accidents. Around the bars those crosses sprouted like thickets.

That Hudson was named Miss Molly, and it logged two hundred twenty thousand miles while never burning a clutch. Through the years it wore into the respectable look that comes to old machinery. It was rough as a cob, cracked glass on one side, and primer over dents. It had the tough and ready look of a hunting hound about its business. I was a good deal younger then, but not so young that I was fearless. The burial had something to do with mystery, and brother Jesse did his burying at midnight.

Through fluke or foresight, brother Jesse had got hold of eighty acres of rangeland that wasn't worth a shake. There wasn't enough of it to run stock, and you couldn't raise anything on it except a little hell. Jesse stuck an old housetrailer out there, stacked hay around it for insulation in Montana winters, and hauled in just enough water to suit him. By the time his Hudson died he was ready to go into trade.

3

"Jed," he told me the night of the burial, "I'm gonna make myself some history, despite this damn Democrat administration." Over beside the housetrailer the Hudson sat looking like it was about ready to get off the mark in a road race, but the poor thing was a goner. Moonlight sprang from between spring clouds, and to the westward the peaks of mountains glowed from snow and moonlight. Along highway 2 some hotrock wound second gear on an old flathead Ford. You could hear the valves begin to float.

"Some little darlin' done stepped on that boy's balls," Jesse said about the driver. "I reckon that's why he's looking for a ditch." Jesse sighed and sounded sad. "At least we got a nice night. I couldn't stand a winter funeral."

"Road Dog?" I said about the driver of the Ford, which shows just how young I was at the time.

"It ain't The Dog," Jesse told me. "The Dog's a damn survivor."

=

You never knew where Brother Jesse got his stuff, and you never really knew if he was anybody's brother. The only time I asked, he said, "I come from a close knit family such as your own," and that made no sense. My own father died when I was twelve, and my mother married again when I turned seventeen. She picked up and moved to Wisconsin.

No one even knew when, or how, Jesse got to Montana territory. We just looked up one day and there he was as natural as if he'd always been here, and maybe he always had.

His eighty acres began to fill up. Old printing presses stood gap-mouthed like spinsters holding conversation. A salvaged greenhouse served for storing dog food, engine parts, chromium hair dryers from 1930's-beauty-shops, dimestore pottery, blades for hay cutters, binder twine, an old gas-powered cross-cut saw, seats from a schoolbus, and a bunch of other stuff not near as useful.

A couple of tabbies lived in that greenhouse, but the Big Cat stood outside. It was an old D6 bulldozer with a shovel, and Jesse stoked it up from time to time. Mostly, it just sat there. In summers it provided shade for Jesse's dogs: Potato was brown and fat and not too bright, while Chip was little and fuzzy. Sometimes they rode with Jesse, and sometimes stayed home. Me or Mike Tarbush fed them. When anything big happened you could count on those two dogs to get underfoot. Except for me, they were the only ones who attended the funeral.

"If we gotta do it," Jesse said mournfully, "we gotta." He wound up the Cat, turned on the headlights, and headed for the gravesite which was an embankment overlooking highway 2. Back in those days Jesse's hair still shone black, and it was even blacker in the darkness. It dangled around a face that carried an Indian forehead and a Scotsman's nose. Denim stretched across most of the six feet of him, and he wasn't rangy, he was thin. He had feet to match his height, and his hands seemed bigger than his feet; but the man could skin a Cat.

I stood in moonlight and watched him work. A little puff of flame dwelt in the stack of the bulldozer. It flashed against the darkness of those distant mountains. It burbled hot in the cold spring moonlight. Jesse made rough cuts pretty quick, moved a lot of soil, then started getting delicate. He shaped and reshaped that grave. He carved a little from one side, backed the dozer, found his cut not satisfactory. He took a spoonful of earth to straighten things, then fussed with the grade leading into the grave. You could tell he wanted a slight elevation, so the Hudson's nose would be sniffing toward the road. Old Potato-dog had a hound's ears, but not a hound's good sense. He started baying at the moon.

It came to me that I was scared. Then it came to me that I was scared most of the time, anyway. I was nineteen, and folks talked about having a war across the sea. I didn't want to hear about it. On top of the war talk, women were driving me crazy; the ones who said 'no' and the ones who said 'yes.' It got downright mystifying just trying to figure out which was worse. At nineteen it's hard to know how to act. There were whole weeks when I could pass myself off as a hellion, then something would go sour. I'd get hit by a streak of conscience and start acting like a missionary.

"Jed," Jesse told me from the seat of the dozer, "go rig a tow on Miss Molly." In the headlights, the grave now looked like a garage dug into the side of that little slope. Brother Jesse eased the Cat back in there to fuss with the grade. I stepped slow toward the Hudson, wiggled under, and fetched the towing cable around the frame. Potato howled. Chip danced like a fuzzy fury, and started chewing on my boot like he's trying to drag me from under the Hudson. I'm on my back trying to kick Chip away and secure the cable. Then I like to died from fright.

Nothing else in the world sounds anywhere near like a Hudson starter. It's a combination of whine and clatter and growl. If I'd been dead a thousand years you could stand me right up with a Hudson starter. There's threat in that sound. There's also the promise that things can get pretty rowdy, pretty quick.

The starter went off. The Hudson jiggled. In the one-half second it took to get from under that car I thought of every bad thing I ever did in my life. I was headed for hell, certain sure. By the time I was on my feet there wasn't an ounce of blood showing anywhere on me. When the old folks say, 'white as a sheet,' they're talking about a guy under a Hudson.

Brother Jesse climbed from the Cat and gave me a couple of shakes.

"She ain't dead," I stuttered. "The engine turned over. Miss Molly's still thinking speedy." From highway 2 came the wail of Mike Tarbush's '48 Roadmaster. Mike loved and cussed that car. It always flattened out at around eighty.

"There's still some sap left in the batt'ry," Jesse said about the Hudson. "You probably caused a short." He dropped the cable around the hitch on the dozer. "Steer her," he said.

The steering wheel still felt alive, despite what Jesse said. I crouched behind the wheel as the Hudson got dragged toward the grave. Its brakes locked twice, but the towing cable held. The locked brakes caused the car to side-slip. Each time Jesse cussed. Cold spring moonlight made the shadowed grave look like a cave of darkness.

The Hudson bided its time. We got it lined up, then pushed it backwards into the grave. The hunched front fenders spread beside the snarly grill. The front bumper was the only thing about that car that still showed clean and uncluttered. I could swear Miss Molly moved in the darkness of the grave, about to come charging onto highway 2. Then she seemed to make some kind of decision, and sort of settled down. Jesse gave the eulogy.

"This here car never did nothing bad," he said. "I must have seen a million crap-crates, but this car wasn't one of them. She had a second gear like hydramatic, and you could wind to 70 before you dropped to third. There wasn't no top end to her, at least I never had the guts to find it. This here was a 100 mile-an-hour car on a bad night, and God-knows-what on a good'n." From highway 2 you could hear the purr of Matt Simon's '56 Dodge, five speeds, what with the overdrive, and Matt was scorching.

Potato howled long and mournful. Chip whined. Jesse scratched his head, trying to figure a way to end the eulogy. It came to him like a blessing. "I can't prove it," he said, "'cause no one could. But, I expect this car has passed The Road Dog maybe a couple of hundred times." He made like he was going to cross himself, then remembered he was Methodist. "Rest in peace," he said, and he said it with eyes full of tears. "There ain't that many who can comprehend The Dog." He climbed back on the Cat and began to fill the grave.

Next day Jesse mounded the grave with real care. He erected a marker, although the marker was more like a little signboard:

1947–1961
Hudson coupe—'Molly'
220,023 miles on straight eight cylinder
Died of busted crankshaft
Beloved in the memory of
Jesse Still

=

Montana roads are long and lonesome, and highway 2 is lonesomest. You pick it up over on the Idaho border where the land is mountains. Bear and cougar still live pretty good, and beaver still build dams. The highway runs beside some pretty lakes. Canada is no more than a jump away; it hangs at your left shoulder when you're headed east.

And can you roll those mountains? Yes, oh yes. It's two lane all the way across, and twisty in the hills. From Libby you ride down to Kalispell, then pop back north. The hills last 'til the Blackfoot reservation. It's rangeland into Cut Bank, then to Havre. That's just about the center of the state.

Just let the engine howl from town to town. The road goes through a dozen, then swings south. And there you are at Glasgow and the river. By Wolf Point you're in cropland, and it's flat from there until Chicago.

I almost hate to tell about this road, because Easterners may want to come and visit. Then they'll do something dumb at a blind entry. The state will erect more metal crosses. Enough folks die up here already. And, it's sure no place for rice grinders, or tacky Swedish station wagons, or high priced German crap crates. This was always a V8 road, and V12 if you had 'em. In the old, old days there were even a few V16s up here. The top end on those things came when friction stripped the tires from too much speed.

=

Speed or not, brakes sure sounded as cars passed Miss Molly's grave. Pickup trucks fishtailed as men snapped them to the shoulder. The men would sit in their trucks for a minute, scratching their heads like they couldn't believe what they'd just seen. Then they'd climb from the truck, walk back to the grave, and read the marker. About half of them would start holding their sides. One guy even rolled around on the ground, he was laughing so much.

"These old boys are laughing now," Brother Jesse told me, "but I predict a change in attitude. I reckon they'll come around before first snowfall."

With his car dead, Jesse had to find a set of wheels. He swapped an old hay rake and a gang of discs for a '49 Chevrolet.

"It wouldn't pull the doorknob off a cathouse," he told me. "It's just to get around in while I shop."

The whole deal was going to take some time. Knowing Jesse, I figured he'd go through half a dozen trades before finding something comfortable. And, I was right.

He first showed up in an old Packard hearse that once belonged to a funeral home in Billings. He'd swapped the Chev for the hearse, plus a gilt-covered coffin so gaudy it wouldn't fit anybody but a radio preacher. He swapped the hearse to Sam Winder, who aimed to use it for hunting trips. Sam's dogs wouldn't go anywhere near the thing. Sam opened all the windows and the back door, then took the hearse up to speed trying to blow out all the ghosts. The dogs still wouldn't go near it. Sam said 'to hell with it' and pushed it into a ravine. Every rabbit and fox and varmint in that ravine came bailing out, and nobody has gone in there ever since.

Jesse traded the coffin to old man Jefferson who parked the thing in his woodshed. Jefferson was supposed to be on his last legs, but figured he wasn't ever, never, going to die if his poor body knew it would be buried in that monstrosity. It worked for several years, too, until a bad winter came along and he split it up for firewood. But, we still remember him.

Jesse came out of those trades with a '47 Pontiac and a Model T. He sold the Model T to a collector, then traded the Pontiac and forty bales of hay for a '53 Studebaker. He swapped the Studebaker for a ratty pickup and all the equipment in a restaurant that went bust. He peddled the equipment to some other poor fellow who was hell-bent to go bust in the restaurant business. Then he traded the pickup for a motorcycle, plus a '51 Plymouth that would just about get out of its own way. By the time he peddled both of them he had his pockets full of cash and was riding shank's mare.

"Jed," he told me, "let's you and me go to the big city." He was pretty happy, but I remembered how scared I'd been at the funeral. I admit to being skittish.

From the center of north Montana there weren't a championship lot of big cities. West was Seattle, which was sort of rainy and mythological. North was Winnipeg, a cow town. South was Salt Lake City. To the east . . .

"The hell with it," Brother Jesse said, "we'll go to Minneapolis."

It was about a thousand miles. Maybe fifteen hours, what with the roads. You could sail Montana and North Dakota, but those Minnesota cops were humorless.

I was shoving a sweet old '53 Desoto. It had a good bit under the bonnet, but the suspension would make a grown man cry. It was a beautiful beast, though. Once you got up to speed that front end would track like a cat. The upholstery was like brand new. The radio worked. There wasn't a scratch or ding on it. I had myself a banker's car, and there I was, only 19.

"We may want to loiter," Jesse told me. "Plan on a couple of overnights."

I had a job, but told myself that I was due for vacation; and so screw it. Brother Jesse put down food for the tabbies, and whistled up the dogs. Potato hopped into the back seat in his large, dumb way. He looked expectant. Chip sort of hesitated. He made a couple of jumps straight up, then backed down and started barking. Jesse scooped him up and shoved him in with old Potato-dog.

"The upholstery," I hollered. It was the first time I ever stood up to Jesse.

Jesse got an old piece of tarp to put under the dogs. "Pee and you're a goner," he told Potato.

We drove steady through the early summer morning. The Desoto hung in around eighty, which was no more than you'd want considering the suspension. Rangeland gave way to cropland. The radio plugged away with western music, beef prices, and an occasional preacher saying 'grace' and 'gimmie.' Highway 2 rolled straight ahead, sometimes rising gradual, so that cars appeared like rapid running spooks out of the blind entries. There'd be a little flash of sunlight from a windshield. Then a car would appear over the rise, and usually it was wailing.

We came across a hell of a wreck just beyond Havre. A new Mercury station wagon rolled about fifteen times across the landscape. There were two nice-dressed people and two children. Not one of them ever stood a chance. They rattled like dice in a drum. I didn't want to see what I was looking at.

Bad wrecks always made me sick, but not sick to puking. That would not have been manly. I prayed for those people under my breath and got all shaky. We pulled into a crossroads bar for a sandwich and a beer. The dogs hopped out. Plenty of hubcaps were nailed on the wall of the bar. We took a couple of them down, and filled them with water from an outside tap. The dogs drank and peed.

"I've attended a couple myself," Brother Jesse said about the wreck. "Drove a Terraplane off a bridge back in '53. Damn near drowned." Jesse wasn't about to admit to feeling bad. He just turned thoughtful.

"This here is a big territory," he said to no one in particular. "But you can get across her if you hustle. I reckon that Merc was loaded wrong, or blew a tire." Beyond the windows of the bar eight metal crosses lined the highway. Somebody had tied red plastic roses on one of them. Another one had plastic violets and forget-me-nots.

We lingered a little. Jesse talked to the guy at the bar, and I ran a rack at the pool table. Then Jesse bought a six pack while I headed for the can. Since it was still early in the day the can was clean; all the last night's pee and spit mopped from the floor. Somebody had just painted the walls. There wasn't a thing written on them, except that Road Dog had signed in.

Road Dog
How are things in Glocca Mora?

His script was spidery and perfect, like an artist who drew a signature. I touched the paint and it was still tacky. We had missed The Dog by only a few minutes.

=

Road Dog was like Jesse in a way. Nobody could say exactly when he showed up, but one day he was there. We started seeing the name 'Road Dog' written in what Matt Simons called 'a fine, Spencerian hand.' There was always a message attached, and Matt called them 'cryptic.' The signature and messages flashed from the walls of cans in bars, truck stops, and roadside cafes through four states.

We didn't know Road Dog's route at first. Most guys were tied to work or home or laziness. In a year or two, though, Road Dog's trail got mapped. His fine hand showed up all along highway 2, trailed east into North Dakota, dropped south through South Dakota, then ran back west across Wyoming. He popped north through Missoula and climbed the state until he connected with highway 2 again. Road Dog, whoever he was, ran a constant square of road that covered roughly two thousand miles.

Sam Winder claimed Road Dog was a communist who taught social studies at U. of Montana. "Because," Sam claimed, "that kind of writing comes from Europe. That writing ain't U.S.A."

Mike Tarbush figured Road Dog was a retired cartoonist from a newspaper. He figured nobody could spot The Dog, because The Dog slipped past us in a Nash, or some other old granny car.

Brother Jesse suggested that Road Dog was a truck driver, or maybe a gypsy, but sounded like he knew better.

Matt Simons supposed Road Dog was a traveling salesman with a flair for advertising. Matt based his notion on one of the cryptic messages:

Road Dog
Ringling Bros. Barnum and Toothpaste

I didn't figure anything. Road Dog stood in my imagination as the heart and soul of highway 2. When night was deep and engines blazed, I could hang over the wheel and run down that tunnel of two lane into the night.

The nighttime road is different than any other thing. Ghosts rise around the metal crosses, and ghosts hitchhike along the wide berm. All the mysteries of the world seem normal after dark. If imagination shows dead thumbs aching for a ride, those dead folk only prove the hot and spermy goodness of life. I'd overtake some taillights, grab the other lane, and blow doors off some partygoer who tried to stay out of the ditches. A man can sing and cuss and pray. The miles fill with dreams of power, and women, and happy, happy times.

Road Dog seemed part of that romance. He was the very soul of mystery; a guy who looked at the dark heart of the road and still flew free enough to make jokes and write that fine hand.

In daytime it was different, though. When I saw Road Dog signed in on the wall of that can, it just seemed like a real bad sign.

=

The guy who owned the bar had seen no one. He claimed he'd been in the back room putting bottles in his cold case. The Dog had come and gone like a spirit.

Jesse and I stood in the parking lot outside the bar. Sunlight laid earthy and hot across new crops. A little puff of dust rose from a side road. It advanced real slow, so you could tell it was a farm tractor. All around us, meadowlarks and tanagers were whooping it up.

"We'll likely pass him," Jesse said, "if we crowd a little." Jesse pretended he didn't care, but anyone would. We loaded the dogs, and even hung the hubcaps back up where we got them, because it was what a gentleman would do. The Desoto acted as eager as any Desoto could. We pushed the top end, which was 89, and maybe 92 downhill. At that speed brakes don't give you much, so you'd better trust your steering and your tires.

If we passed The Dog we didn't know it. He might have parked in one of the towns, and of course we dropped a lot of revs passing through towns; that being neighborly. What with a little loafing, some pee stops, and general fooling around, we did not hit Minneapolis until a little after midnight. When we checked into a motel on the strip Potato was sleepy and grumpy. Chip looked relieved.

"Don't fall in love with that bed," Jesse told me. "Some damn salesman is out there waitin' to do us in. It pays to start early."

Car shopping with Jesse turned out as fascinating as anybody could expect. At 7 a.m. we cruised the lots. Cars stood in silent rows like advertising men lined up for group pictures. It being Minneapolis, we saw a lot of high-priced iron. Cadillacs and Packards and Lincolns sat beside Buick convertibles, hemi-Chryslers, and Corvettes ("nice c-hars," Jesse said about the Corvettes, "but no room to 'em. You couldn't carry more than one sack of feed.") Hudsons and Studebakers hunched along the back rows. On one lot was something called 'Classic Lane.' A Model A stood beside a '37 International pickup. An L29 Cord sat like a tombstone, which it was because it had no engine. But, glory be, beside the Cord nested a '39 LaSalle coupe just sparkling with threat. That LaSalle might have snookered Jesse, except something highly talented sat buried deep in the lot.

It was the last of the fast and elegant Lincolns, a '54 coupe as snarly as any man could want. The '53 model had taken the Mexican Road Race. The '54 was a refinement. After that, the marque went downhill. It started building cars for businessmen and rich grannies.

Jesse walked round and round the Lincoln, which looked like it was used to being cherished. Matchless and scratchless. It was a little less than fire engine red, with a white roof and a grill that could shrug off a cow. That Linc was a solid set of fixings. Jesse got soft lights in his eyes. This was no Miss Molly, but this was Miss somebody. There were a lot of crap crates running out there, but this Linc wasn't one of them.

"You prob'ly can't even get parts for the damn thing," Jesse murmured, and you could tell he was already scrapping with a salesman. He turned his back on the Lincoln. "We'll catch a bite to eat," he said. "This may take a couple days."

I felt sort of bubbly. "The Dog ain't gonna like this," I told Jesse.

"The Dog is gonna love it," he said. "Me and The Dog knows that road."

By the time the car lots opened at 9 a.m. Jesse had a trader's light in his eyes. About all that needs saying is that never before, or since, did I ever see a used car salesman cry.

The poor fellow never had a chance. He stood in his car lot most of the day while me and Jesse went through every car lot on the strip. We waved to him from a sweet little '57 Cad, and we cruised past real smooth in a mama-san '56 Imperial. We kicked tires on anything sturdy while he was watching, and we never even got to his lot until fifteen minutes before closing. Jesse and I climbed from my Desoto. Potato and Chip tailed after us.

"I always know when I get to Minneapolis," Jesse said to me, but loud enough the salesman could just about hear. "My woman wants to lay a farmer, and my dogs start pukin.'" When we got within easy hearing range Jesse's voice got humble. "I expect this fella can help a cowboy in a fix."

I followed, experiencing considerable admiration. In two sentences Jesse had his man confused.

Potato was dumb enough that he trotted right up to the Lincoln. Chip sat and panted, pretending indifference. Then he ambled over to a ragged-out Pontiac and peed on the tire. "I must be missing something," Jesse said to the salesman, "because that dog has himself a dandy nose." He looked at the Pontiac. "This thing got an engine?"

We all conversed for the best part of an hour. Jesse refused to even look at the Lincoln. He sounded real serious about the LaSalle, to the point of running it around a couple of blocks. It was a darling. It had ceramic covered manifolds to protect against heat and rust. It packed a long stroke V8 with enough torque to bite rubber in second gear. My Desoto was a pretty thing, but until that LaSalle I never realized that my car was a total pussycat. When we left the lot the salesman looked sad. He was late for supper.

"Stay with what you've got," Jesse told me as he climbed in my Desoto. "The clock has run on that LaSalle. Let a collector have it. I hate it when something good dies for lack of parts."

I wondered if he was thinking of Miss Molly.

"Because," Jesse said, and kicked the tire on a silly little Volkswagen, "the great, good cars are dying. I blame it on the Germans."

Next day we bought the Lincoln and made the salesman feel like one proud pup. He figured he foisted something off on Jesse that Jesse didn't want. He was so stuck on himself that he forgot that he had asked a thousand dollars, and come away with five-fifty. He even forgot that his eyes were swollen, and that maybe he crapped his pants.

We went for a test drive, but only after Jesse and I crawled around under the Linc. A little body lead lumped in the left rear fender, but the front end stood sound. Nobody had pumped any sawdust into the differential. We found no water in the oil, or oil in the water. The salesman stood around, admiring his shoeshine. He was one of those easterners who can't help talking down to people, especially when he's trying to be nice. I swear he wore a white tie with little red ducks on it. That Minnesota sunlight made his red hair blond, and his face pop with freckles.

Jesse drove real quiet until he found an interesting stretch of road. The salesman sat beside him. Me and Potato and Chip hunkered in the back seat. Chip looked sort of nauseated, but Potato was pretty happy.

"I'm afraid," Jesse said regretful, "that this thing is gonna turn out to be a howler. A fella gets a few years on him and he don't want a screamy car." Brother Jesse couldn't have been much more than thirty, but he tugged on his nose and ears like he was ancient. "I sure hope," he said real mournful, "that nobody stuck a boot in any of these here tires." Then he poured on some coal.

There was a most satisfying screech. That Linc took out like a roadrunner in heat. The salesman's head snapped backward, and his shoulders dug into the seat. Potato gave a happy, happy woof and stuck his nose out the open window. I felt like yelling hosannah, but knew enough to keep my big mouth shut. The Linc shrugged off a couple of cars that were conservatively motoring. It wheeled past a hay truck as the tires started humming. The salesman's freckles began to stand up like warts while the airstream howled. Old Potato kept his nose sticking through the open window and the wind kept drying it. Potato was so dam' dumb he tried to lick it wet while his nose stayed in the airstream. His tongue blew sideways.

"It ain't nothing but speed," Jesse complained. "Look at this here steering." He jogged the wheel considerable, which at ninety got even more considerable. The salesman's tie blew straight backward. The little red ducks matched his freckles. "Jee-sus-Chee-sus," he said, "Eight hundred and slow down." He braced himself against the dash.

When it hit the century mark the Linc developed a little float in the front end. I expect all of us were thinking about the tires.

You could tell Jesse was jubilant. The Linc still had some pedal left.

"I'm gettin' old," Jesse hollered above the wind. "This ain't no car for an old man."

"Seven hundred," the salesman said, "And Mother-of-God, slow it down."

"Five-fifty," Jesse told him, and dug the pedal down one more notch.

"You got it," the salesman hollered. His face twisted up real tear-y. Then Potato got all grateful and started licking the guy on the back of the neck.

So Jesse cut the speed and bought the Linc. He did it diplomatic, pretending he was sorry he'd made the offer. That was kind of him. After all, the guy was nothing but a used car salesman.

=

We did a second night in that motel. The Linc and Desoto sat in an all-night filling station. Lube, oil change, and wash, because we were riding high. Jesse had a heap of money left over. In the morning we got new jeans and shirts, so as to ride along like gentlemen.

"We'll go back through South Dakota," Jesse told me. "There's a place I've heard about."

"What are we looking for?"

"We're checking on The Dog," Jesse told me, and would say no more.

We eased west to Bowman, just under the North Dakota line. Jesse sort of leaned into it, just taking joy from the whole occasion. I flowed along as best the Desoto could. Potato rode with Jesse, and Chip sat on the front seat beside me. Chip seemed rather easier in his mind.

A roadside cafe hunkered among tall trees. It didn't even have a neon sign. Real old-fashioned.

"I heard of this place all my life," Jesse said as he climbed from the Linc. "This here is the only outhouse in the world with a guest registry." He headed toward the rear of the cafe.

I tailed along, and Jesse, he was right. It was a palatial privvy built like a little cottage. The men's side was a three-holer. There was enough room for a standup desk. On the desk was one of those old-fashioned business ledgers like you used to see in banks.

"They're supposed to have a slew of these inside," Jesse said about the register as he flipped pages. "All the way back to the early days."

Some spirit of politeness seemed to take over when you picked up that register. There was hardly any bad talk. I read a few entries:

On this site, May 16th, 1971,
James John Johnson (John-John)

cussed hell out of his truck.

I came, I saw, I kinda liked it.
　　　—Bill Samuels, Tulsa

This place *does* know squat.
　　　—Pauley Smith, Ogden

This South Dakota ain't so bad,
but I sure got the blues,

17

I'm working in Tacoma,
'cause my kids all need new shoes.
—Sad George

Brother Jesse flipped through the pages. "I'm even told," he said, "that Teddy Roosevelt crapped here. This is a fine old place." He sort of hummed as he flipped. "Uh, huh," he said, "The Dog done made his pee spot." He pointed to a page:

Road Dog
Run and run as fast as you can
you can't catch me, I'm the Gingerbread Man.

Jesse just grinned. "He's sorta upping the ante, ain't he. You reckon this is getting serious?" Jesse acted like he knew what he was talking about, but I sure didn't.

II

We didn't know, as we headed home, that Jesse's graveyard business was about to take off. That wouldn't change him, though. He'd almost always had a hundred dollars in his jeans anyway, and was usually a happy man. What changed him was Road Dog and Miss Molly.

The trouble started a while after we crossed the Montana line. Jesse ran ahead in the Lincoln, and I tagged behind in my Desoto. We drove highway 2 into a western sunset. It was one of those magic summers where rain sweeps in from British Columbia just regular enough to keep things growing. Rabbits get fat and foolish, and foxes put on weight. Rattlesnakes come out of ditches to cross the sun-hot road. It's not sporting to run over their middles. You have to take them in the head. Redwings perch on fenceposts, and magpies flash black and white from the berm where they scavenge road kills.

We saw a hell of a wreck just after Wolf Point. A guy in an old Kaiser came over the back of a rise and ran under a tanker truck that burned. Smoke rose black as a plume of crows, and we saw it five miles away. By the time we got there the truck driver stood in the middle of the road all white and shaking. The guy in the Kaiser sat behind the wheel. It was fearful to see how fast fire can work, and just terrifying to see bones hanging over a steering wheel. I remember thinking the guy no doubt died before any fire started, and we were feeling more than he was.

That didn't help. I said a prayer under my breath. The truck driver wasn't to blame, but he took it hard as a Presbyterian. Jesse tried to comfort him without much luck. The road melted and stank and began to burn. Nobody was drinking, but it was certain-sure we were all more sober than we'd ever been in our lives. Two deputies showed up. Cars drifted in easy, because of the smoke. In a couple of hours there were probably twenty cars lined up on either side of the wreck.

"He must have been asleep or drunk," Jesse said about the driver of the Kaiser. "How in hell can a man run under a tanker truck?"

When the cops reopened the road, night hovered over the plains. Nobody cared to run much over sixty, even beneath a bright moon. It seemed like a night to be superstitious; a night when there was a deer or pronghorn out there just ready to jump into your headlights. It wasn't a good night to drink, or shoot pool, or mess around in strange bars. It was a time for being home with your woman, if you had one.

On most nights ghosts do not show up beside the metal crosses, and they sure don't show up in owl light. Ghosts stand out on the darkest, moonless nights, and only then when bars are closed and the only thing open is the road.

I never gave it a thought. I chased Jesse's taillights, which on that Lincoln were broad up-and-down slashes in the dark. Chip sat beside me, sad and solemn. I rubbed his ears to perk him, but he just laid down and snuffled. Chip was sensitive. He knew I felt bad over that wreck.

The first ghost showed up on the left berm and fizzled before the headlights. It was a lady ghost, and a pretty old one judging from her long white hair and long white dress. She flicked on and off in just a flash, so maybe it was a road dream. Chip was so depressed he didn't even notice, and Jesse didn't either. His steering and his brakes didn't wave to me.

Everything stayed straight for another ten miles, then a whole peck of ghosts stood on the right berm. A bundle of crosses shone all silvery-white in the headlights. The ghosts melted into each other. You couldn't tell how many, but you could tell they were expectant. They looked like people lined up for a picture show. Jesse never gave a sign he saw them. I told myself to get straight. We hadn't had much sleep in the past two nights, and did some drinking the night before. We'd rolled near two thousand miles.

Admonishing seemed to work. Another twenty minutes passed, maybe thirty, and nothing happened. Wind chased through the open windows of the Desoto, and the radio gave mostly static. I kicked off my boots because that helps you stay awake; the bottoms of the feet being sensitive. Then a single ghost showed up on the right hand berm, and boy-howdy.

Why anybody would laugh while being dead has got to be a puzzle. This ghost was tall with Indian hair like Jesse's, and I could swear he looked like Jesse, the spitting image. This ghost was jolly. He clapped his hands and danced. Then he gave me the old road sign for 'roll 'em'; his hand circling in the air as he danced. The headlights penetrated him, showed tall grass solid at the roadside, and instead of legs he stood on a column of mist. Still, he was dancing.

It wasn't road dreams. It was hallucination. The nighttime road just fills with things seen or partly seen. When too much scary stuff happens, it's time to pull her over.

I couldn't do it, though. Suppose I pulled over, and suppose it wasn't hallucination? I recall thinking that a man don't ordinarily care for preachers until he needs one. It seemed like me and Jesse were riding through the Book of Revelations. I dropped my speed, then flicked my lights a couple times. Jesse paid it no attention, and then Chip got peculiar.

He didn't bark, he chirped. He stood up on the front seat, looking out the back window, and his paws trembled. He shivered, chirped, shivered, and went chirp, chirp, chirp. Headlights in back of us were closing fast.

I've been closed on plenty of times by guys looking for a ditch. Headlights have jumped out of night and fog and mist when nobody should be pushing forty. I've been overtaken by drunks and suiciders. No set of headlights ever came as fast as the ones that began to wink in the mirrors. This highway 2 is a quick, quick road, but it's not the salt flats of Utah. The crazy man behind me was trying to set a new land speed record.

Never confuse an idiot. I stayed off the brakes and coasted, taking off speed and signaling my way onto the berm. The racer could have my share of the road. I didn't want any part of that boy's troubles. Jesse kept pulling away as I slowed. It seemed like he didn't even see the lights. Chip chirped, then sort of rolled down on the floorboards and cried.

For ninety seconds I feared being dead. For one second I figured it already happened. Wind banged the Desoto sideways. Wind whooped, the way it does in winter. The headlights blew past. What showed was the curve of a Hudson fender—the kind of curve you'd recognize if you'd been dead a million years—and what showed was the little squinchy shapes of a Hudson's taillights; and what showed was the slanty door post like a nail running kitty corner; and what showed was slivers of reflection from cracked glass on the rider's side; and what sounded was the drumbeat of a straight eight engine wanging like a locomotive gone wild; the thrump, bumpa, thrum of a crankshaft whipping in its bed. The slaunch-forward form of Miss Molly wailed, and showers of sparks blew from the tailpipe as Miss Molly rocketed.

Chip was not the only one howling. My voice rose high as the howl of Miss Molly. We all sang it out together, while Jesse cruised three, maybe four miles ahead. It wasn't two minutes before Miss Molly swept past that Linc like it was foundationed in cement. Sparks showered like the 4th of July, and Jesse's brake lights looked pale beside the fireworks. The Linc staggered against wind as Jesse headed for the berm. Wind smashed against my Desoto.

Miss Molly's taillights danced as she did a jig up the road, and then they winked into darkness as Miss Molly topped a rise, or disappeared. The night went darker than dark. A cloud scudded out of nowhere and blocked the moon.

Alongside the road the dancing ghost showed up in my headlights, and I could swear it was Jesse. He laughed like at a good joke, but he gave the old road sign for 'slow it down'; his hand palm down like he's patting an invisible pup. It seemed sound advice, and I blamed near liked him. After Miss Molly, a happy ghost seemed downright companionable.

"Shitfire," said Jesse, and that's all he said for the first five minutes after I pulled in behind him. I climbed from the Desoto and walked to the Linc. Old Potato dog sprawled on the seat in a dead faint, and Jesse rubbed his ears trying to warm him back to consciousness. Jesse sat over the wheel like a man who has just met Jesus. His hand touched gentle on Potato's ears, and his voice sounded reverent. Brother Jesse's conversion wasn't going to last, but at the time it was just beautiful. He had the lights of salvation in his eyes, and his skinny shoulders weren't shaking too much. "I miss my c'har," he muttered finally, and blinked. He wasn't going to cry if he could help. "She's trying to tell me something," he whispered. "Let's find a bar. Miss Molly's in car heaven, certain sure."

We pulled away, found a bar, and parked. We drank some beer and slept across the car seats. Nobody wanted to go back on that road.

=

When we woke to a morning hot and clear, Potato's fur had turned white. It didn't seem to bother him much, but for the rest of his life he was a lot more thoughtful.

"Looks like mashed Potato," Jesse said, but he wasn't talking a whole lot. We drove home like a couple of old ladies. Guys came scorching past, cussing at our granny-speed. We figured they could get mad and stay mad, or get mad and get over it. We made it back to Jesse's place about 2 in the afternoon.

A couple of things happened quick. Jesse parked beside his house trailer, and the front end fell out of the Lincoln. The right side went down, thump, and the right front tire sagged. Jesse turned even whiter than me, and I was bloodless. We had posted over a hundred miles an hour in that thing. Somehow, when we crawled around underneath inspecting it, we missed something. My shoulders and legs shook so hard I could barely get out of the Desoto. Chip was polite. He just yelped with happiness about being home, but he didn't trot across my lap as we climbed from the car.

Nobody could trust their legs. Jesse climbed out of the Linc and leaned against it. You could see him chewing over all the possibilities, then arriving at the only one that made sense. Some hammer mechanic bolted that front end together with no lock nut, no cotter pin, no lock washer, no lock-nothin'. He just wrenched down a plain old nut, and the nut worked loose.

"Miss Molly knew," Jesse whispered. "That's what she was trying to tell." He felt a lot better the minute he said it. Color came back to his face. He peered around the corner of the house trailer, looking toward Miss Molly's grave.

Mike Tarbush was over there with his '48 Roadmaster. Matt Simons stood beside him, and Matt's '56 Dodge sat beside the Roadmaster looking smug; which that model Dodge always did.

"I figger," Brother Jesse whispered, "that we should keep shut about last night. Word would just get around that we were alkies." He pulled himself together, arranged his face like a horse trying to grin, and walked toward the Roadmaster.

Mike Tarbush was a man in mourning. He sat on the fat trunk of that Buick and gazed off toward the mountains. Mike wore extra-large of everything, and still looked stout. He sported a thick red mustache to make up for his bald head. From time to time he bragged about his criminal record which amounted to three days in jail for assaulting a pool table. He threw it through a bar window.

Now his mustache drooped, and Mike seemed small inside his clothes. The hood of the Roadmaster gaped open. Under that hood things couldn't be worse. The poor thing had thrown a rod into the next county.

Jesse looked under the hood and tsked. "I know what you're going through," he said to Mike. He kind of petted the Roadmaster. "I always figured Betty Lou would last a century. What happened?"

There's no call to tell about a grown man blubbering, and especially not one who can heave pool tables. Mike finally got straight enough to tell the story.

"We was chasing The Dog," he said. "At least I think so. Three nights ago over to Kalispell. This Golden Hawk blew past me sittin'." Mike watched the distant mountains like he'd seen a miracle, or else like he was expecting one to happen. "That sonovabitch shore can drive," he whispered in disbelief. "Blown out by a dam' Studebaker."

"But a very swift Studebaker," Matt Simons said. Matt is as small as Mike is large, and Matt is educated. Even so, he's set his share of fenceposts. He looks like an algebra teacher, but not as delicate.

"Betty Lou went on up past her flat spot," Mike whispered. "She was tryin'. We had ninety on the clock, and The Dog left us sitting." He patted the Roadmaster. "I reckon she died of a broken heart."

"We got three kinds of funerals," Jesse said, and he was sympathetic. "We got the no-frills type, the regular-type, and the extra-special. The extra-special comes with flowers." He said it with a straight face, and Mike took it that way. He bought the extra-special, and that was sixty-five dollars.

Mike put up a nice marker:

1948–1961
Roadmaster two-door—Betty Lou
Gone to Glory while chasing The Dog
She was the best friend of Mike Tarbush

=

Brother Jesse worked on the Lincoln until the front end tracked rock solid. He named it Sue Ellen, but not *Miss* Sue Ellen, there being no way to know if Miss Molly was jealous. When we examined Miss Molly's grave the soil seemed rumpled. Wildflowers, that Jesse sowed on the grave, bloomed in midsummer. I couldn't get it out of my head that Miss Molly was still alive, and maybe Jesse couldn't either.

Jesse explained about the Lincoln's name. "Sue Ellen is a lady I knew in Pocatello. I expect she misses me." He said it hopeful, like he didn't really believe it.

It looked to me like Jesse was brooding. Night usually found him in town, but sometimes he disappeared. When he was around he drove real calm and always got home before midnight. The wildness hadn't come out of Jesse, but he had it on a tight rein. He claimed he dreamed of Miss Molly. Jesse was working something out.

And so was I, awake or dreaming. Thoughts of the Road Dog filled my nights, and so did thoughts of the dancing ghost. As summer deepened, restlessness took me wailing under moonlight. The road unreeled before my headlights like a magic line that pointed to places under a warm sun where ladies laughed and fell in love. Something went wrong, though. During that summer the ladies stopped being dreams and became only imagination. When I told Jesse, he claimed I was just growing up. I wished for once Jesse was wrong. I wished for a lot of things, and one of the wishes came true. It was Mike Tarbush, not me, who got in the next tangle with Miss Molly.

Mike rode in from Billings where he'd been car shopping. He showed up at Jesse's place on Sunday afternoon. Montana lay restful. Birds hunkered on wires, or called from high grass. Highway 2 ran watery with sunlight, deserted as a road ever could be. When Mike rolled a '56 Merc up beside the Linc it looked like old home week at a Ford dealership.

"I got to look at something," Mike said when he climbed from the Mercury. He sort of plodded over to Miss Molly's grave and hovered. Light breezes blew the wildflowers sideways. Mike looked like a bear trying to shake confusion from its head. He walked to the Roadmaster's grave. New grass sprouted reddish-green. "I was sober," Mike said. "Most Saturday nights, maybe I ain't, but I was sober as a deputy."

For a while nobody said anything. Potato sat glowing and white and thoughtful. Chip slept in the sun beside one of the tabbies. Then Chip woke up. He turned around three times and dashed to hide under the bulldozer.

"Now tell me I ain't crazy," Mike said. He perched on the front fender of the Merc, which was blue and white and adventuresome. "Name of Judith," he said about the Merc. "A real lady." He swabbed sweat from his bald head. "I got blown out by Betty Lou and Miss Molly. That sound reasonable?" He swabbed some more sweat, and looked at the graves which stood like little speed bumps on the prairie. "Nope," he answered himself, "that don't sound reasonable a-tall."

"Something's wrong with your Mercury," Jesse said, real quiet. "You got a bad tire, or a hydraulic line about to blow, or something screwy in the steering."

He made Mike swear not to breathe a word. Then he told about Miss Molly and about the front end of the Lincoln. When the story got over, Mike looked like a halfback hit by a twelve man line.

"Don't drive another inch," Jesse said. "Not until we find what's wrong."

"That car already cracked a hundred," Mike whispered. "I bought it special to chase one sumbitch in a Studebaker." He looked toward Betty Lou's grave. "The Dog did that."

The three of us went through that Merc like men panning gold. The trouble was so obvious we missed it for two hours while the engine cooled. Then Jesse caught it. The fuel filter rubbed its underside against the valve cover. When Jesse touched it the filter collapsed. Gasoline spilled on the engine and the sparkplugs. That Merc was getting set to catch on fire.

"I got to wonder if The Dog did it," Jesse said about Betty Lou after Mike drove away. "I wonder if the Road Dog is the Studebaker type."

=

Nights started to get serious, but any lonesomeness on that road was only in a man's head. As summer stretched past its longest days and sunsets started earlier, ghosts rose beside crosses before daylight hardly left the land. We drove to work and back, drove to town and back. My job was steady at a filling station, but it asked day after day of the same old thing. We never did any serious wrenching; no engine rebuilds or transmissions, just tuneups and flat tires. I dearly wanted to meet a nice lady, but no woman in her right mind would mess with a pump jockey.

Nights were different, though. I figured I was going crazy, and Jesse and Mike were worse. Jesse finally got his situation worked out. He claimed Miss Molly was protecting him. Jesse and Mike took the Linc and the Merc on long runs, just wringing the howl out of those cars. Some nights they'd flash past me at speeds no sane man would try in darkness. Jesse was never a real big drinker, and Mike stopped altogether. They were too busy playing road games. It got so the state cop never tried to chase them. He just dropped past Jesse's place next day and passed out tickets.

The dancing ghost danced in my dreams, both asleep and driving. When daylight left the land I passed metal crosses and remembered some of the wrecks.

Three crosses stood on one side of the railroad track, and four crosses on the other side. The three happened when some Canadian cowboys lost a race with a train. It was too awful to remember, but on most nights those guys stood looking down the tracks with startled eyes.

The four crosses happened when one-third of the senior class of '59 hit that grade too fast on prom night. They rolled a damned old Chevrolet. More bodies by Fisher. Now the two girls stood in their long dresses looking wistful. The two boys pretended that none of it meant nothin'.

Further out the road things had happened before my time. An Indian ghost most often stood beside the ghost of a deer. In another place a chubby old rancher looked real picky and angry.

The dancing ghost continued unpredictable. All the other ghosts stood beside their crosses, but the dancing ghost showed up anywhere he wanted, anytime he wanted. I'd slow the Desoto as he came into my lights, and he was the spitting image of Jesse.

"I don't want to hear about it," Jesse said when I tried to tell him. "I'm on a roll. I'm even gettin' famous."

He was right about that. People up and down the line joked about Jesse and his graveyard business.

"It's the very best kind of advertising," he told me. "We'll see more action before snow flies."

"You won't see snow fly," I told him, standing up to him a second time. "Unless you slow down and pay attention."

"I've looked at heaps more road than you," he told me, "and seeing things is just part of the night. That nighttime road is different."

"This is starting to happen at last light."

"I don't see no ghosts," he told me, and he was lying. "Except Miss Molly once or twice." He wouldn't say anything more.

And Jesse was right. As summer ran on more graves showed up near Miss Molly. A man named Mcguire turned up with a '41 Cad.

1941–1961
Fleetwood Coupe—Annie
304,018 miles on flathead V8
She was the luck of the Irishman
Pat Mcguire

And Sam Winder buried his '47 Packard.

1947–1961
Packard 2-door—Lois Lane
Super Buddy of Sam Winder
Up Up and Away

And Pete Johansen buried his pickup.

1946–1961
Ford pickup — Gertrude
211,000 miles give or take
Never a screamer
but a good pulling truck.
Pete Johansen put up many a day's work with her.

=

Montana roads are long and lonesome, and along the highline is lonesomest of all. From Saskatchewan to Texas nothing stands tall enough to break the wind which begins to blow cold and clear toward late October. Rains sob away toward the middlewest, and grass turns goldish-amber. Rattlesnakes move to high ground where they will winter. Every creature on God's plains begins to fat-up against the winter. Soon it's going to be 30 below and the wind blowing.

Four wheel drive weather. Internationals and Fords, with Dodge crummy-wagons in the hills; cars and trucks will line up beside houses, garages, sheds, with electric wires leading from plugs to radiators and blocks. They look like packs of nursing pups. Work will slow, then stop. New work turns to accounting for the weather. Fuel, emergency generators, hay bale insulation. Horses and cattle and deer look fuzzy beneath thick coats. Check your battery. If your rig won't start, and you two miles from home, she won't die—but you might.

School buses creep from stop to stop, and bundled kids look like colorful little bears trotting through late afternoon light. Snowy owls come floating in from northward, while folks go to church on Sunday against the time when there's some better amusement. Men hang around town, because home is either empty or crowded, depending on if you're married. Folks sit before television watching the funny, goofy, unreal world where everybody plays at being sexy and naked, even when they're not.

And 19 years old is lonesome, too. And work is lonesome when nobody much cares for you.

=

Before winter set in, I got it in my head to run the Road Dog's route. It was September. Winter would close us down pretty quick. The trip would be a luxury. What with room rent, and gas, and eating out, it was payday to payday with me. Still, one payday would account for gas and sandwiches. I could sleep across the seat. I hocked a Marlin 30-30 to Jesse for twenty bucks. He seemed happy with my notion. He even went into the greenhouse and came out with an arctic sleeping bag.

"In case things get vigorous," he said, and grinned. "Now get on out there and bite The Dog."

It was a happy time. Dreams of ladies sort of set themselves to one side as I cruised across the eternal land. I came to love the land that autumn, in a way that maybe ranchers do. The land stopped being something that a road ran across. Canadian honkers came winging in vees from the north. The great Montana sky stood easy as eagles. When I'd pull over and cut the engine, sounds of grasshoppers mixed with birdcalls. Once, a wild turkey, as smart as any domestic turkey is dumb, talked to himself and paid me not the least mind.

The Dog showed up right away. In a cafe in Malta:

Road Dog
"It was all a hideous mistake."
—Christopher Columbus

In a bar in Tampico:

Road Dog
Who's afraid of the big bad Woof?

In another bar in Culbertson:

Road Dog
Go East young man, go East

I rolled Williston and dropped south through North Dakota. The Dog's trail disappeared until Watford City where it showed up in the can of a filling station:

Road Dog
Atlantis and Sargasso
Full fathom five thy brother lies

And in a joint in Grassy Butte:

Road Dog
Ain't Misbehavin'

That morning in Grassy Butte I woke to a sunrise where the land lay bathed in rose and blue. Silhouettes of grazing deer mixed with silhouettes of cattle. They herded together peaceful as a dream of having your own place, your own woman, and you working hard; and her glad to see you coming home.

In Bowman The Dog showed up in a nice restaurant:

Road Dog
The Katzenjammer Kids minus one

Ghosts did not show up along the road, but the road stayed the same. I tangled with a bathtub Hudson, a '53, outside of Spearfish in South Dakota. I chased him into Wyoming like being dragged on a string. The guy played with me for twenty miles, then got bored. He shoved more coal in the stoker and purely flew out of sight.

Sheridan was a nice town back in those days, just nice and friendly; plus I started to get sick of the way I smelled. In early afternoon I found a five dollar motel with a shower. That gave me the afternoon, the evening, and next morning if it seemed right. I spiffed up, put on a good shirt, slicked down my hair and felt just fine.

The streets lay dusty and lazy. Rancher's pickups stood all dented and workworn before bars, and an old Indian sat on hay bales in the back of one of them. He wore a flop hat, and he seemed like the eyes and heart of the prairie. He looked at me like I was a splendid puppy that might someday amount to something. It seemed okay when he did it.

I hung around a soda fountain at the five and dime because a girl smiled. She was just beautiful. A little horsey-faced, but with sun-blond hair, and with hands long-fingered and gentle. There wasn't a chance of talking because she stood behind the counter for lady's underwear. I pretended to myself that she looked sad when I left.

It got onto late afternoon. Sunlight drifted in between buildings, and shadows overreached the streets. Everything was normal, and then everything got scary.

I was just poking along, looking in store windows, checking the show at the movie house, when ahead of me Jesse walked toward a Golden Hawk. He was maybe a block and a half away, but it was Jesse sure as God made sunshine. It was a Golden Hawk. There was no way of mistaking that car. Hawks were high-priced sets of wheels, and Studebaker never sold that many.

I yelled and ran. Jesse waited beside the car looking sort of puzzled. When I pulled up beside him he grinned.

"It's happening again," he said, and his voice sounded amused but not mean. Sunlight made his face reddish, but shadow put his legs and feet in darkness. "You believe me to be a gentleman named Jesse Still." Behind him shadows of buildings told that night was on its way. Sunset happens quick on the prairies.

And I said, "Jesse, what in the hell are you doing in Sheridan?"

And he said, "Young man, you are not looking at Jesse Still." He said it quiet and polite, and he thought he had a point. His voice was smooth and cultured, so he sure didn't sound like Jesse. His hair hung combed-out, and he wore clothes that never came from a drygoods. His jeans were soft looking and expensive. His boots were tooled. They kind of glowed in the dusk. The Golden Hawk didn't have a dust speck on it, and the interior had never carried a tool, or a car part, or a sack of feed. It just sparkled. I almost believed him, and then I didn't.

"You're fooling with me."

"On the contrary," he said real soft, "Jesse Still is fooling with *me*, although he doesn't mean to. We've never met." He didn't exactly look nervous, but he looked impatient. He climbed in the Stude and started the engine. It purred like racing tune. "This is a large and awfully complex world," he said, "and Mr. Still will probably tell you the same. I've been told we look like brothers."

I wanted to say more, but he waved real friendly and pulled away. The flat and racey backend of the Hawk reflected one slash of sunlight, then rolled into shadow. If I'd had a hot car I'd have gone out hunting him. It wouldn't have done a lick of good, but doing something would be better than doing nothing.

I stood sort of shaking and amazed. Life had just changed somehow, and it wasn't going to change back. There wasn't a thing in the world to do, so I went to get some supper.

The Dog had signed in at the cafe:

Road Dog
The Bobbsey Twins Attend The Motor Races

And—I sat chewing roast beef and mashed potatoes.

And—I saw how the guy in the Hawk might be lying, and that Jesse was a twin.

And—I finally saw what a chancy, dicey world this was, because without meaning to, exactly; and without even knowing it was happening, I had just run up against the Road Dog.

=

It was a night of dreams. Dreams wouldn't let me go. The dancing ghost tried to tell me Jesse was triplets. The ghosts among the crosses begged rides into nowhere, rides down the long tunnel of night that ran past lands of dreams but never turned off to those lands. It all came back, the crazy summer, the running, running, running behind the howl of engines. The Road Dog drawled with Jesse's voice, and then The Dog spoke cultured. The girl at the five and dime held out a gentle hand, then pulled it back. I dreamed of a hundred roadside joints, bars, cafes, old-fashioned filling stations with grease pits. I dreamed of winter wind, and the dark, dark days of winter; and of nights when you hunch in your room because it's a chore too big to bundle up and go outside.

I woke to an early dawn and slurped coffee at the bakery which kept open because they had to make morning donuts. The land lay all around me, but it had nothing to say. I counted my money and figured miles.

I climbed in the Desoto thinking I had never got around to giving it a name. The road unreeled toward the west. It ended in Seattle where I sold my car. Everybody said there was going to be a war, and I wasn't doing anything, anyway. I joined the Navy.

III

What with him burying cars and raising hell, Jesse never wrote to me in summer. He was surely faithful in winter, though. He wrote long letters printed in a clumsy hand. He tried to cheer me up, and so did Matt Simons.

The Navy sent me to boot camp and diesel school, then to a motor pool in San Diego. I worked there three and a half years, sometimes even working on ships if the ships weren't going anywhere. A sunny land and smiling ladies lay all about, but the ladies mostly fell in love by ten at night and got over it by dawn. Women in the bars were younger and prettier than back home. There was enough clap to go around.

"The business is growing like jimson weed," Jesse wrote toward Christmas of '62. "I buried fourteen cars this summer, and one of them was a kraut." He wrote a whole page about his morals. It didn't seem right to stick a crap crate in the ground beside real cars. At the same time it was bad business not to. He opened a special corner of the cemetery and pretended it was exclusive for foreign iron.

"And Mike Tarbush got to drinking," he wrote. "I'm sad to say we planted Judith."

Mike never had a minute's trouble with that Merc. Judith behaved like a perfect lady until Mike turned upside down. He backed across a parking lot at night, rather hasty, and drove backwards up the guywire of a power pole. It was the only rollover wreck in history that happened at twenty miles an hour.

"Mike can't stop discussing it," Jesse wrote. "He's never caught The Dog, neither, but he ain't stopped trying. He wheeled in here in a beefed up '57 Olds called Sally. It goes like stink and looks like a hereford."

Home seemed far away, though it couldn't have been more than thirty-six hours by road for a man willing to hang over the wheel. I wanted to take a leave and drive home, but knew it better not happen. Once I got there I'd likely stay.

"George Pierson at the feed store says he's going to file a paternity suit against Potato," Jesse wrote. "The pups are cute and there's a family resemblance."

It came to me then why I was homesick. I surely missed the land, but even more I missed the people. Back home folks were important enough that you knew their names. When somebody got messed up or killed you felt sorry. In California nobody knew nobody. They just swept up broken glass and moved right along. I should have meshed right in. I had made my rating and was pushing a rich man's car, a '57 hemi Chrysler; but never felt it fit.

"Don't pay it any mind," Jesse wrote when I told about meeting Road Dog. "I've heard about a guy who looks the same as me. Sometimes stuff like that happens."

And, that was all he ever did say.

1963 ended happy and hopeful. Matt Simons wrote a letter. Sam Winder bought a big Christmas card and everybody signed it with little messages. Even my old boss at the filling station signed 'Merry Xmas Jed—Keep It Between The Fenceposts.' My boss didn't hold it against me that I left. In Montana a guy is supposed to be free to find out what he's all about.

Christmas of '63 saw Jesse pleased as a bee in clover. A lady named Sarah moved in with him. She waitressed at the cafe, and Jesse's letter ran pretty short. He'd put twenty-three cars under that year, and bought more acreage. He ordered a genuine marble gravestone for Miss Molly. "Sue Ellen is a real darling," Jesse wrote about the Linc. "That marker like-to weighed a ton. We just about bent a back axle bringing it from the railroad."

From Christmas of '63 to January of '64 was just a few days, but they marked an awful downturn for Jesse. His letter was more real to me than all the diesels in San Diego.

He drew black borders all around the pages. The letter started out okay, but went downhill. "Sarah moved out and into a rented room," he wrote. "I reckon I was just too much to handle." He didn't explain, but I did my own reckoning. I could imagine that it was Jesse, plus two cats and two dogs trying to get into a ten-wide-fifty trailer, that got to Sarah. "I think she misses me," he wrote, "but I expect she'll have to bear it."

Then the letter got just awful.

"A pack of wolves came through from Canada," Jesse wrote. "They picked off old Potato like a berry from a bush. Me and Mike found tracks, and a little blood in the snow."

I sat in the summery dayroom surrounded by sailors shooting pool and playing ping pong. I imagined the snow and ice of home. I imagined old Potato nosing around in his dumb and happy way, looking for rabbits, or lifting his leg. Maybe he even wagged his tail when that first wolf came into view. I sat blinking tears, ready to bawl over a dog, and then I did, and to hell with it.

The world was changing and it wouldn't change back. I put in for sea duty one more time, and the Chief Warrant who ramrodded that motor pool turned it down again. He claimed we kept the world safe by wrenching engines.

=

"The '62 Dodge is emerging as the car of choice for people in a hurry." Matt Simons wrote that in February '64, knowing I'd understand that nobody could tell which cars would be treasured until they had a year or two on them. "It's an extreme winter," he wrote, "and it's taking its toll on many of us. Mike has now learned not to punch a policeman. He's doing ten days. Sam Winder managed to roll a Jeep, and neither he, nor I, can figure out how a man can roll a Jeep. Sam has a broken arm, and lost two toes to frost. He was trapped under the wreck. It took awhile to pull him out. Brother Jesse is in the darkest sort of mood. He comes and goes in an irregular manner, but the Linc sits outside the pool hall on most days.

"And for myself," Matt wrote, "I think come summer I'll drop some revs. My flaming youth seems to be giving way to other interests. A young woman named Nancy started teaching at the school. Until now I thought I was a confirmed bachelor."

A postcard came the end of February. The postmark said Cheyenne, Wyoming, way down in the southeast corner of the state. It was written fancy. Nobody could mistake that fine, spidery hand. It read:

Road Dog

Run and run as fast as he can,

He can't find who is the Gingerbread Man

The picture on the card had been taken from an airplane. It showed an oval racetrack where cars chased each other round and round. I couldn't figure why Jesse sent it, but it had to be Jesse. Then it came to me that Jesse was the Road Dog. Then it came to me that he wasn't. The Road Dog was too slick. He wrote real delicate, and Jesse only printed real clumsy. On the other hand, the Road Dog didn't know me from Adam's off ox. Somehow it *had* to be Jesse.

"We got snow nut-deep to a tall palm tree," Jesse wrote at about the same time, "and Chip is failing. He's off his feed. He don't even tease the kitties. Chip just can't seem to stop mourning."

I had bad premonitions. Chip was sensitive. I feared he wouldn't be around by the time I got back home, and my fear proved right. Chip held off until the first warm sun of spring and then he died while napping in the shade of the bulldozer. When Jesse sent a quick note telling me, I felt pretty bad, but had been expecting it. Chip had a good heart. I figured now he was with Potato, romping in the hills somewhere. I knew that was a bunch of crap, but that's just the way I chose to figure it.

=

They say a man can get used to anything, but maybe some can't. Day after day, and week after week, California weather nagged. Sometimes a puny little dab of weather dribbled in from the

Pacific, and people hollered it was storming. Sometimes temperatures dropped toward the fifties, and people trotted around in thick sweaters and coats. It was almost a relief when that happened, because everybody put on their shirts. In three years I'd seen more woman-skin than a normal man sees in a lifetime, and more tattoos on men. The Chief Warrant at the motor pool had the only tattoo in the world called 'worm's eye view of a pig's butt in the moonlight'.

In autumn '64, with one more year to pull, I took a two week leave and headed north just chasing weather. It showed up first in Oregon with rain, and more in Washington. I got hassled on the Canadian border by a distressful little guy who thought, what with the war, that I wanted political asylum.

I chased on up to Calgary where matters got chill and wholesome. Wind worked through the mountains, like it wanted to drive me south toward home. Elk and moose and porcupines went about their business. Red tail hawks circled. I slid on over to Edmonton, chased on east to Saskatoon, then dropped south through the Dakotas. In Williston I had a terrible want to cut and run for home, but didn't dare.

The Road Dog showed up all over the place, but the messages were getting strange. At a bar in Amidon:

Road Dog
Taking Kentucky Windage

At a hamburger joint in Belle Fourche:

Road Dog
Chasing his tail

At a restaurant in Redbird:

Road Dog
Flea and flee as much as we can
We'll soon find who is the Gingerbread Man

In a pool room in Fort Collins:

Road Dog
Home home on derange

Road Dog, or Jesse, was too far south. The Dog had never showed up in Colorado before. At least nobody ever heard of such. My leave was running out. There was nothing to do except sit over the wheel. I dropped on south to Albuquerque, hung a right, and headed back to the big city. All along the road I chewed a dreadful fear for Jesse. Something bad was happening, and that didn't seem fair because something good went on between me and the Chrysler. We reached an understanding. The Chrysler came alive and began to hum. All that poor car had ever needed was to look at road. It had been raised among traffic and poodles, but needed long sight-distances and bears.

=

When I got back, there seemed no way out of writing a letter to Matt Simons, even if it was borrowing trouble. It took evening after evening of gnawing the end of a pencil. I hated to tell about Miss Molly, and about the dancing ghost, and about my fears for Jesse. A man is supposed to keep his problems to himself.

At the same time, Matt was educated. Maybe he could give Jesse a hand if he knew all of it. The letter came out pretty thick. I mailed it thinking Matt wasn't likely to answer real soon. Autumn deepened to winter back home, and everybody would be busy.

So I worked and waited. There was an old White Mustang with a fifth wheel left over from the last war. It was a lean and hungry looking animal, and slightly marvelous. I overhauled the engine, then dropped the tranny and adapted a tenspeed Roadranger. When I got that truck running smooth as a Baptist's mouth, the Navy surveyed it and sold it for scrap.

"Ghost cars are a tradition," Matt wrote toward the back of October, "and I'd be hard pressed to say they are not real. I recall being passed by an Auburn boat-tail about 3 a.m. on a summer day. That happened ten years ago. I was about your age, which means there was not an Auburn boat-tail in all of Montana. That car died in the early '30s.

"And we all hear stories of huge old headlights overtaking in the mist; stories of Mercers and Duesenbergs and Bugattis. I try to believe the stories are true, because, in a way, it would be a shame if they were not.

"The same for road ghosts. I've never seen a ghost who looked like Jesse. The ghosts I've seen might not have been ghosts. To paraphrase an expert, they may have been a trapped beer-belch, an undigested hamburger, or blowing mist. On the other hand, maybe not. They certainly seemed real at the time.

"As for Jesse—we have a problem here. In a way we've had it for a long while, but only since last winter have matters become solemn. Then your letter arrives and matters become mysterious. Jesse has— or had—a twin brother. One night when we were carousing he told me that, but he also said his brother was dead. Then he swore me to a silence I must now break."

Matt went on to say that I must never, never say anything. He figured something was going on between brothers. He figured it must run deep.

"There is something uncanny about twins," Matt wrote. "What great matters are joined in the womb? When twins enter the world they learn and grow the way all of us do; but some communication (or communion) surely happens before birth. A clash between brothers is a terrible thing. A clash between twins may spell tragedy."

Matt went on to tell how Jesse was going over the edge with road games, only the games stayed close to home. All during the summer Jesse would head out, roll fifty or a hundred miles, and come home scorching like drawn by a string. Matt guessed the postcard I'd gotten from Jesse in February was part of the game, and it was the last time Jesse had been very far from home. Matt figured Jesse used tracing paper to imitate the Road Dog's writing. He also figured Road Dog had to be Jesse's brother.

"It's obvious," Matt wrote, "that Jesse's brother is still alive, and is only metaphorically dead to Jesse. There are look-alikes in this world, but you have reported identical twins."

Matt told how Jesse drove so crazy even Mike would not run with him. That was bad enough, but it seemed the graveyard had sort of moved in on Jesse's mind. That graveyard was no longer just something to do. Jesse swapped around until he came up with a tractor and mower. Three times that summer he trimmed the graveyard and straightened markers. He dusted and polished Miss Molly's headstone.

"It's past being a joke," Matt wrote, "or a sentimental indulgence. Jesse no longer drinks, and no longer hells around in a general way. He either runs road or tends the cemetery. I've seen other men search for a ditch, but never in such bizarre fashion."

Jesse had been seen on his knees praying before Miss Molly's grave.

"Or perhaps he was praying for himself, or for Chip," Matt wrote. "Chip is buried beside Miss Molly. The graveyard has to be seen to be believed. Who would ever think so many machines would be so dear to so many men?"

Then Matt went on to say he was going to 'inquire in various places' that winter. "There are ways to trace Jesse's brother," Matt wrote, "and I am very good at that sort of research." He said it was about the only thing he could still do for Jesse.

"Because," Matt wrote, "I seem to have fallen in love with a romantic. Nancy wants a June wedding. I look forward to another winter alone, but it will be an easy wait. Nancy is rather old-fashioned, and I find that I'm old-fashioned as well. I will never regret my years spent helling around, but am glad they are now in the past."

Back home winter deepened. At Christmas a long letter came from Jesse and some of it made sense. "I put 18 cars under this summer. Business fell off because I lost my hustle. You got to scooch around a good bit, or you don't make contacts. I may start advertising.

"And the tabbies took off. I forgot to slop them regular, so now they're mousing in a barn on Jimmy Come Lately Road. Mike says I ought to get another dog, but my heart ain't in it."

Then the letter went into plans for the cemetery. Jesse talked some grand ideas. He thought a nice wrought iron gate might be showy, and bring in business. He thought of finding a truck that would haul 'deceased' cars. "On the other hand," he wrote, "if a guy don't care enough to find a tow, maybe I don't want to plant his iron." He went on for a good while about morals, but a lawyer couldn't understand it. He seemed to be saying something about respect for Miss Molly, and Betty Lou, and Judith. "Sue Ellen is a real hummer," he wrote about the Linc. "She's got two hundred thousand I know about, plus whatever went on before."

Which meant Jesse was piling up about seventy thousand miles a year, and that didn't seem too bad. Truck drivers put up a hundred thousand. Of course, they make a living at it.

Then the letter got so crazy it was hard to credit.

"I got the Road Dog figured out. There's two little kids. Their mama reads to them and they play tag. The one that don't get caught gets to be the Gingerbread Man. This all come together because I ran across a bunch of kids down on the Colorado line. I was down that way to call on a lady I once knew but she moved and I said what the hell and hung around a few days and that's what clued me to The Dog. The kids were at a Sunday School picnic, and I was napping across the carseat. Then a preacher's wife came over and saw I wasn't drunk, but the preacher was there too, and they invited me. I eased over to the picnic and everybody made me welcome. Anyway, those kids were playing, and I heard the gingerbread business, and I figure The Dog is from Colorado."

The last page of the letter was just as scary. Jesse took kids' crayons and drew the front ends of the Linc and Miss Molly. There was a tail that was probably Potato's, sticking out from behind the picture of Miss Molly, and everything was centered around the picture of a marker that said R.I.P. Road Dog.

But—there weren't any little kids. Jesse had not been to Colorado. Jesse had been tending that graveyard, and staying close to home. Jesse played make-believe, or else Matt Simons lied; and there was no reason for Matt to lie. Something bad, bad wrong was going on with Jesse.

There was no help for it. I did my time and wrote a letter every month or six weeks pretending everything was normal. I wrote about what we'd do when I got home, and about the Chrysler. Maybe that didn't make much sense, but Jesse was important to me. He was a big part of what I remembered about home.

At the end of April a postcard came, this time from Havre. "The Dog is after me. I feel it." It was just a plain old postcard. No picture.

Matt wrote in May, mostly his own plans. He busied himself building a couple of rooms onto his place. "Nancy and I do not want a family right away," he wrote, "but someday we will." He wrote a bubbly letter, with a feel of springtime to it.

"I almost forgot my main reason for writing," the letter said. "Jesse comes from around Boulder, Colorado. His parents are long dead, ironically in a car wreck. His mother was a schoolteacher, his father a librarian. Those people, who lived such quiet lives, somehow produced a hellion like Jesse, and Jesse's brother. That's the factual side of the matter.

"The human side is so complex it will not commit to paper. In fact, I do not trust what I know. When you get home next fall we'll discuss it."

The letter made me sad and mad. Sad because I wasn't getting married, and mad because Matt didn't think I'd keep my mouth shut. Then I thought better of it. Matt didn't trust himself. I did what any gentleman would do, and sent him and Nancy a nice gravy boat for the wedding.

In late July Jesse sent another postcard. "He's after me, I'm after him. If I ain't around when you get back don't fret. Stuff happens. It's just a matter of chasing road."

Summer rolled on. The Navy released 'non essential personnel' in spite of the war. I put four years in the outfit and got called nonessential. Days choked past like a rig with fouled injectors. One good thing happened. My old boss moved his station to the outskirts of town and started an IH dealership. He straight-out wrote how he needed a diesel mechanic. I felt hopeful thoughts, and dark ones.

In September I became a veteran who qualified for an overseas ribbon, because of work on ships that later on went somewhere. Now I could join the Legion Post back home, which was maybe the pay-off. They had the best pool table in the county.

"Gents," I said to the boys at the motor pool, "it's been a distinct by-God pleasure enjoying your company, and don't never come to Montana 'cause she's a heartbreaker." The Chrysler and me lit out like a kyoodle of pups.

It would have been easier to run Salt Lake, then climb the map to Havre, but notions pushed. I slid east to Las Cruces then popped north to Boulder with the idea of tracing Jesse. The Chrysler hummed and chewed up road. When I got to Boulder the notion turned hopeless. There were too many people. I didn't even know where to start asking.

It's no big job to fool yourself. Above Boulder it came to me how I've been pointing for Sheridan all along, and not even Sheridan. I pointed toward a girl who smiled at me four years ago.

I found her working at a hardware, and she wasn't wearing any rings. I blushed around a little bit, then got out of there to catch my breath. I thought of how Jesse took whatever time was needed when he bought the Linc. It looked like this would take a while.

My pockets were crowded with mustering out pay and money for unused leave. I camped in a ten dollar motel. It took three days to get acquainted, then we went to a show and supper afterward. Her name was Linda. Her father was a Mormon. That meant a year of courting, but it's not all that far from North Montana to Sheridan.

I had to get home and get employed, which would make the Mormon happy. On Saturday afternoon, Linda and I went back to the same old movie, but this time we held hands. Before going home she kissed me once, real gentle. That made up for those hard times in San Diego. It let me know I was back with my own people.

I drove downtown all fired-up with visions. It was way too early for bed, and I cared nothing for a beer. A run down cafe sat on the outskirts. I figured pie and coffee.

The Dog had signed in. His writing showed faint, like the wall had been scrubbed. Newer stuff scrabbled over it.

Road Dog
Tweedle Dum and Tweedle Dee
Lonely pups as pups can be
For each other had to wait
Down beside the churchyard gate

The cafe sort of slumbered. Several old men lined the counter. Four young gearheads sat at a table and talked fuel injection. The old men yawned and put up with it. Faded pictures of old racing cars hung along the walls. The young guys sat beneath a picture of the Bluebird. That car held the land speed record of 301.29 m.p.h. This was a racer's cafe, and had been for a long, long time.

The waitress was graying and motherly. She tsked and tished over the old men as much as she did the young ones. Her eyes held that long-distance prairie look, a look knowing wind and fire and hard times; stuff that either breaks people or leaves them wise. Matt Simons might get that look in another twenty years. I tried to imagine Linda when she became the waitress' age, and it wasn't bad imagining.

Pictures of quarter-mile cars hung back of the counter, and pictures of street machines hung on each side of the door. '50's hotrods scorched beside worked-up stockers. Some mighty rowdy iron crowded that wall. One picture showed a Golden Hawk. I walked over, and in one corner was the name 'Still'—written in the Road Dog's hand. It shouldn't have been scary.

I went back to the counter shaking. A nice looking old gent nursed coffee. His hands wore knuckles busted by a thousand slipped wrenches. Grease was worked-in deep around his eyes, the way it gets after years and years when no soap made will touch it. You could tell he'd been a steady man. His eyes were clear as a kid.

"Mister," I said, "and beg pardon for bothering you. Do you know anything about that Studebaker?" I pointed to the wall.

"You ain't bothering me," he said, "but I'll tell you when you do." He tapped the side of his head like trying to ease a gear in place, then he started talking engine specs on the Stude.

"I mean the man who owns it."

The old man probably liked my haircut, which was short. He liked it that I was raised right. Young guys don't always pay old men much mind.

"You still ain't bothering me." He turned to the waitress. "Sue," he said, "has Johnny Still been in?"

She turned from cleaning the pie case, and she looked toward the young guys like she feared for them. You could tell she was no big fan of engines. "It's been the better part of a year, maybe more." She looked down the line of old men. "I was fretting about him just the other day . . ." She let it hang. Nobody said anything. "He comes and goes so quiet, you might miss him."

"I don't miss him a hell of a lot," one of the young guys said. The guy looked like a duck, and had a voice like a sparrow. His fingernails were too clean. That proved something.

"Because Johnny blew you out," another young guy said. "Johnny *always* blew you out."

"Because he's crazy," the first guy said. "There's noisy-crazy and quiet-crazy. The guy is a spook."

"He's going through something," the waitress said, and said it kind. "Johnny's taken a lot of loss. He's the type who grieves." He looked at me like she expected an explanation.

"I'm friends with his brother," I told her. "Maybe Johnny and his brother don't get along."

The old man looked at me rather strange. "You go back quite a-ways," he told me. "Jesse's been dead a good long time."

I thought I'd pass out. My hands started shaking, and my legs felt too weak to stand. Beyond the window of the cafe red light came from a neon sign, and inside the cafe everybody sat quiet waiting to see if I was crazy too. I sort of picked at my pie. One of the young guys moved real uneasy. He loafed toward the door, maybe figuring he'd need a shotgun. The other three young ones looked confused.

"No offense," I said to the old man, "but Jesse Still is alive. Up on the highline. We run together."

"Jesse Still drove a damn old Hudson Terraplane into the South Platte River in spring of '52, maybe '53." The old man said it real quiet. "He popped a tire when not real sober."

"Which is why Johnny doesn't drink," the waitress said. "At least I expect that's the reason."

"And now you are bothering me." The old man looked to the waitress, and she was as full of questions as he was.

Nobody ever felt more hopeless or scared. These folks had no reason to tell this kind of yarn. "Jesse is sort of roughhouse." My voice was only whispering. It wouldn't make enough sound. "Jesse made his reputation helling around."

"You've got that part right," the old man told me, "and youngster, I don't give a tinker's dam if you believe me or not, but Jesse Still is dead."

I saw what it had to be, but seeing isn't always believing. "Thank you, mister," I whispered to the old man, "and thank you ma'am," to the waitress. Then I hauled out of there leaving them with something to discuss.

=

A terrible fear rolled with me, because of Jesse's last postcard. He said he might not be home, and now that could mean more than it said. The Chrysler bettered its reputation, and we just flew. From the Montana line to Shelby is eight hours on a clear day. You can wail it in seven, or maybe six and a half if a deer doesn't tangle with your front end. I was afraid, and confused, and getting mad. Me and Linda were just to the point of hoping for an understanding, and now I was going to get killed running over a porcupine or into a heifer. The Chrysler blazed like a hound on a hot scent. At eighty, the pedal kept wanting to dig deep and really howl.

The nighttime road yells danger. Shadows crawl over everything. What jumps into your headlights may be real, and maybe not. Metal crosses hold little clusters of dark flowers on their arms, and the land rolls out beneath the moon. Buttes stand like great ships anchored in the plains, and riverbeds run like dry ink. Come spring they'll flow, but in September all flow is in the road.

The dancing ghost picked me up on highway 3 outside Comanche, but this time he wasn't dancing. He stood on the berm and no mist tied him in place. He gave the old road sign for 'roll 'em.' Beyond Columbia he showed up again. His mouth moved like he was yelling me along, and his face twisted with as much fear as my own.

That gave me reason to hope. I'd never known Jesse to be afraid like that, so maybe there was a mistake. Maybe the dancing ghost wasn't the ghost of Jesse. I hung over the wheel and forced myself to think of Linda. When I thought of her I couldn't bring myself to get crazy. Highway 3 is not much of a road, but that's no bother. I can drive anything with wheels over any road ever made. The dancing ghost kept showing up and beckoning, telling me to scorch. I told myself the damn ghost had no judgment, or he wouldn't be a ghost in the first place.

That didn't keep me from pushing faster, but it wasn't fast enough to satisfy the roadside. They came out of the mist, or out of the ditches; crowds and clusters of ghosts standing pale beneath a weak moon. Some of them gossiped with each other. Some stood yelling me along. Maybe there was sense to it, but I had my hands full. If they were trying to help they sure weren't doing it. They just made me get my back up, and think of dropping revs.

Maybe the ghosts held a meeting and studied out the problem. They could see a clear road, but I couldn't. The dancing ghost showed up on highway 12 and gave me 'thumbs up' for a clear road. I didn't believe a word of it, and then I really didn't believe what showed in my mirrors. Headlights closed like I was standing. My feelings said that all of this had happened before; except last time there was only one set of headlights.

It was Miss Molly and Betty Lou that brought me home. Miss Molly overtook, sweeping past with a lane change smooth and sober as an Adventist. The high, slaunch-forward form of Miss Molly thrummed with business. She wasn't blowing sparks or showing off. She wasn't playing Gingerbread Man or tag.

Betty Lou came alongside so I could see who she was, then Betty Lou laid back a half mile. If we ran into a claim-jumping deputy, he'd have to chase her first; and more luck to him. Her headlights hovered back there like angels.

Miss Molly settled down a mile ahead of the Chrysler and stayed that distance, no matter how hard I pressed. Twice before Great Falls she spotted trouble, and her squinchy little brakelights hauled me down. Once it was an animal, and once it was busted road surface. Miss Molly and Betty Lou dropped me off before Great Falls, and picked me back up the minute I cleared town.

We ran the night like rockets. The roadside lay deserted. The dancing ghost stayed out of it, and so did the others. That let me concentrate, which proved a blessing. At those speeds a man don't have time to do deep thinking. The road rolls past, the hours roll, but you've got a racer's mind. No matter how tired you should be, you don't get tired until it's over.

I chased a ghost car northward while a fingernail moon moved across the sky. In deepest night the land turned silver. At speed you don't think, but you do have time to feel. The further north we pushed, the more my feelings went to despair. Maybe Miss Molly thought the same, but everybody did all they could.

The Chrysler was a howler, and Lord knows where the top end lay. I buried the needle. Even accounting for speedometer error, we burned along in the low half of the second century. We made highway 2 and Shelby around three in the morning, then hung a left. In just about no time I rolled home. Betty Lou dropped back and faded. Miss Molly blew sparks and purely flew out of sight. The sparks meant something. Maybe Miss Molly was still hopeful. Or, maybe she knew we were too late.

=

Beneath that thin moon, mounded graves looked like dark surf across the acreage. No lights burned in the trailer, and the Linc showed nowhere. Even under the scant light you could see snowy tops of mountains, and the perfectly straight markers standing at the head of each grave. A tent, big enough to hold a small revival, stood not far from the trailer. In my headlights a sign on the tent read 'chapel.' I fetched a flashlight from the glove box.

A dozen folding chairs stood in the chapel, and a podium served as an altar. Jesse had rigged up two sets of candles, so I lit some. Matt Simons had written that the graveyard had to be seen to be believed. Hanging on one side of the tent was a sign reading 'shrine,' and all along that side hung roadmaps, and pictures of cars, and pictures of men standing beside their cars. There was a special display of odometers, with little cards beneath them: 330,938 miles, 407,000 miles, 'half a million miles more or less'. These were the championship cars, the all-time best at piling up road, and those odometers would make even a married man feel lonesome. You couldn't look at them without thinking of empty roads and empty nights.

Even with darkness spreading across the cemetery, nothing felt worse than the inside of that tent. I could believe that Jesse took it serious, and had tried to make it nice, but couldn't believe anyone else would buy it.

The night was not too late for owls, and nearly silent wings swept past as I left the tent. I walked to Miss Molly's grave, half expecting ghostly headlights. Two small markers stood beside a real fine marble headstone.

Potato
Happy-go-sloppy and good.
Rest In Peace Wherever You Are

Chip
A dandy little sidekicker
Running With Potato

From a distance I could see piled dirt where the dozer had dug new graves. I stepped cautious toward the dozer, not knowing why, but knowing it had to happen.

Two graves stood open like little garages, and the front ends of the Linc and the Hawk poked out. The Linc's front bumper shone spotless, but the rest of the Linc looked tough and experienced. Dents and dings crowded the sides, and cracked glass starred the windows.

The Hawk stood sparkly, ready to come roaring from the grave. Its glass shone washed and clean before my flashlight. I thought of what I heard in Sheridan, and thought of the first time I'd seen the Hawk. It hadn't changed. The Hawk looked like it had just been driven off a showroom floor.

Nobody in his right mind would want to look in those two cars, but it wasn't a matter of 'want.' Jesse, or Johnny—if that's who it was—had to be here someplace. It was certain-sure he needed help. When I looked, the Hawk sat empty. My flashlight poked against the glass of the Linc. Jesse lay there, taking his last nap across a car seat. His long black hair had turned to gray. He had always been thin, but now he was skin and bones. Too many miles, and no time to eat. Creases around his eyes came from looking at road, but now the creases were deep like an old man's. His eyes showed that he was dead. They were only open a little bit, but open enough.

=

I couldn't stand to be alone with such a sight. In less than fifteen minutes I stood banging on Matt Simon's door. Matt finally answered, and Nancy showed up behind him. She was in her robe. She stood taller than Matt, and sleepier. She looked blond and Swedish. Matt didn't know whether to be mad or glad. Then I got my story pieced together, and he really woke up.

"Dr. Jekyll has finally dealt with Mr. Hyde," he said in a low voice to Nancy. "Or, maybe the other way around." To me he said,

"That may be a bad joke, but it's not ill meant." He went to get dressed. "Call Mike," he said to me. "Drunk or sober, I want him there."

Nancy showed me the phone. Then she went to the bedroom to talk with Matt. I could hear him soothing her fears. When Mike answered he was sleepy and sober, but he woke up stampeding.

Deep night and a thin moon is a perfect time for ghosts, but none showed up as Matt rode with me back to the graveyard. The Chrysler loafed. There was no need for hurry.

I told Matt what I'd learned in Sheridan.

"That matches what I heard," he said, "and we have two mysteries. The first mystery is interesting, but it's no longer important. Was John Still pretending to be Jesse Still, or was Jesse pretending to be John?"

"If Jesse drove into a river in '53, then it has to be John." I didn't like what I said, because Jesse was real. The best actor in the world couldn't pretend that well. My sorrow choked me, but I wasn't ashamed.

Matt seemed to be thinking along the same lines. "We don't know how long the game went on," he said real quiet. "We never will know. John could have been playing at being Jesse way back in '53."

That got things tangled and I felt resentful. Things were complicated enough. Me and Matt had just lost a friend, and now Matt was talking like that was the least interesting part.

"Makes no difference whether he was John or Jesse," I told Matt. "He was Jesse when he died. He's laying across the seat in Jesse's car. Figure it anyway you want, but we're talking about Jesse."

"You're right," Matt said, "Also, you're wrong. We're talking about someone who was both." Matt sat quiet for a minute figuring things out. I told myself it was just as well that he'd married a schoolteacher. "Assume, for the sake of argument," he said, "that John was playing Jesse in '53. John drove into the river, and people believed they were burying Jesse.

"Or, for the sake of argument, assume that it was Jesse in '53. In that case the game started with John's grief. Either way, the game ran for many years." Matt was getting at something, but he always has to go roundabout.

"After years, John, or Jesse, disappeared. There was only a man who was both John and Jesse. That's the reason it makes no difference who died in '53."

Matt looked through the car window into the darkness like he expected to discover something important. "This is a long and lonesome country," he said. "The biggest mystery is: Why? The answer may lie in the mystery of twins, or it may be as simple as a man reaching into the past for happy memories. At any rate, one brother dies, and the survivor keeps his brother alive by living his brother's life, as well as his own. Think of the planning, the elaborate schemes, the near self-deception. Think of how often the roles shifted. A time must have arrived when that lonely man could not even remember who he was."

The answer was easy, and I saw it. Jesse, or John, chased the road to find something they'd lost on the road. They lost their parents and each other. I didn't say a damn word. Matt was making me mad, but I worked at forgiving him. He was handling his own grief, and maybe didn't have a better way.

"And so he invented the Road Dog," Matt said. "That kept the personalities separate. The Road Dog was a metaphor to make him proud. Perhaps it might confuse some of the ladies, but there isn't a man ever born who wouldn't understand it."

I remembered long nights and long roads. I couldn't fault his reasoning.

"At the same time," Matt said, "the metaphor served the twins. They could play road games with the innocence of children, maybe even replay memories of a time when their parents were alive and the world seemed warm. John played the Road Dog, and Jesse chased; and, by God, so did the rest of us. It was a magnificent metaphor."

"If it was that blamed snappy," I said, "how come it fell to pieces? For the last year it seems like Jesse's been running away from The Dog."

"The metaphor began to take over. The twins began to defend against each other," Matt said. "I've been watching it all along, but couldn't understand what was happening. John Still was trying to take over Jesse, and Jesse was trying to take over John."

"It worked for a long time," I said, "and then it didn't work. What's the kicker?"

"Our own belief," Matt said. "We all believed in the Road Dog. When all of us believed, John was forced to become stronger."

"And Jesse fought him off?"

"Successfully," Matt said. "All this year, when Jesse came firing out of town, rolling fifty miles, and firing back, I thought it was Jesse's problem. Now I see that John was trying to get free, get back on the road, and Jesse was dragging him back. This was a struggle between real men, maybe titans in the oldest sense, but certainly not imitations."

"It was a guy handling his problems."

"That's an easy answer. We can't know what went on with John," Matt said, "but we know some of what went on with Jesse. He tried to love a woman, Sarah, and failed. He lost his dogs which doesn't sound like much, unless your dogs are all you have. Jesse fought defeat by building his other metaphor which was that damned cemetery." Matt's voice got husky. He'd been holding in his sorrow, but his sorrow started coming through. It made me feel better about him.

"I think the cemetery was Jesse's way of answering John, or denying that he was vulnerable. He needed a symbol. He tried to protect his loves and couldn't. He couldn't even protect his love for his brother. That cemetery is the last bastion of Jesse's love." Matt looked like he was going to cry, and I felt the same.

"Cars can't hurt you," Matt said. "Only bad driving hurts you. The cemetery is a symbol for protecting one of the few loves you can protect. That's not saying anything bad about Jesse. That's saying something with sadness for all of us."

I slowed to pull onto Jesse's place. Mike's Olds sat by the trailer. Lights were on in the trailer, but no other lights showed anywhere.

"Men build all kinds of worlds in order to defeat fear and loneliness," Matt said. "We give and take as we build those worlds. One must wonder how much Jesse, and John, gave in order to take the little that they got."

We climbed from the Chrysler as autumn wind moved across the graveyard and felt its way toward my bones. The moon lighted faces of grave markers, but not enough that you could read them. Mike had the bulldozer warming up. It stood and puttered, and darkness felt best and Mike knew it. The headlights were off. Far away on highway 2 an engine wound tight and squalling, and it seemed like echoes of engines whispered among the graves. Mike stood huge as a grizzly.

"I've shot horses that looked healthier than you two guys," he said, but said it sort of husky.

Matt motioned toward the bulldozer. "This is illegal."

"Nobody ever claimed it wasn't." Mike was ready to fight if a fight was needed. "Anybody who don't like it can turn around and walk."

"I like it," Matt said. "It's fitting and proper. But, if we're caught there's hell to pay."

"I like most everything and everybody," Mike said, "except the government. They paw a man to death while he's alive, then keep pawing his corpse. I'm saving Jesse a little trouble."

"They like to know that he's dead and what killed him."

"Sorrow killed him," Mike said. "Let it go at that."

Jesse killed himself, timing his tiredness and starvation just right, but I was willing to let it go, and Matt was too.

"We'll go along with you," Matt said. "But, they'll sell this place for taxes. Somebody will start digging sometime."

"Not for years and years. It's deeded to me. Jesse fixed up papers. They're on the kitchen table." Mike turned toward the trailer. "We're going to do this right, and there's not much time."

We found a blanket and a quilt in the trailer. Mike opened a kitchen drawer and pulled out snapshots. Some looked pretty new, and some were faded: a man and woman in old fashioned clothes, a picture of two young boys in Sunday suits, pictures of cars and roadsigns, and pictures of two women who were maybe Sue Ellen and Sarah. Mike piled them like a deck of cards, snapped a rubber band around them, and checked the trailer. He picked up a pair of pale yellow sunglasses that some racers use for night driving. "You guys see anything else?"

"His dogs," Matt said. "He had pictures of his dogs."

We found them under a pillow, and it didn't pay to think why they were there. Then we went to the Linc and wrapped Jesse real careful in the blanket. We spread the quilt over him, and laid his stuff on the floor beside the accelerator. Then Mike remembered something. He half unwrapped Jesse, went through his pockets, then wrapped him back up. He took Jesse's keys and left them hanging in the ignition.

The three of us stood beside the Linc, and Matt cleared his throat.

"It's my place to say it," Mike told him. "This was my best friend." Mike took off his cap. Moonlight lay thin on his bald head:

"A lot of preachers will be glad this man is gone, and that's one good thing you can say for him. He drove nice people crazy. This man was a hellion pure and simple; but what folks don't understand is hellions have their place. They put everything on the line over nothing very much. Most guys worry so much about dying they never do any living. Jesse was so alive with living he never gave dying any thought. This man would roll 90 just to get to a bar before it closed." Mike kind of choked up and stopped to listen. From the graveyard came the echoes of engines, and from highway 2 rose the thrum of a straight-eight crankshaft whipping in its bed. Dim light covered the graveyard, like a hundred sets of parking lights and not the moon.

"This man kept adventure alive, when every place else it's dying. There was nothing ever smug or safe about this man. If he had fears he laughed. This man never hit a woman or crossed a friend. He did tie the can on Betty Lou one night, but can't be blamed. It was really The Dog who did that one. Jesse never had a problem until he climbed into that Studebaker."

So Mike had known all along. At least Mike knew something.

"I could always run even with Jesse," Mike said, "but I never could beat The Dog. The Dog could clear any track. And in a damn Studebaker."

"But a very swift Studebaker," Matt muttered, like a Holy Roller answering the preacher.

"Bored and stroked and rowdy," Mike said, "and you can say the same for Jesse. Let that be the final word. Amen."

IV

A little spark of flame dwelt at the stack of the dozer, and distant mountains lay white-capped and prophesied winter. Mike filled the graves quick. Matt got rakes and a shovel. I helped him mound the graves with only moonlight to go on, while Mike went to the trailer. He made coffee.

"Drink up and git," Mike told us when he poured the coffee. "Jesse's got some friends who need to visit, and it will be morning pretty quick."

"Let them," Matt said. "We're no hindrance."

"You're a smart man," Mike told Matt, "but your smartness makes you dumb. You started to hinder the night you stopped driving beyond your headlights." Mike didn't know how to say it kind, so he said it rough. His red mustache and bald head made him look like a pirate in a picture.

"You're saying that I'm getting old." Matt has known Mike long enough not to take offense.

"Me too," Mike said, "but not that old. When you get old you stop seeing them. Then you want to stop seeing them. Then you want to want to stop seeing them. You get afraid for your hide."

"You stop imagining?"

"Shitfire," Mike said, "you stop seeing. Imagination is something you use when you don't have eyes." He pulled a cigar out of his shirt pocket and was chawing it before he ever got it lit. "Ghosts have lost it all. Maybe they're the ones the Lord didn't love well enough. If you see them, but ain't one, maybe you're important."

Matt mulled that, and so did I. We've both wailed a lot of road for some sort of reason.

"They're kind of rough," Matt said about ghosts. "They hitch rides but don't want 'em. I've stopped for them and got laughed at. They fool themselves, or maybe they don't."

"It's a young man's game," Matt said.

"It's a game guys got to play. Jesse played the whole deck. He was who he was, whenever he was it. That's the key. That's the reason you slug cops when you gotta. It looks like Jesse died old, but he lived young longer than most. That's the real mystery. How does a fella keep going?"

"Before we leave," I said, "how long did you know that Jesse was The Dog?"

"Maybe a year and a half. About the time he started running crazy."

"And never said a word?"

Mike looked at me like something you'd wipe off your boot. "Learn to ride your own fence," he told me. "It was Jesse's business." Then he felt sorry for being rough. "Besides," he said, "we were having fun. I expect that's all over now."

Matt followed me to the Chrysler. We left the cemetery feeling tired and mournful. I shoved the car onto highway 2, heading toward Matt's place.

"Wring it out once for old times?"

"Putter along," Matt said. "I just entered the putter-stage of life, and may as well practice doing it."

In my mirrors a stream of headlights showed, then vanished one by one as cars turned into the graveyard. The moon had left the sky. Over toward South Dakota was a suggestion of first faint morning light. Mounded graves lay at my elbow, and so did Canada. On my left the road south ran fine and fast as a man can go. Mist rose from the roadside ditches, and maybe there was movement in the mist, maybe not.

=

There's little more to tell. Through fall and winter and spring and summer I drove to Sheridan. The Mormon turned out to be a pretty good man, for a Mormon. I kept at it, and drove through another autumn and another winter. Linda got convinced. We got married in the spring, and I expected trouble. Married people are supposed to fight, but nothing like that ever happened. We just worked hard, got our own place in a few years, and Linda birthed two girls. That disappointed the Mormon, but was a relief to me.

And in those seasons of driving, when the roads were good for twenty mile an hour in snow, or eighty under sun, the road stood empty except for a couple times. Miss Molly showed up once early on to say a bridge was out. She might have showed up another time. Squinchy little taillights winked one night when it was late and I was highballing. Some guy jack-knifed a Freightliner, and his trailer lay across the road.

But I saw no other ghosts. I'd like to say that I saw the twins, John and Jesse standing by the road, giving the high sign or dancing, but it never happened.

I did think of Jesse, though, and thought of one more thing. If Matt was right, then I saw how Jesse had to die before I got home. He had to, because I believed in Road Dog. My belief would have been just enough to bring John forward, and that would have been fatal too. If either one of them became too strong, they both of them lost. So Jesse had to do it.

The graveyard sank beneath the weather. Mike tended it for awhile, but lost interest. Weather swept the mounds flat. Weed-covered markers tumbled to decay and dust, so that only one marble headstone stands solid beside highway 2. The marker doesn't bend before the winter winds, nor does the little stone that me and Mike and Matt put there. It lays flat against the ground. You have to know where to look:

> Road Dog
> 1931–1965
> 2 million miles more-or-less
> Run and run as fast as we can
> We never can catch the Gingerbread Man

And now, even the great good cars are dead, or most of them. What with gas prices and wars and rumors of wars the cars these days are all suspensions. They'll corner like a cat, but don't have the scratch of a cat; and maybe that's a good thing. The state posts fewer crosses.

Still, there are some howlers left out there, and some guys are still howling. I lie in bed of nights and listen to the scorch of engines along highway 2. I hear them claw the darkness, stretching lonesome at the sky, scatting across the eternal land; younger guys running as young guys must; chasing each other, or chasing the land of dreams, or chasing into ghostland while hoping it ain't true—guys running into darkness chasing each other, or chasing something—chasing road.

Support Your Local Griffin

THE GRIFFIN IS AN EXOTIC CREATURE COMPOSED OF ONE-HALF LION, one-half eagle. Because of these mixed media, ornithologists are in disagreement about the griffin.

You will not, for example, find the griffin listed in *The Sibley Guide to Birds*. This is a pure piece of arrogance on the part of the National Audubon Society . . . but then, the society does not recognize the pterodactyl, either.

I am getting a little sick of people running around ignoring the griffin. And the pterodactyl. And, even, the unicorn. I am tired as all-get-out of people who go around hollering about bears (oh, pah, bears), and rhinos they have tamed (oh, tish, rhinoceros), and platinum blondes (oh, yawn). When someone tells me that he keeps sharks in his hot tub I am bored. I detest this continuing sophism that would convince us that the mamba is in every way superior to the common hoop snake. Fah. Give me a sensible, well-ordered hoop snake any time.

The whole sorry problem is caused by this century's craze for science. People think that everything must be explained. They want every creature catalogued, embalmed in museums, put on display . . . and named Alfred. People believe that if science cannot show them a griffin, then griffins do not exist.

Well, smarties, you are now in trouble. One of my best friends is a griffin. He lives in my chimney and his name is Hector. Hector is a magic griffin. He can shrink himself to about the size of a doughnut, and he can puff himself up to around the girth of your average rocket ship.

When he is doughnut-sized he looks a lot like my pet cat. When he is rocketing, the whole town nigh gets blown away in the wind from his wings. This, as anyone around here can tell you, usually happens in winter.

Hector will be exactly 2600 years old next Tuesday. I am giving him a party. The guests will be a couple of hoop snakes named Gloria and Lester, plus a unicorn named Uzz, and three pterodactyls named Prester John, Caligula, and Sam.

For his birthday Hector is getting an evil charm purchased (after a lot of mayhem) from an obscure tribe in Australia. Hector needs that charm because he is just too good-natured. In 2600 years, and with all the opportunity in the world, Hector has eaten no more than 400 to 500 politicians. It is scarcely enough. He knows it. He knows that I know it. It is the only dark secret in his life that will make him blush.

At first he tried to alibi. He claimed that the average politician has such bad taste . . . but, of course, that is no excuse. Anyone who lives for 2600 years cannot think it can be done without a certain amount of suffering.

There are advantages to associating with a griffin. For one thing, you never have chimney fires. Every time Hector fluffs up his feathers, and gives his tail a twitch, stuff tumbles out of that chimney faster than banalities at a Sunday School picnic.

In addition, griffins are interesting company. Having lived so long, Hector, even with his flaws, can tell you that a Republican tastes the same as a Commissar, and a Democrat greatly resembles a six-weeks-dead camel.

I think we should all quit thinking about bears, and begin thinking about griffins. To push this idea, I am proclaiming the week before election as National Griffin Week. Support your local griffin, friends. It may be our last chance.

A Poet in the School:
Or, The Mystery of the
Missing Mouse

ALAS, CLAYMORE

Not since Peter Rabbit got into old man MacGregor's cabbage patch had there been such a fuss in the first grade. Jerome's best friend, Sally, said so. Jerome would never have thought of calling Mr. MacGregor 'old man'; but when he stopped to think about it, Jerome figured Mr. MacGregor probably was.

The fuss happened because during Thanksgiving holiday a new bear arrived. No one knew where from. Plus, the stuffed mouse was missing. When the first grade came back after holiday, back to the chalk-smelling, paste-smelling and blunt-scissors classroom the bear sat on the table that held colored blocks, tinker toys, the stuffed rabbit named Henry; and which also held the paper mache alligator Candace. The raggedy mouse named Claymore had once sat on the table but he was no longer there.

Claymore was stolen or maybe kidnapped by Mr. Keeper the janitor, and taken to the dump. Jerome did not believe that. He liked Mr. Keeper. Sally threw a fit, and Jerome helped. Jerome was going to miss Claymore pretty bad.

The bear was a growly-type, carpety fur; dark brown carpety, and he wore a red beret. The bear was leaner and more sinewy than other bears, although it had a pot belly. For the first three days the bear talked to no one except the goldfishes who lived in a tank beside the sunny window. And it didn't talk much to them. The fish were named Ebb and Flow and Waterbury.

The teacher was Mrs. Keeper. She was a pill. She was fat and wore orange flowery dresses. She carried an orange and pink flowery satchel that bulged like a biscuit. She was the wife of Mr. Keeper the janitor. When Jerome asked what happened to Claymore the mouse Mrs. Keeper looked sad. Jerome could tell she was trying to think of something to say. "What mouse?" she said.

Mrs. Keeper did not like the new bear and anybody could see that. At least Jerome told himself anybody could, and he told his best friend Sally that anybody could see that too.

Sally was a rotten kid and proud of it. During Show and Tell, Sally had once held up a busted piece of bannister and said she came from a broken home. She happily announced that she had managed to break it all by herself. Sally said, but privately, that Mrs. Keeper stayed in the classroom during recess so she could pick her nose.

"That new bear is watching Mrs. Keeper," Sally whispered. "That bear is going to tell the principal about all the nose picking that goes on around here."

Sally was taller than Jerome, and she was not chubby like Jerome. Sally was downright skinny. She had blue eyes, and one of them sort of looked off to the left when she was thinking about being ornery. When she talked about the new bear, though, her eyes looked straight ahead and were dreamy. Sally's browny-tan hair was cut short. She did not have pigtails like other girls.

"I don't approve of finks," Sally whispered, "but I do like that bear."

Jerome was pretty sure he knew what 'approve' meant, but he was not sure about 'fink'. It had something to do with television programs about brave and kindly policemen who were all your friends, and who shot people. Jerome's father watched those programs in the evening when Jerome was in bed, listening.

On Thursday the bear cleared its throat, a firm 'harrumph'.

"Do you ever have a substitute teacher," the bear asked Jerome. The bear spoke in a loud, growly voice. It did not seem to care that Mrs. Keeper had a rule against talking in the classroom. "An *intelligent* substitute?"

"No," Sally whispered to the bear, and Sally was mad and sad. "The only *person* who is ever missing around here is Claymore the mouse."

"Oh dear," said the bear. Then it muttered a few things under its breath, words that Jerome had never even heard on television. Then the bear turned back to its conversation with the fish.

Mrs. Keeper tapped her foot and looked at Sally. Jerome understood that Mrs. Keeper had heard Sally, but had not even heard the bear. He looked around. No one was watching. It seemed to him that only he and Sally heard the bear.

On Friday Mrs. Keeper announced that there would be a 'name the bear ' contest. Over the weekend everyone was to think of a name for the new bear. On Monday Mrs. Keeper would decide which name was best.

"Are you a girl," Sally whispered to the bear, "or are you a boy." Sally did not just come right out and say that only girls could be rotten kids, but she sounded that way. She even sounded hopeful.

"You are a girl," the bear said to Sally, "and you are a boy," the bear said to Jerome. "Me, I'm a poet."

"What is a poet," Jerome whispered, even if Mrs. Keeper was tapping her foot and looking at him.

"A poet," said the bear, "is a sort of sublime detective. A poet treads the mists of reflection. A poet makes solid the tenuous fabric of dreams."

"A detective is just what we need," said Sally. "Somebody's got to figure out what happened to Claymore the mouse."

"The case might amuse me," the bear said as it turned back to a conversation with the fish. "While you infants spend your weekend watching reruns of *Spider Man* I begin work on the problem."

Requirements For Becoming A Poet

Jerome liked Saturday mornings best. He would wake up a long time before his mother and father. His mother always left a bowl of cereal for him. He would sit and eat his cereal and watch how the gray, misty light covering the lawn went away, and the sun began to make colors in the trees and on the top of the fence. In the winter there were not very many birds and all of them were little except the crows. There were sparrows and Oregon juncos and rufous-sided towhees that scratched sideways when they ate seeds from the feeder. His mother told him what the birds were named.

After the sun was up, or anyway after the sky was light, he would go and watch television. If there was no rain he would play outside with Sally in the afternoon. If it was raining Sally might come to his house to play.

This Saturday morning Jerome watched *Spider Man and The Klutzy Kritter*. He watched *Galapagos Goose* and *The Purple Baron Goes to Hollywood*. He watched *The Strawberry Benders* and *Beast From The Sewer* and *Barbie Meets The Eastside Strangler*. He got most excited about *Beast From The Sewer* because the beast looked a lot like the paper mache alligator Candace.

When cartoons were over some noisy men on television began to talk about a football game. Jerome's father came into the living room. Jerome's father was bigger than Mr. Keeper. He was louder than Mr. Keeper, but he was not as loud as Mrs. Keeper. Jerome liked his father, even if there was not much room on the sofa after his father sat down. Once during Show and Tell Jerome had taken a heavy red tool to class to show how his father was a plumber. That same night his father yelled that a man's pipe wrench was a man's pipe wrench, and you just couldn't *check it out* like a library book. On Saturdays Jerome's father watched football games and drank beer.

Beer was bad. Mrs. Keeper said so. Jerome did not understand, because his father always talked to him more on Saturdays. Jerome's father smoked cigars. Mrs. Keeper said that smoking was bad even if the cigars smelled fat and nice. When Jerome's father came home from work he was usually pretty dirty and sometimes smelly. Mrs. Keeper said those things were bad.

"What's a poet," Jerome said to his father. His father blinked, then turned the knob on the television. "Sparkle sparkle little twink, how the hell you are I think." Jerome's father chuckled. "That's a poet."

Cussing was bad. Mrs. Keeper said so.

"I'm going to be one," Jerome said. "So is Sally."

"You're going to get a lobotomy," Jerome's father said, but he said it most kindly. "Poets never have any money, and they all have dandruff, and they are bums. Forget about being a poet."

"What's a lobot-o- . . . ?"

"Every poet has one," Jerome's father said. "Game's starting."

Jerome felt warm and comfortable sitting beside his father. Sometimes his father held Jerome on his lap.

Jerome would snuggle down, smelling the cigar and beer smells. He would feel safe and warm. Sometimes he would take a little nap, but the naps did not last. One of the football players would do something wonderful. That would make his father bounce around.

"We have a new bear at school," Jerome said. "The bear is a poet."

"That sounds about right," his father said. "All the good poets are dead ones, except the ones who are bears." His arm hugged Jerome. "Fifty-two yard field goal. That guy couldn't kick a Georgia peach hard enough to bust it. "

On Becoming A Fireman

Jerome's mother was not fat like Mrs. Keeper, but lately when she took Jerome on her lap and read stories there was less lap. Jerome's mother said that Jerome would have a baby sister pretty soon. Jerome did not know if that was a good idea. Sally had a baby brother, but Sally said the baby was not working out.

"What's a poet?" Jerome said to his mother.

She was standing in the kitchen. The radio was playing. She hummed along with a song on the radio. Her hair was browner than Sally's, and she had a big nose and freckles. Her hair was tied up in a green bandanna. Jerome thought she was prettier than anybody.

"A poet makes stories with rhymes," his mother said. "I read poetry to you all the time. 'Black sheep black sheep have you any wool/yes sir yes sir three bags full' Wool and full are rhymes."

"I'm going to be one. So is Sally."

"Maybe you'll be a fireman."

"I'm going to be both."

"That is a very good idea," his mother told him. "Are you going to Sally's, or is she coming here?"

"Going."

"Coat weather." His mother looked at the thermometer hanging outside by the bird feeder. "Get your coat and hat."

"We're not going to be bears. We're going to get married."

"That is another very good idea," his mother said, "and you must be sure to tell me when, but you still have to wear your coat and hat."

"Next Saturday."

"I intend to have the baby next Saturday," his mother said. "You'll have to put it off awhile."

It was chilly as he went down the sidewalk and maybe there wasn't any rain, but the mist was thick like rain. He stuck out his tongue and let the mist tickle it. He was so busy letting the mist tickle his tongue that he almost ran into Mr. Feet who was the mailman. "Your face is going to freeze that way," Mr. Feet said. "Then what are you going to do?" Sometimes Mr. Feet was nice, sometimes he was a grump.

"Be a poet."

"Rejects," said Mr. Feet. "Friends of the post office. If we don't have poets I ain't got a job." Today Mr. Feet was being a grump.

"And wear a red hat and drink beer and smoke cigars and cuss," Jerome told him.

"And get rejected," Mr. Feet said. "Spend all your money on stamps and beer and cigars. By golly, you even sound like a poet."

"Do you have a letter for me?" Sometimes Mr. Feet gave him a letter, but it never had his name on it. It almost always said 'Occupant'.

"I have just the thing," Mr. Feet said. He searched through his bag. "Read this."

"Do you a - - - - - - - - to - - - -?"

"Do you have a restless urge to write?" Mr. Feet said. "That's the kind of letters poets get."

Mr. Feet was no fun so Jerome kept on walking to Sally's house. He folded up the letter and put it in his coat pocket. Mrs. Keeper said that littering was bad.

The Secret Fort and The Evil Weed

"Sally is outside," Sally's mother said. Sally's mother was tall and skinny. She had long black hair. Sometimes Sally said her mother was Mexican. Sometimes Sally said her mother was a Choctaw.

Sometimes Sally said her mother was a Rosicrucian. Jerome didn't understand the difference, but he liked Sally's mother.

The new baby wasn't really so new anymore. It sat in a highchair in the kitchen. It was wearing a bib and diapers. The baby had a little dab of black hair and an orange streak of strained carrots on its bib. Sally said that it wasn't much of a baby but Jerome thought it looked about right.

"... said she was going to play with a new friend," Sally's mother told Jerome.

Jerome blinked and felt bad.

"Baby, baby," Sally's mother said to Jerome, "a person can have a new friend. That doesn't mean they don't like their old friends."

Jerome felt better.

"She asked me what was a poet," Sally's mother said. Jerome felt even better. Sally was playing with the new bear. It seemed a little goofy, because bears were supposed to stay at school.

"What is a poet," Jerome said.

"A poet is like a painter, only a poet draws pictures with words. 'The Angels bustle in the Hall-/Softly my Future climbs the Stair/I fumble at My Childhood' s prayer/So soon to be a Child no more-' that' s a poet."

"And drink beer and smoke cigars and cuss and wear red hats?"

"I don't think that one did," Sally's mother said softly, "but maybe she should of." Sally's mother turned to look at the baby, her voice even softer. "Butcher, baker, candlestick maker; what will it be? I hope it goes well for you," she said to the baby. To Jerome she said, "Try the secret fort. I expect they are there."

The secret fort was a place that only Sally and Jerome knew about. It was in a woods back of Sally's house. Some trees had fallen down, and some other trees drooped over them. In the summer the fort was a cool and quiet place that the birds liked. Sally and Jerome would fight Indians and make up stories. Once they found a dead bird and held a funeral.

In the winter the fort was not shady because the leaves were off the trees. The fort was pretty wet from rain. In the winter they took popcorn to the fort and fed the squirrels.

Sometimes the squirrels and the crows got to jawing at each other about the popcorn.

Jerome knew that Sally was playing with the new bear because he saw a little spot of red as he got close to the fort. When he got even closer he saw that the bear seemed bigger, almost as big as Sally. In school the bear had not been much bigger than the stuffed rabbit Henry. He decided that poets could make themselves bigger whenever they wanted.

"Good afternoon, urchin," the bear said in a growly voice. "We are examining your battlements."

Jerome saw Sally who stood beside the bear. Sally looked like Sally never looked. Sally looked impressed. She did not look ornery at all.

"Your tents of white now pitched before the gates,

And gentle flags of amity displayed,

I doubt me not the governor will yield."

"What?"

"I was declaiming about the fort," the bear growled. "I spoke the words of the sainted Marlowe."

"Been carrying on like that," Sally said.

"What is your name," Jerome asked. "We have to be in the 'name the bear' contest."

The bear pushed its red hat forward. The hat nearly covered the bear's button eyes. "What is my name," the bear growled.

"Gruff," Sally said.

"Correct," said the bear. "My name is Gruff because I am gruff."

It seemed like a perfect name to Jerome.

"We'll never win," Sally said. "Mrs. Keeper will never say Gruff is best. She'll say that 'Patty Cake' is best.

"Mrs. Keeper," said Gruff, "is unfortunately an obese and dictatorial termagant."

"She sure is," said Sally as if she understood, while Jerome looked confused.

"Fat old poop," Gruff explained to Jerome. "However, it is not good policy for me to undermine your authority figures. Let us simply say that Mrs. Keeper leads an unfortunate existence."

"She used to be nice," Jerome said.

"Have you found Claymore the mouse?"

"In good time," Gruff said. Gruff squatted down behind one of the fallen trees. He looked out across the field which was before the woods. "If I were mounting an attack on this fort," Gruff said,

"I would bring my unicorns in from that direction." He pointed toward Sally's house. "Over that way . . ." and he pointed toward Jerome's house, "I would fly air cover with an umbrella of griffins. Beneath that cover I'd place a squad of wooly mammoths escorting fifty hand-picked trolls. This place could be overrun."

Jerome felt like he was about to cry. "However," said Gruff, "Jerome and Sally would not allow that to happen."

Jerome felt better.

"Because," Gruff explained, "as all the unicorns and griffins and mammoths and trolls were converging, Jerome and Sally would begin a tea party. Everybody would sit down to tea and cookies and they would all become good friends. That is the best way to defend a fort."

"Claymore is a little bitty mouse," Sally said. "Why would Mr. Keeper pick on a little bitty mouse?"

Gruff stood back up and adjusted his hat. Now that Gruff was bigger the carpety fur was even more carpety. Gruff was not the kind of bear that anyone would just want to walk up to and hug.

"Mr. Keeper did not pick on Claymore," Gruff said. "My investigation is far from complete, but I already know that the culprit is not Mr. Keeper who has depth."

"He didn't do it?" Jerome was glad. Jerome thought Mr. Keeper had always been nice.

"And speaking of tea and cookies, and speaking of Claymore, I find that I will need a cookie," Gruff said. He seemed to be listening to his own words. "Two cookies," Gruff said.

It was easy to get the cookies. Sally and Jerome went to Sally's house, and Sally's mother gave each of them a cookie. Then they went to Jerome's house. Jerome's mother gave each of them a cookie. Jerome's father was taking a nap on the sofa. A cigar sat in ashtray, barely used.

"This is a rare treat," Gruff said about the cigar. "Each of us may now eat a cookie."

There was one cookie left over.

"This is bait," Gruff explained. "I have a theory about the missing Claymore." Gruff turned to Jerome. "Please give my thanks to your father for the cigar. You brains have furthered Claymore's cause. I will see you in school on Monday."

Garibaldi and The Children's Hour

On Monday after the children were in school and the fathers went to work Sally's mother and Jerome's mother visited at Jerome's house. They drank coffee and watched the birds at the feeder.

"Pulled the old double-cookie scam again on Saturday," Sally's mother said about the children. Her long black hair was tied back. She wore a little red bow to hold it together. "Should we tell them not to be devious?"

"We'd better tell them not to smoke cigars," Jerome's mother said. "One of Jim's cigars turned up missing. Jerome gave it to the new bear." Jerome's mother giggled. "I know they didn't smoke it because nobody urped."

"A bear who is a poet," Sally's mother said. "They're at an age when they have invisible friends. It's just that I never heard of two kids sharing the same invisible friend."

"Maybe they're both afraid of the same things," Jerome's mother said. "We've got the new baby coming. You had yours last year."

"My Sally-kid is jealous" Sally's mother said. "On Sunday she bit the baby on his big toe. The baby yelled murder, and Michael yelled at Sally. Gave her a pat on the butt. More yelling. I went to the living room and watched football."

"Pat on the butt."

"Michael is a panty-waist," Sally's mother said. "*I* used to smack her harder burping her."

"And Mrs. Keeper is no help," Jerome's mother said.

"It's bad enough the kids are jealous. I'm afraid she'll end up making them hate school."

"She used to be wonderful," Sally's mother said. "At least the women with older kids say so."

"I used to be wonderful," Jerome's mother said. "Now I just tote watermelons."

"Ninth month is lousy."

"What's this business about red hats?"

"Sally wants a red hat," Sally's mother said. "As near as I can tell what she wants is a red beret."

"That's it," Jerome's mother said. "Like Garibaldi. *That's* what he was trying to describe."

"Garibaldi was the red shirts, not hats. I'll make up a couple of red berets," Sally's mother said. "You just get busy and have that kid."

"Garibaldi in the first grade," Jerome's mother said. "I'll bet Mrs. Keeper has a fit."

'Poop' For Short

Mrs. Keeper had her first fit during Show and Tell when Sally said she was an unwanted child.

Sally showed her teeth. They were the teeth she used to bite her baby brother on the toe. Sally pulled down her jeans and showed her pants. She was showing the spot on her hindey where her father beat her with a ballbat and a great big whip.

"Sit down," Mrs. Keeper said. "Pull up your jeans first." Mrs. Keeper turned to a goody-two-shoes named Annabel. "Go get Mr. Keeper," she said to Annabel. To Sally she said, "That was unladylike. Nothing is more unladylike than that."

Gruff chuckled. Gruff was sitting on the table between the stuffed rabbit Henry and the paper mache alligator Candace. Gruff was still carpety, but he was shrunk. He was the same size as when he first came to school.

Sally stuck out her tongue at Gruff. Mrs. Keeper could not hear Gruff. She yelled at Sally. Sally turned, and Sally's tongue was sticking right out at Mrs. Keeper. Some of the children laughed. Gruff laughed.

"It would certainly be unladylike for Mrs. Keeper to expose *her* hindey," Gruff said with another chuckle. "In fact, it would be downright overwhelming."

Two of the children who had laughed were now listening hard. Johnnie-red-head was listening, but the other Johnnie, the one with yellow hair, was not. A girl named Wong Li was listening. She was smiling.

"I am a poet," Gruff continued, "and poets are notoriously over-sensitive in matters of good taste. Thus, I may say with some authority that an exposed hindey does not seem like a hanging offense."

Sally looked happy. Gruff was on her side.

Gruff tried to look gruff but did not do good at it.

Gruff chuckled. "In the case of Mrs. Keeper's hindey, what I just said was a pun; and a very good pun, and maybe everything would be just opposite in the case of Mrs. Keeper's hindey."

Wong Li giggled. Johnnie-red-head laughed. So did the stuffed rabbit Henry.

"Good show," Henry said to Gruff, "a really good go there, old bear."

"You can talk," Jerome whispered to Henry. "You never talked before."

"Never had a thing to say before," Henry said in a voice that was not loud, but it was loud for a rabbit.

Now a girl named Sandy whispered to Jerome. "Can you hear that bear."

"We played together all weekend," Jerome whispered.

"That bear's name is Gruff." Jerome looked at all of the other children. He counted on his fingers. Jerome and Sally and Johnny-red-head and Wong Li and Sandy. All five of them could hear the bear. The rest of the children could not.

When Mr. Keeper arrived Mrs. Keeper did not even speak. She pointed at Sally. She handed Mr. Keeper a note. Mr. Keeper winked at Sally when Mrs. Keeper was not looking. "I prithee give me leave to go from hence," he snickered. Sally went with Mr. Keeper. They went to the principal's office.

Mrs. Keeper threw her second fit during the 'name the bear' contest. Sally was at the principal's office, and Jerome knew that Sally was sitting in a corner thinking cuss. That happened when you went to the principal's office.

Jerome and Wong Li and Johnnie-red-head and Sandy all said the bear's name was Gruff. Goody-two-shoes Annabel said the bear's name was Rugby.

"Bad pun," said the stuffed rabbit Henry. He flopped his ears and gave a big sigh. "She is an exterior sort of person," said Candace the paper mache alligator in a raspy, papery voice. "Goody-two-shoes types always are."

"You can talk," Jerome whispered to Candace. "You never did before."

"I talk all the time," Candace said, "you never listened before."

Another girl said the bear's name was Rosalyn.

A boy said the bear's name was Fire Chief because of the red hat.

Another boy said the bear s name was Captain Marvel.

A girl said the bear's name was Douglas Fur.

"Not bad," growled Gruff.

"Jolly good," said Henry.

A girl said the bear's name was Poopsy.

"It's garbage time," growled Gruff. "Now we've descended to Poopsy."

"Poop for short," said Waterbury from the fish tank. "Really, now." The voice giggled and burbled. Ebb and Flow hummed along as Waterbury sang.

Mrs. Keeper will take Poopsy
As a name that not too oopsy
Shorten Poopsy down to Poop
Mrs. Keeper will yell and whoop.

"Your meter's off, " growled Gruff. "read 'will go whoop.' I despise a cracked meter."

"I'm new at this business," Waterbury said apologetically. He blushed so orange that he was almost red.

Mrs. Keeper said that the new bear's name was Percy, and that was the end of it. She said that the children had suggested some very good names, but the bear's name was really Percy.

"The bear's name is Percy," Gruff said in a simpery little voice. "The bear is not a romantic poet." The bear abhors romantic poets."

"The bear's name is Percy," said Gruff in a hollow voice. "Although the bear goes 'this and that' on the shades of Wordsworth and Perce Shelley. The bear is really taking a bath on this one."

"It isn't fair," Jerome said. "Me and Johnnie-red-head and Wong Li and Sandy know that ain't right." He gulped. He had said ain't.

"Take your chair and sit in the corner," Mrs. Keeper told Jerome. "The bear's name is Percy."

A Mouse Is Down

On Tuesday Jerome and Sally wore their red berets to school. Mrs. Keeper made them put the berets in the cloakroom, and Sally and

Mrs. Keeper had a fight. Sally said why do we put our hats in the cloakroom and Gruff doesn't.

"Percy," Mrs. Keeper said.

"Gruff," Sally said.

Then Gruff said something under his breath that made the stuffed rabbit Henry blush.

That same day Gruff explained to Jerome and Sally how Mr. Keeper had not kidnapped Claymore the mouse.

"There were witnesses," Gruff said. "The rabbit Henry, and the alligator Candace, and the three fish were watching. Claymore had an adventure."

"That is a droll way of putting it," said Henry the rabbit. "While I do not watch *Spider Man* reruns, I believe the accurate description says that Claymore was 'offed.'"

Both Johnnie-red-head and Johnnie-yellow-hair gasped. Now Johnnie-yellow-hair was hearing the animals too.

"Or," said Henry, "one might say 'we have a mouse down '—or one might say 'Claymore bit the big one'—or, as the English would say, 'toodle-oooh Claymore.'"

"Rabbits should jump," Gruff observed. That is the nature of rabbits. Rabbits should not jump to conclusions."

"Claymore jumped to a hasty conclusion," said the paper mache alligator Candace. "Claymore was tired of the first grade. This was his fourth year in first grade. He was greedy. He was sick of eating crumbs from peanut butter and jelly sandwiches. He swore if he touched another twinkie it would put knots in his tail. "

"I reconstructed events leading to the disappearance of Claymore," said Gruff. "Claymore wanted an adventure, and yes, he was greedy. His biggest task was to get through the doorway unobserved. Mrs. Keeper always keeps the door closed . . . ."

"During recess Mrs. Keeper takes her flowery satchel and hides in the cloakroom," one of the fish trilled. "She hums and eats and cusses."

Jerome did not believe the fish. He looked at the rabbit Henry. "She doesn't cuss," Henry said, "most days."

"When Mrs. Keeper goes home at night she always closes the door," Gruff said. "The only one who comes to the room is Mr. Keeper the janitor."

"And he always closes the door," the three fish hummed. "But on what may have been the fatal day . . ." and Gruff paused dramatically, "at least on the day of moment, Mr. Keeper left the classroom and closed the door. Then Mrs. Keeper came back to the classroom. She left the door ajar. She walked past this table and to the cloakroom. She entered the cloakroom . . . ." Gruff paused even more dramatically.

"And," said Henry the rabbit, "that is when Claymore yelled, 'The Hell with it boys, I'm *out* of here.'"

"He jumped," said Candace sadly. "We heard a muffled scream and that is the last that is known of Claymore."

"Now that all interruptions are over," said Gruff, "I will continue my case. I will prove deductively that Claymore must still be in this room. But first, my investigation.

"There is a stuffed calico cat named Susan in the third grade. I interviewed her as a prime suspect. I theorized that the cat entered the classroom behind Mrs. Keeper. As Mrs. Keeper passed the table the cat waited. Claymore jumped. The cat took a nap after devouring Claymore, then sneaked back to third grade in the dead of night."

"A pretty theory," Gruff continued, "but it came to naught. Susan had an unshakable alibi for the evening in question. She was at the home of a student. The student's mother was sewing Susan's head back on, because Susan had been involved in a pillow fight."

Jerome whispered to Sally that he could hardly wait 'til they got to third grade.

"I then sought inductive evidence," said Gruff. "I tried to induce Claymore to reveal his presence. "This was accomplished by spreading cookie crumbs all over the cloakroom floor. For," Gruff continued, "had Claymore been in the classroom he would have been seen. The crumbs were spread after Mr. Keeper swept. On the following morning the crumbs were still there. However," and Gruff paused again, "Yesterday, Monday—and before Mr. Keeper swept—the crumbs were gone."

"Greedy Mrs. Keeper," said Candace.

"Claymore is in the cloakroom," Jerome whispered to Sally.

Gruff looked at Candace and shook his head. "You are no judge of character," Gruff said sadly." If Mrs. Keeper saw crumbs she would just yell for Mr. Keeper to clean them up."

"If you and Sally do not stop whispering," Mrs. Keeper said to Jerome," I'll have to send you both to the principal."

Then she turned to the rest of the class. "Johnnie and Johnnie and Sandy and Wong Li what is *wrong* with you today? All of you are usually so good."

"Gruff is telling about what happened to Claymore," Sandy said.

"Percy," Mrs. Keeper said, "The new bear's name is Percy."

"We have to have an English lesson pretty soon," Gruff growled. "There is going to be a glorious joust during English."

"It is a pretty name for a pretty bear," said Mrs. Keeper.

"A pritttty name for a pritttty bear," Gruff grumbled. "Well I have seen some pritttty bears, Madame, and I am not the bear of whom you speak. Wouldst joust?"

The Horny Butterfly

On Wednesday Jerome and Sally wore their red berets to school. Johnnie-red-head wore his red beret to school, and Sandy wore her red beret to school. Wong Li wore a red scarf to school. Johnnie-yellow-hair wore a red shirt to school. A quiet little boy named Peter wore a red tie and red socks, and a girl named Mary Lou wore a red bandanna.

Gruff was happy. Gruff pushed the red beret forward. It came down just above the button eyes. "Sink me that ship, master gunner," Gruff muttered. "Split her, rend her, tear her in twain."

Mrs. Keeper was mad. Jerome did not know why. Mrs. Keeper was so mad she even forgot to put her big flowered satchel in the cloak room. She was so mad she even forgot to be nice to goody-two-shoes Annabel.

"We will not read today," Mrs. Keeper said. "We will make pictures with words."

"That is a courageous woman," Gruff muttered. "Have I missed something?"

"Like Spider Man?" Sally said.

"Spider Man always fights battles he can win," Gruff said. "That is not courage. Mrs. Keeper, however, sets forth on a deep and turbulent sea."

"Some of those pictures you have already heard," Mrs. Keeper said. "Like, 'A bolt from the blue.'"

"Cliché," Gruff said, "although it is used as an example. 'Like a mouse overboard' might suit our cause."

"Madder than a wet hen," said Mrs. Keeper. "Can you see the picture of a wet chicken? Can you imagine how mad that chicken would be?"

"Cliché," said Sally. "Although it is used as an example." Sally was trying to sound just like Gruff.

"Madder than a stuffed rabbit," said Henry. Then he said, "Oh dear, that doesn't sound exactly right."

"A fish out of water," Mrs. Keeper said.

"This party is getting rough," Waterbury said. "Rough as a trout among tadpoles."

"Rough as an alligator in a hot tub," said Candace. "Like Garibaldi at the Republican Convention," Gruff sniffed. "C'mon, let's get on with it."

"Cliché," said Sally, "Cliché, cliché, cliché." Sally liked the new word.

Mrs. Keeper did not like the new word. "Sally will make a picture," Mrs. Keeper said. "Since Sally knows all about clichés she will make a new picture."

"A paradise of swallows," Gruff muttered. "Throw that one at her."

Sally did. Mrs. Keeper gasped. "That is wonderful," she said, "where did you hear that?"

"Gruff told me."

"You have a very creative mother," Mrs. Keeper said, and that seemed to explain something but nobody could figure out what. Mrs. Keeper forgot that Gruff's name was supposed to be Percy.

"Softer than a rabbit's bottom," said Henry. He chuckled.

"I say," he said, "I believe I'm catching on to this."

"Boo," said Candace.

"Hiss," said Waterbury.

"Painted bunting pretty," said Mrs. Keeper.

"Not bad alliteration," said Gruff, "give her 'condominiums like a harmonica.'"

Jerome did, although he had a hard time saying condomim-imimum.

Mrs. Keeper gasped. "Where did you hear that?"

"Gruff told me."

Mrs. Keeper stood before the class and for a little while she did not look so fat. She looked excited.

"Slippery as a brigade of fishworms," said Waterbury.

"Yum," hummed Ebb and Flow.

"Warm as the spots on a giraffe," said Mrs. Keeper.

"Hey, hey," said Gruff, "now we're cracking. Wong Li, give her 'a rosary of stars.'"

Wong Li did.

Mrs. Keeper looked like she was about to cry, but she did not look sad.

"Scratchy as a towhee," Jerome said, and he realized that he had made that one up himself.

"Very good, toddler," Gruff said. "That is very good indeed."

"Orange as strained carrots on a baby," Sally said. Then she looked surprised because she had made one up herself.

"It appears," said Gruff in a happy voice, "that the speed limit has been raised back up to seventy. Give her, 'a cacophony of carousels.'"

Johnnie-red-head said it, but he stumbled over 'cat-cat-phoney.'

Mrs. Keeper actually *was* crying, but she was smiling too. "You never heard of cacophony in your life," she said to Johnnie-red-head, "but magic happens. I'd forgotten that magic happens."

"It's called passive resistance," Gruff said to Henry. " It's a way of fighting so that everybody wins."

"Passive as a snoozing rabbit," said Henry.

"Very good," said Candace, "Henry seems to be catching on."

"Henry is sparkly as a butterfly in heat," Gruff said. "Whoops!" Gruff yelled. "Don't say that one. That one will get us all kicked out."

It was too late. Jerome had already said it.

Mrs. Keeper actually giggled. "I'm not mad at you at all," she said to Jerome, "but you will have to explain that to the principal."

Goody-two-shoes Annabel stood up. She was going to go find Mr. Keeper.

"Jerome can find Mr. Keeper all by himself," Mrs. Keeper said. "I think Mr. Keeper would like to talk to Jerome."

A Poet Unmasked

"As one poet to another," Mr. Keeper said, "I do enjoy your butterfly line. It is only slightly pornographic."

Mr. Keeper and Jerome sat on the stair steps outside the principal's office.

"I thought you are a janitor," Jerome said.

Mr. Keeper reached in the pocket of his jacket, and he pulled out a red beret. At least it had been red sometime. Now it was faded. It looked like Waterbury the goldfish when Waterbury blushed. "In my day," Mr. Keeper said, "I could zip out similes with the best of 'em. Iambs came as natural as speech."

"You are not a janitor?"

"I'm a janitor on the side," Mr. Keeper said. "Poets often are."

"I'm glad you did not take Claymore to the dump."

"Oh dear, " said Mr. Keeper, "that greedy Claymore. I did not take him to the dump. Claymore would love to be taken to the dump. The dump is not unlike mouse heaven."

"Did Claymore say that?"

"Did you ever hear a mouse whine," Mr. Keeper asked. "We all have our duty, and Claymore's duty is to the first grade. Every day after school Claymore whined to be taken to the dump. Claymore cared aught for duty."

"Is Mrs. Keeper's duty to the first grade?"

"Yes," said Mr. Keeper in an unhappy voice, "as is mine. But Mrs. Keeper is sad and eats too much. That is because the first grade no longer spends much time watching birds and fairies. The first grade no longer looks for trolls and unicorns. Spider Man is easy to find, but elves are not. "

Jerome gulped.

"However," Mr. Keeper said cheerfully, "some things changed in first grade today. Mrs. Keeper is excited again. I'll bet she goes to recess instead of sitting in the cloakroom, eating."

"Will Claymore come back?"

"That depends," Mr. Keeper said. "If the first grade keeps thinking about poets, Claymore will be forced to come back. Gruff will tell you why. In fact, I expect Gruff already knows the entire sordid tale of Claymore."

"Are you sad like Mrs. Keeper?"

"When the first grade stopped thinking about frogs who are princes, my hat began to fade."

"I'll think about birds," Jerome said. He stood up. "All the time in the principal's office."

"That will make Mrs. Keeper very happy," Mr. Keeper said.

"It will also make me very happy, because fat as she is, I am rather more fond of Mrs. Keeper than you might imagine."

The Last Bedad

Thursday was the *reddest* day. Almost every child had some kind of red hat. Those who had no hat wore something red. Johnnie-yellow-hair even wore a red clown nose but it kept falling off. Even goody-two-shoes Annabel was wearing a little red bow. Mrs. Keeper called the new bear Gruff.

"Leg over leg, the dog got to Dover," said Henry the rabbit.

"Cliché," said Gruff. "Besides, the subject today is arithmetic. Besides, I'm busy with observations. Tomorrow I will reveal the whereabouts of the recalcitrant Claymore."

Mrs. Keeper talked about twos. Twos were wonderful things. When Mrs. Keeper talked about adding twos, Jerome saw how to do it right away. It was just like building blocks. He said so.

"It *is* just like building blocks," said Mrs. Keeper. "Show us."

Jerome went to the table for blocks. He snapped two together. "A two," he said. He snapped another two together.

"A two," he said.

He snapped the twos together. "Two twos," he said, "not just four ones. I could make a whole house out of twos," he bragged.

"People do," said Mrs. Keeper. "They call them bricks, and that was very very good, Jerome."

"Bravo, ragamuffin," said Gruff.

All the children expected Mrs. Keeper to stay in at recess. They did not think she would come outside for recess two days in a row.

Mrs. Keeper surprised them. She left her flowery satchel sitting by her desk. She did not pick it up and take it to the cloakroom.

Instead she put on her coat and everybody followed. Mrs. Keeper showed them an Indian dance you could do outdoors.

On Friday Mrs. Keeper came to school and she was wearing a red beret. Sally thought it looked like a redbird sitting on a pig's back end. Jerome was shocked. He thought Mrs. Keeper looked pretty in the hat.

"Wait 'til you get a baby sister," Sally said. "You will know about back ends."

"Somebody bite your toe?" asked Gruff. He said it in a snickery, funny way. Pretty soon Sally was laughing. Sally thought Mrs. Keeper looked all right.

Friday was when everybody talked about other places.

This Friday Mrs. Keeper told them about children who live in Spain. She showed pictures of dancers. She showed a man swinging a red cape, and the picture of a cow with horns.

"Bloody bastards," Henry the rabbit said, "Bedad."

"Your label," said Gruff, and not unkindly, "says 'made in Hong Kong'. Hong Kong is no longer a British protectorate. So let's can the 'bedad'."

"Jolly well right," said Candace to Henry. "Kindly can the 'bedad'."

"Topping good suggestion," said Waterbury.

"Splendid, really."

"Unless," said Gruff, "you *feel* like a tweed rabbit. In which case it is self-expression."

"Smashing," Henry said, but he did not say 'bedad', and it never said it ever again.

"Because," said Gruff, "in the case of the missing Claymore, self-expression of a crude sort is at the bottom of the mystery." Gruff attempted to look stern, but then sniggered. "There is such a thing as poetic license, and then there is licentious license."

Jerome was so interested in Spain that he almost did not hear Gruff. "Claymore?" Jerome said.

"Muchacho," said Gruff. "Pay attention. Our time is no longer much."

"A flamingo dancer," Sally said. "With a long red dress and red flowers in my hair." Sally's eyes were looking straight at Mrs. Keeper, and Sally's eyes were dreamy.

"Flamenco," growled Gruff. "Gringa."

"From those bleeders who brought you the Inquisition," said the stuffed rabbit Henry. "The Armada. The Popish enterprises . . . ," and then Henry stopped talking because he saw that no one heard him anymore.

"Pretend," Gruff said with an absolute roar, "that you are a bull fighter." Gruff made snickety-snick noises. They were the kind of noises that Jerome's father made at Thanksgiving. Jerome's father went snickety-snick with a knife when he sharpened the carving knife on a stone stick.

"Pretend," Gruff said with an absolutely bigger roar, "that Mrs. Keeper's flowery satchel is a bull."

Jerome looked at Mrs. Keeper's flowery satchel. It seemed to be moving a little.

"Take this sword," Gruff roared, and then went "snickety-snick, snickety-snick."

"Oh help," screamed a voice from Mrs. Keeper's flowery satchel. "Oh, don't, oh, please."

A fat gray streak rapidly turned into a fat gray bubble as it fled from the flowery satchel and rolled over and over across the floor. It screamed as it rolled.

"That," said Gruff, "is the fattest and most wanton looking mouse I have ever seen." He turned to Henry. "May I present Claymore."

"Henry isn't talking anymore," said Candace. "But yep, that's our Claymore. That's our boy."

The first grade had not been so relieved since Peter Rabbit got away from Mr. MacGregor's cabbage patch. Everybody had to pet Claymore. Nobody heard Claymore yelling. Claymore was yelling, "Don't hug me, for God's sake *don't hug me.*"

"If they hug him he'll urp," Candace predicted.

"Serve him right," said Waterbury. Then Waterbury began to complain. "Serve *them* right if they get urped on. It seems that they no longer hear me."

"Ah," said Gruff, "and here is the prodigal himself." Mrs. Keeper sat Claymore back on the table.

"I owe it all to sloth and greed," Claymore said happily. He rolled on his back. His tummy was so round that even if he raised his head and his tail, he could not see the tip of his tail. "I owe it mostly to greed," he explained with a good deal of satisfaction, "but sloth has its place and should receive some credit."

"You fell into Mrs. Keeper's satchel. That accounts for the muffled scream," said Candace.

"Scared hell out me," said Claymore. "Then I realized I'd fallen square onto a cheese sandwich. Potato chips on the side."

"And so you stayed there," said Waterbury. "Riding back and forth between school and Mrs. Keeper's house."

"A moveable feast," said Claymore. "I coulda et forever, man. Mrs. Keeper didn't miss a crumb. She kept that satchel loaded."

"A doomed enterprise, nonetheless," said Gruff. "Mrs. Keeper is no longer stuffing herself during recess. You may have been too busy to notice, but for the last two days nothing new has been tossed into that satchel.

"I knew what had to be happening," Gruff continued.

"Your reputation preceded you. There are no mouse holes in the cloakroom, so you could not be hiding. I trusted your greed to keep you close to your supplier. The only time I was thrown off was when you ate the cookie crumbs."

"Why?" asked Candace. "It looks like he'll eat anything. In fact, it looks like he has."

"Because he would have had to stray from the sanctuary of Mrs. Keeper's flowery satchel," Gruff said.

"Goody-two-shoes Annabel swept up those crumbs when she went to the supply closet for chalk," said Claymore. "I didn't give a hang for those crumbs."

"Zounds," said the stuffed rabbit Henry. "That's my last word. You'll hear no more from me. Zounds."

"And so it ends," said Gruff. "And it ends well." He turned to the fish tank. "Ebb and Flow and Waterbury, worthy thanes. Candace," and he turned to Candace, "Our rudder in some heavy seas . . . ."

"Cliché," said the stuffed rabbit Henry. "That's my last word. You'll hear no more from me. Cliché."

"And stout hearted Henry," Gruff said. He looked about. Mrs. Keeper was smiling. Claymore was holding his tummy and groaning. The first grade looked like the red sparkles one finds on a Christmas cookie. The first grade was busy listening to Mrs. Keeper.

Except for Jerome and Sally. Jerome and Sally were whispering. Tomorrow was Saturday. Jerome and Sally were planning to get up at daylight and go to the secret fort. They were planning to practice all day. Surely by night, they would be the world's best flamingo dancers.

Epilogue

Since it was so late in the year, after Thanksgiving, the days were short. By the time Mr. Keeper got around to cleaning up the first grade classroom the sun was a red glow in the windows. Mr. Keeper moved around the classroom in the dim light. He was too stooped to be a young man, but he moved too easily to be an old man. He emptied waste baskets. He swept. He brushed the chalk board. He sprinkled food for Ebb and Flow and Waterbury. Mr. Keeper's shadow got more and more invisible as the darkness grew. Mr. Keeper did everything so easily that anyone watching him would say that he loved the classroom.

Mr. Keeper finished just before his shadow sank all the way into the dark floor. He looked around to make sure he had done all of his work. Then he went to the front of the classroom and picked up Mrs. Keeper's chair. He brought the chair back to the animal table. He sat in the chair and watched the animals.

"When I asked you here," he said to Gruff, "I didn't know whether it would work or not. As one poet to another, I must say that you are a magnificent bear."

"No I'm not," said Gruff. "I'm not cuddly and I'm not nice. I'm not a very good bear at all."

"The bear we needed . . . ," Mr. Keeper murmured.

"Not a good bear," said Gruff, "and not a good teacher. I'm not even sure I'm a good poet. "

"Ah hah, " said Mr. Keeper. "I know what ails you. A big job just completed. It is what the sainted Conrad called 'revulsion in the face of the completed fact'. In other words, you've got the blues."

"Times like this," Gruff said helplessly, "you want to call them back and explain what you *really* meant."

"That's teaching," said Mr. Keeper. "Brother, that's teaching, that ain't only poetry."

"Hurts bad enough to be poetry," Gruff muttered.

"Take it from an old hand," said Mr. Keeper, and he looked fondly through the darkening windows to the dark trees beyond. "You don't teach them a thing they'll remember. They are busy growing up, busy with happy and unhappy things like baby brothers. By tomorrow half of them will not even remember you. What they will remember is that when they were kids there was somebody who stood for something. A few will even remember what that something was."

"Poetry."

"Don't crap me with poetry," Mr. Keeper said. "Poetry is nothing but life and love on the hoof. A poet ropes it and takes it and shapes it. What are you, a nihilist?"

"A confused bear," Gruff said. "A bear with a call, and tomorrow morning early a bear who is headed out to some burg on the other side of the state. Farm town. Class in trouble. "

"Lot of Mexican farm laborers over that way."

"I got a little red cape," said Gruff. "Got a goddamn Zorro hat with silver trim. Got a book of Spanish poetry."

"And got the blues," said Mr. Keeper.

"Who learned what?" Gruff looked at the fish tank. "Hey, fish."

There was no answer. The fish were eating fish food.

"I learned something," Gruff said. "I learned something about humility. Not at all sure that's a good thing for a poet to know."

"Think it over for a few years," Mr. Keeper said.

"Meanwhile, you said 'a class in trouble'. Was this class in trouble?"

"Yes. No. I don't know."

"The teacher was in trouble," Mr. Keeper said. "Just as much trouble as you've got now, and for a lot the same reasons."

"Gotcha," Gruff said. "That helps. Maybe that's why I'm headed to the apple and alfalfa belt." Gruff took off his red beret. He handed it to Mr. Keeper. "Yours is kind of fadey," he said apologetically. "Plus I've got that Zorro hat. "

"We'll trade," said Mr. Keeper. He pulled his faded hat from his pocket and passed it to Gruff.

"This hat is full of cigars," Gruff said in an amazed voice. He sniffed. "Fresh cigars."

"For the road," Mr. Keeper said.

The Girl in the Orange Hat

In San Francisco's Golden Gate Park there is an outdoor amphitheatre where a band plays every Sunday in fine weather. My wife and I always attend the concert.

It is a good place. The program is a mixture of classical, folk, show tunes and pop. It does not require great commitment from the listener, serving me as a leisure time before the inanities of the coming week at the gallery. There I will sell noisy art to noisy people, and only occasionally put a dearly bought painting in the hands of someone who respects the work.

A good place. Sea gulls make slanting wheels in the air, squawking and white against a flat and unfathomable blue. There is sound and color; the band, people's chatter, and occasional individual performances on sitar, guitar or flute. Street people come wearing tiny brass bells, beads and round eyeglasses. They tinkle past.

The bandmen's uniforms are black with gold trim and their instruments are gold. The band shell is washed gray concrete. It is framed by the silver and green eucalyptus which rise more than two hundred feet to intercept the wheeling gulls. A concession sells popcorn and hotdogs. There is a picnic smell. It is a large city's aspiration to our memories of small-town bandstands and Saturday nights.

My wife and I bring a blanket to sit on the lawn near one of the high-splashing fountains. Except on very hot days it is a sensual pleasure to be warmed by direct sunlight. We watch each other. At

85

thirty (eight years younger than I) my wife is both beautiful and beautifully proportioned. I can imagine her living in some antique time, sacrificing flowers to Mayan gods. When she dozes on the blanket I sometimes sketch her. Children gather and often wake her with cries:

"Hey, neat!"

"Hey, mister. Draw my dog."

The rest of the people are more sophisticated. They do not trouble us. When my wife wakes it is never to loss. We watch the diversity of people who pass. My wife is a poet. You would easily recognize her name. She is a watcher, a creator whose need to express sometimes confounds me. There is a troubling undercurrent in some of her work. Fear, perhaps, or shyness. At other times she internalizes the world and writes of it indignantly. Her best work is courageous, but sometimes she uses only the courage of compulsion.

Many people at the concerts are old. Pensioners. They sit on benches beneath carefully pruned sycamores that stand in long rows to form a canopy of leaves. Some tourists come, attracted from the nearby Japanese tea garden. Many families attend. There are always girls looking for husbands and men looking for girls. They are shy on these days, perhaps because the band evokes a sense of earlier days which held the strictures of thou-shalt-not. They glance covertly at each other and seem trying to bolster their courage to express mutual longing. The wiser or more desperate girls have pet dogs on leashes. The dogs are good emissaries. Marriages are surely arranged by poodle, dachshund, and beagle.

There is a lonesomeness present. Not lonely. I always believe that the people will be lonely again on Monday morning when they return to their jobs through the big-city traffic. No. Lonesome, which I take to mean as not being at home and not being on loving ground. A great number of people in San Francisco were reared hundreds or thousands of miles away. The westward migration is larger than ever. I look at them and wonder why they came; their only tie to Cleveland or Wheeling, the telephone cables across the Rockies, the familiar handwriting on a letter. Then I think that they had no notion when they came of walking through a park on Sunday, walking through murmuring crowds where their singleness has a Goya starkness; the effect of unmasked sunlight flooding white concrete. They pre-empt the scenery.

Worse, the families are that way. They come together, men and women and children, with dogs and an occasional cat. They move privately and speak of private matters. There is no sense of community. Instead, there is fragmentation so that the crowd becomes units of one with feet that point outward and lips that speak away. I feel these things generally. In the specifics they are not always true. Sometimes there is a special occasion, Irish-American day, Hungarian day. Then there is a feeling of community that makes the starkness of the alone people a special painfulness to watch.

It was that way with the girl in the orange hat. She is a tall girl of slight figure who is eternally twenty-eight because she has not dared to become older.

When we first saw her we were sitting on the lawn. I was sketching. The girl came down steps leading in the direction of the art museum which houses the Brundage collection. The collection is a proud mix of good and bad. See it if possible.

She came slowly, magnificently postured. At first I did not see. My wife directed my attention.

"Look," she said, "Sacagawea. I love her." My wife's inheritance is a mix of Mexican-Spanish-Indian. Enough to help her beauty. Enough also to make her conscious of the beauty in either distinct or modified racial traits. She looks for particularity of beauty.

"Sacagawea was probably short and fat," I told her. "She had white babies." I regretted my speech. My wife's enthusiasm was registering as I spoke. Perhaps the sunlight made my mind lazy. I tried to call it back.

"The lower lip . . . ."

"Is perfect," she told me. We have been married long enough for her to know what constitutes apology. A gift for understanding. Men place trust as well as speak of it when they marry. I understand good fortune.

The girl was splendid. Her heritage probably lay in North Carolina or Oklahoma, if Cherokee. If not, then Creek or from one of the tall and beautiful peoples of the Northeast. I have seen it before, but seldom, the serenity implied by features. Rounded high cheeks, deep eyes, and an unusual small excessiveness about the mouth that is not sensuous but hints of thrill. A classical nose, a fine forehead, she would be a fit subject to be painted by genius. A second rate painter would tremble.

Her hair was black. Soft, long and black. It was the classical notion of Indian hair and she had been good enough to leave it that way. Her color was frail white. Translucent. Third generation. Fourth generation.

"By Indian parents, by parents the same," my wife murmured. "Look at her walk, it didn't come from the avenues."

And it did not. The posture did not come from schoolyard playgrounds where tall girls stoop to their self-consciousness. There was absolute fluidity in the walk. It was as smooth as the joyous movement of an otter.

The girl did not seem joyous. There was a passive reserve. It was not until she passed near and we saw her eyes that we pondered interior questions. Her eyes were dark and intense, eyes that I saw as filled with brooding and confusion. If she painted I would know. The deep things come out and rough up the conception. Even Renoir. The girl passed and was soon lost in the crowd, although for a time we could trace her by the flash of her orange knit dress and the small orange hat low against her dark hair.

"It is necessary to love," my wife said as we walked from the park to find our car. She seemed trying to remain detached but her voice was sad. "We all feel what that girl knows, or most do who have learned to sense as well as think. It's cruel to be alone."

"You always know too much." I smiled and dug for my keys, watching her because she was speaking and because she is beautiful. Her hair is also long. Her hair is dark; deep, and it fills my face when I love her. It fills my mind when I think of her.

"You don't have to meet someone to know them," she said.

She pleases me with story telling. It is her gift.

We drove across Geary, then California, and through the Presidio. There are easier ways to get to North Beach but none better.

"She is more than thirty," my wife said. "She was raised in a small town or near a small town where there was no one except family. It's possible she did not enter school at the proper age. Maybe that still makes her afraid."

"Why?"

"Maybe she had nothing to wear. Perhaps there was no school. There may have been discrimination."

"Of course." From the top of the Presidio the bay was like a blue exclamation above the trees and yellow stuccoed army houses. "Look," I pointed. An aircraft carrier nosed from behind distant buildings, this according to the perspective.

"I know all about her."

"I meant the carrier, they do not come here often."

"I am telling about the girl." Her voice was not pressing, not sharp, and the edge in it was an asking.

"Does it mean that much?" I was surprised.

"Yes. Without you, she is me. Except for a few years of age and some general supposing I've just described what you already know of me."

"And I did not notice." It was alarming. Loving someone, you forget that they have lived beyond you, lived in other places at other times.

"My father was short and half-Mexican and had religion and children."

"His daughter became a poet."

"I take credit for that," she said, "and remember that the truth of a poem is not always consciously in the poet. There are deeper layers of the mind, and some of those layers are hungry."

"The girl has touched you deeply." I spoke quietly. The traffic was very heavy. My attention was constantly diverted.

"What does she want to misunderstand, or not know about people like us?"

"Us?" We were nearly home.

She would say nothing more. I parked the Porsche, we drank cappuccino and went to our apartment. That evening I listened to Bach who is fundamental and good. My wife worked in her room. The next day I went to the gallery.

It was to be one of my most successful weeks. I placed true work that was not bought on speculation. I worked on my copy of a Wyeth. My love is art and Americans make art. Wyeth and Arthur Miller have not been exceeded. I love beauty, an appreciator. That night my wife was absent. She works one night a week in adult education programs.

Aloneness is good sometimes. From our apartment it is possible to see a great part of San Francisco and the bay. With the arguable exceptions of Athens and Madrid it is the most beautiful city in the world.

I stood at the large windows. The bay was purple and green in the last lustre of fading light. The island lay like a stone. From the Marin County side lights began to appear. The Golden Gate, subject of thousands of poor paintings, stood defying paint in the smooth sheen of purpling water. Lights appeared on the Richmond Bridge. Turning, but not moving to the windows on the other side, I could see reflections of light in the tops of a few tall buildings. Our apartment is over the city. It would be necessary to cross the room to gaze into the streets where traffic, sex, and the famous restaurants spelled the occupations and excitements of the nighttime city.

Some of my wife's work lay on a low table. I picked it up. Unfinished. Very abrupt, as she sometimes writes in anger or fear.

> Vacuity sits in state surveying plunder,
> and our lives are spent in dreams of Mercedes,
> of tampered forests with selected trees,
> that complement our roads . . . .

A fragment. We have spoken of this before, there is a bitterness in her about unnatural things that I do not understand. The constructions of men may be either ignored or used. A fine piece of engineering may be an exquisite thing. Precision automobiles are not the same as dishwashers. I do not understand her resentment.

When she returned I was glad. We went out for a late dinner. On the following Sunday we returned to the park.

We arrived early. The park seemed newly washed. Large sprinklers were still watering, the liquid arcs throwing crystal shatterings in the sunlight. We walked through the arboretum, allowing time for the grass to dry and the crowds to gather. My wife was abstracted. I respect her moods. Once, and I did not call her attention, there was a flash of orange far away on a cross path. We were to see the girl a little later.

She arrived about halfway through the band program, and she

arrived with company. A younger man. It made me wish we had gone elsewhere. My wife was stunned.

They came down the same steps, passing between the ornamental plantings that border the short slopes. The flowers were orange and yellow and red. They would have framed her perfectly, except for the man. Her hat was again orange, but a different hat. She wore a light orange suit and she was a gentleness, a contrast to the man.

He was about thirty, dressed in expensive and tasteless clothes, an efficient haircut, and his eyes were not kind. His face was tense. His laugh loud. Doubtless a hard and honest worker; one who knew jokes, and resenting it, told them with near defiance because he did not understand the resentment.

"No," my wife said. She turned to me. "Stop her."

"You can't stop people from talking and walking together."

"I'll stop her." She stood, walked to the couple and spoke to them. The man looked like a plastic pressing of a poor sculpture beside the woman. For one shocking moment I was unable to distinguish between the two women, unable to believe that I knew one less intimately than the other.

The couple was nearly amazed. I am a San Franciscan and know San Franciscans. We may even applaud the unorthodox but we do not intrude on one another. It was slightly embarrassing, and then my wife returned with them. Three outlanders. Two were beautiful.

The girl's name was Marie. I thought of Catholic missions. The man's name was Jim and they had just met.

He appraised me and spoke of his job while watching my wife. I watched both women in turn.

"Have you just arrived in the city," I asked her. The band was playing a march. The man was humming.

"Nearly a year." She was very close. Her accent held touches of the red-neck South that did not match her low and musical voice. There is a vast range of southern accents.

"What do you want?" The man had stopped humming. He was using the 'no nonsense' voice of someone asking a price.

"To talk," my wife said. "Our custom on Sunday is to try to spend some time with another couple." There was a remarkable hatred in her voice. The Spanish intonations never quite leave. It was low, easily misunderstood, but the girl reacted. Watching. The man leaned forward. Interested. Too interested. I guessed his thought and was repulsed.

"Florida," I said, and turned to the girl.

"Kentucky, near the Tennessee line. I have to go now."

"Wait." My wife reached and nearly touched her. "I want to know you and that is a true thing."

"Chicago," the man said, "and before that Indianapolis." The band crashed and cymbaled to a halt.

"How you must miss the mountains." I spoke carefully. "They are not as rugged as our western chain."

"Mountains?" The man was startled. "In Illinois?"

"No." The girl turned from my wife. Her face was tense, hard, and filled with restraint that would otherwise be tears. "They move like waves and they have trees all the way to the top," she said.

She walked rapidly away. The man followed, caught up with her, and together they passed into the crowd and from our view. The band began a blaring show tune. My wife stood quietly.

"They have only just met," I told her. "The girl is searching, not trapping. There is time for judgment."

"There has been time."

"I hope I understand." I folded the blanket and stood beside her.

"I love her for being beautiful. Unique. I love that."

"I love it too. She is like you."

She looked at me and there were tears and gentleness, her soft hair partly obscuring her face. There was something else. My mind was assailed with a sudden horror. There was also a terrifying, a pagan impression of submission.

We walked in silence across the park. Usually I hold her hand because it is warm and narrow and beautiful. On this day I did not hold her hand and it seemed inestimably precious. The girl in the orange hat would be making initial decisions now, decisions that perhaps could be recalled.

"Then I am failing." My voice was low.

"No. There is very much success. Please, let's smile."

She attempted a smile and I took her hand. We found the car and drove tonelessly through the sunlit streets between tall buildings that seemed monuments to easy and countless successes. The traffic was heavy and fast, continuous surprises of brightly painted steel.

The sun reflected from tall columns of a thousand windows where men spoke of stocks and construction and insurance. I wondered, troubling, uncertain for the first time in our lives together. I tried to imagine just what were her inner and most unspeakable sorrows.

Israel and Earnest

THE ROOM WAS COLD AND THE FIRST WIND OF AUTUMN RATTLED THE window and there was death in that wind which was beautiful and also very sad. Shake, shake, went a hand, and then it went rattle, rattle. I moaned and a voice moaned back.

"Depart, Israel," I said. "It is three o'clock in the morning and the truth of that is dark and severe, although, of course, it is also beautiful and very sad."

"Up!" Israel hollered.

". . . when the sun rises. For now it is three o'clock in the morning."

"Moan," he said. (For those who do not know him, Israel is the ghost whose job it is to haunt my house. He haunts my house beautifully and very truly and well. He is wonderfully good at the haunting and we have been through much together).

"That did it," he said. "That did it, that did-dit."

"Did what, hombre?"

He slapped me awake. "You have to quit reading Hemingway before going to sleep," he explained. "And," he added thoughtfully, "you got to get rid of the damn dog."

"Oooof," I added. "At three o'clock in the morning?" I yawned. Then a flicker of white drifted across the room. It was luminescent. It panted as it drifted.

"Arrrr . . ." I screamed, "a Ghost."

"Where?" Israel yelped and made a dive to get under the bed. Israel is scared silly of ghosts.

"There," I shrieked and pointed. The flicker of white slathered and simpered. It drooled and wagged its invisible tail. It seemed to bounce on its hind legs even if it did not have any. Then the flicker of white nuzzled closer and I began to sneeze.

"Oi," Israel moaned. "They fool me too, and there are tons of them. You have failed me once too often, kid. I'm moving."

"Don't leave me," I whimpered. "What is it?"

"Dog shed," he said. "The dog you so proudly brought home is shedding. Explain yourself."

"A long story."

"I have until dawn."

"A friend downtown . . . ." I began.

"Search for the woman," he interrupted.

"All right," I said. "I met a lady friend downtown. She told me that I was a crude man who owned cats and wrote nothing but cat stories. She said I was sarcastic about dogs."

"Is she pretty?"

"They all are," I sobbed. "Even the ones who are dog lovers. Or maybe them, especially."

"You fool," Israel laughed. "You blighted idiot. This is too much." He rolled around on the floor whooping and laughing. "Jerk," he giggled. "So to impress a lady you bought a dog and a bunch of Hemingway novels . . . ."

"Nothing in the books say a word about shed," I protested. "They are brave and true books and they say nothing about shed."

"I've changed my mind," Israel told me. "I'm not leaving. I'm staying around to see you handle this mess."

"I'll handle it all right. Yes sir. No-doubt-about-it." But, I knew I was in trouble. "I'll learn about dogs and write dog stories and all my readers will know that I am fair and just and not simply a friend of cats."

"Two questions," Israel said. "First, what does a Hemingway dog look like?"

"Lean and ranging and intelligent and serious and brave."

"Second question. And you brought home a Samoyed?"

"Yes."

"You see the difference?"

"That's three questions," I protested. "But, yes, I see the difference. At least I see it now."

"Go back to sleep," Israel told me. "Tomorrow I'll teach you to roll over and fetch . . . and how to use a vacuum."

Halloween 1942

I WAS TEN YEARS OLD IN '42, AND TRAPPED IN THE GERMAN-LUTHERAN wilderness of small town Indiana. Halloween of that year still lives in memory because threats of Hell spouted from every pulpit, while true fires of Hell rose above coal and wood-burning chimneys; and a real ghost walked.

In October of '42 our town lay stunned as Hitler, having leveled Europe, marched on Russia. The Battle of Stalingrad thundered; bloodstained symbol of an adventure that would eventually cost a million, six hundred thousand lives. However, that many people, and more, were already dead before the Nazi thrust.

In that Indiana town, where lived many third and fourth generation Germans, our people wisely concentrated their fears and hatreds on Japan. The Rape of Nanking had worked its way into local thought. Bataan had fallen, and government censorship could not conceal the Bataan Death March. Nor could censors hide the battle of the Java Sea. Government news hawks made much of the Battle of the Coral Sea, but its turn-around-significance would not be understood for years. Jimmy Doolittle led a raid on Tokyo, lost men (of whom some were captured and executed as war criminals.) Attu and Kiska in the Aleutians fell to Japan; and Japan took Correigidor.

Difficult memories, these. It is also difficult to separate feelings about WWII from those of localized wars that have happened since. America would lose 33,529 of her people in Korea, above 60,000 in

97

Vietnam; but in this war 406,000 were lost; and that in a nation of 100 million (today we are 267 million.)

In that small town, Halloween usually progressed with boring predictability. Kids went costumed, soaped windows, and youths sixteen years and up tipped over outhouses (yes, many people still had outhouses.) Occasionally, while stealing pumpkins to smash on porches, a miscreant would run into a farmer who carried a shotgun filled with rock salt. The blast tore the salt to dust, and the dust bored beneath skin so that the unlucky target "scratched where it didn't itch" for weeks. But all of that, as I say, was "ordinarily".

On this Halloween there were sixteen-year-olds, but few eighteen-year-olds, and almost no twenties. Those not in the Army were in the Navy, or the Army Air Corps; and it is with the Air Corps, and a piano, and a witch, that this story begins:

My family's across-the-street-neighbor-lady lives in memory as The Widow, for her last name is lost. She was only a little dumpy, wore plain housedresses, and had become reclusive.

She had a son, Darrell, age eighteen, and a daughter, Janine. When he was alive, Darrell made model airplanes that really flew. During my growing-up, and because of the airplanes, he was one of my heroes. He went to war; an early casualty, his bomber blown to bits with no survivors.

To a ten-year-old, Janine seemed ancient, but I now know she could not have been more than twenty. Even in that small town, where—if anybody thought about art they felt threatened—it was known that Janine was a musical prodigy. On soft summer nights, with windows open, she would play ballads instead of classical exercises. Neighbors gathered on porches, watched lightning bugs, and listened to the best musical renditions that most of them would ever hear. After Darrell was killed there were no more ballads, and the music became subdued.

The witch was Mrs. Lydia Kale. She was, it was rumored, nothing but a fearful old country woman moved to town shortly after WWI; angry and bitter from a life spent in a place so small that people walked to church. No one knew why she came. No one cared.

To a ten-year-old she meant fright. Most people, I believe, remember at least one "mean lady" from their childhoods, but Mrs. Lydia Kale really was mean. She would grab a child, shake and mutter. She would even send curses when a kid passed on the sidewalk. She insulted preachers (no one else dared), and she intimidated adults.

She remains a crazed figure, dressed as dark as night wings. Her hair did not flow in the wind; nothing like that. Her hair was as white as her clothes were black, and her hair was worn in a tight knot at the back of her head. No one knew what she hated most.

These, then, were the players in that Halloween when, dressed in an old bed sheet and wearing a "funny face" (our name for mask) I embarked after a warning:

"Do not," my mother said, "go to any house with a gold star." She was adamant.

During that war, families with sons in the service hung small flags in their windows. A silver star on a blue field meant a man still serving. A gold star meant a man dead. Some houses had both kinds.

What does a ten-year-old know? More, I think, than I believed when I sat down to write this small tale. I remember stepping into a wind-blown, leaf-blown night—7 PM but midnight dark—with dry leaves scurrying.

Something was wrong with the night. Other kids trotted past, laughing and whooping. Older kids hid in shadows, soaping windows, or suddenly appearing as they tried to scare each other. A normal Halloween, but something was wrong with the night.

I could not get in motion. I sat on a step at the side of the house feeling "wrong." An adult would say that he felt depressed, perhaps beleaguered. Children did not then know such words.

I finally understood that it was Darrell. He moved out there in the night, standing in his own yard amidst gusts of wind, flying airplanes. I could, but vaguely, see him. I could feel him. I could even feel the balsa wings fight the wind, rise, and rise higher.

And what the hell did I know about death? All I knew was that Darrell would not hurt me. But he was supposed to be gone. Lost, somewhere in the South Pacific.

There came music in the wind, but only gradually. Janine, when at that keyboard, found comfort beyond religion, beyond philosophy. The music began as light finger exercises and light runs, the kind of practice that lifts wings.

They were, brother and older sister, somehow together. I don't know, and never will, if Janine knew what was happening. I do know that for what seemed a long time I sat waiting. The planes rose into the wind, the rubber bands that drove them somehow never unwinding. They flew and flew. Music lifted them; and Darrell was no more than a moving shadow.

I hope Janine knew. I think Janine knew. Because of what happened.

There was music in the wind, a ghost in the wind, and so who needed a witch? And besides, Mrs. Lydia Kale was a daytime witch who never stepped outdoors at night.

Her clothes were black. Only her white hair was a trace of her slow movement through the wind. It came to me that Mrs. Lydia Kale must be very, very old. Music, or Darrell, pulled her forward. Wind, only strong enough to scatter leaves, seemed to press her back. She had to walk a short block, and yet it took awhile.

Twenty-five years before, back in WWI, our nation had lost 116,000 sons. Tales of that war still covered the town. And, Mrs. Lydia Kale walked slow.

It was a night of shadows. On the darkened back porch, and facing the yard where Darrell flew his planes, The Widow appeared. She moved timidly. The Widow was but a dumpy form, a darker shadow among shadows. The music did not crescendo, but began to rise. Some sort of fury, or anger, or sorrow propelled the music; but Janine was already a master. She had it under control.

The shadows came together, but gradually. Mrs. Lydia Kale walked along the sidewalk, while in the yard the planes rose. I think she saw nothing. I think she wanted to see nothing. The Widow stepped from the back porch, moving slowly to the sidewalk. In that dark night the two forms came together. I could only see the white hair of Mrs. Lydia Kale. It seemed, to a child, that there was but one person out there, white-haired.

I do not know why Darrell appeared, and can't say exactly when he left. Mystery lived in the night, and the two women who seemed to have become only one woman, stood silent. From the house the music became, for a few moments, tender. That must be when Darrell left.

And then the music began to weep. It filtered through the night, through wind, and across the street to ten-year-old ears. The three women held the night, or pressed it back. The young woman wept above her keyboard, wept with her keyboard. The two older women simply held each other and wept.

The Forest Ranger

THE VIEW FROM THE FREEWAY WAS EXCELLENT. BEYOND THE DUSTY trees, mottled and sickly from either fumes or disappointment, lay a narrow strip of San Francisco Bay on which cast-off bottles bobbed and shimmered softly in the diminishing light. The sunset would be sickening.

Near the water was an auto wrecking yard, a big one that processed junkers wholesale; stomping and kicking and mashing and baling them to be stacked on railway flatcars. It was instructional. No fewer than seventy klunks were fitted on each car, like multicolored cans of anchovies. He had been counting them for half an hour.

Traffic moved. He pressed the accelerator and rolled forward twelve feet. He figured that the evening commuter jam was breaking. Only fifteen minutes ago he had moved five feet. He savored the recollection. It had given him a good look at the baler.

With the daily salvation in sight he sat thoughtfully; distinguished, holding down the seat of the Brooks Brothers. He sat in the expensive automobile. He sat listening attentively to the imported radio that was not playing. It was buzzing. He had tuned out the helpful helicopter announcer who advised him to avoid the only road that led home. The idea almost made sense. He tuned back to the station. The announcer was still speaking of congestion. This time it was of the eliminatory tract. He reflected that it was a long way between filling stations and wriggled uncomfortably in his seat. Then he tuned the announcer out and chuckled. A man well under forty should learn exquisite control of all things . . . the girl in the car next to him smiled. He decided that she should go topless.

The parking lot lunged forward. It was dazzling. He was nearly past the baler now and thinking of Yellowstone. The park. Ten years ago, a kid, he had wanted to be a forest ranger. His old man had encouraged him. His old man had been in the insurance game and must have known. Who ever heard of an uptight bear? A squirrel in the wrong bag? What in the hell had happened to them? Him? His old man? In spite of his bladder he chuckled again.

He chuckled with the secret glee of a man content to know an impending revenge, a man to whom the rage of an outraged wife was a trifle. She suspected him of an affair. He allowed her to believe that. It was much cleaner than working with the truth. Besides, he was afraid of making counter-accusations. Maybe only birds and elephants mated for life.

Revenge. He rolled the flavor of the antique word across his tongue. It tasted good. He was now a man. He wondered why automobiles were not fitted with chamber pots. Then he marveled again at the magnificent luck that had served to bring him the means of stunning violence; the means to be the prime adulterer of a way of life that understood adultery to be as healthful as breakfast cereal. His name was Arthur. It had been for three months. Before that it had been Art. He thought on the old days. They were disgusting. Art and Arthur were both fed up.

Three months. Three little months since the huge moving van had pulled up to his door to gulp his possessions; piano, fishing rods, bed (dismantled, dismasted, depleted), rugs, pictures, college artifacts, tables, television, books, record player, potted plants, objects d'art, all . . . gobbled into the maw of the fathomless, unfathomable giant.

He had spoken to the driver. Wiry man. Tough. No fat. "You'll take good care . . . ."

"Of everything," the driver told him. "Except the potted plants. We don't ever guarantee the potted plants."

"The wife . . . ."

"She rides with you."

"Yes," he had admitted, and turned to the truck which fascinated him. "Big."

"Fifty feet long. Over three thousand cubic feet capacity. Up to forty-two thousand gross." The driver had been proud of his machine. They walked through the empty rooms, checking to see that nothing had been left.

"You see a lot of road?"

"Eighty, maybe a hundred thou a year. You going into the business?"

The thought startled him. "No, going to California. Bucked for one grade and got promoted two. Nice surprise. Going to California. Twenty thousand a year."

"Yeah," the driver shook his head in commiseration. "Won't make more myself. But," he brightened, "it's been an off year."

"Can you make that much?" He had been incredulous.

"Sure. But lots of road. Never home. Fella like you it's different. Good money and home every night."

"Uh huh," he said, trying to feel a good-bye. The trees beyond the window were bare. Sterile. The house was empty. There were no whispers. "Listen," he asked, "is it nice there like they say? A little peace . . . ."

"They grow artichokes," the driver told him.

The truck had continued to fascinate him. He and his wife drove the new automobile coast to coast. During most of the first day he stayed with the truck. His wife wanted to check up on the trucker's driving. It was a relief. On the second day he was sleepy and pulled over early.

His wife protested. "If a little guy like him can go, why can't . . . ."

"They take dope," he had offered hopefully, knowing that it was going to be a pretty long trip.

The traffic moved. Two whole car lengths. He checked his watch and congratulated himself on his progress. He was either ten minutes or fifteen hundred feet ahead of schedule.

The trip had started long. At about Minnesota it had shortened. His wife had loved him again by Minnesota. They had taken time to explore the country and ended by exploring each other. Like back in college and then later when they were married.

"Please," she had said. "I love you," she had said. He thought a lot about Minnesota.

In California the biggest change was the weather. That, and artichokes were plentiful. His job was more responsible. He had to push hard from the first. It filled his life. Later there was time for a drink before lunch. The clubs were a little more liberal. The women, maybe. He still went home every night. Now he drove. No more commuted trains. The prestigious new car was a joy on weekends when there was a chance to drive in the hills. Sometimes his wife accompanied him. She was very busy. Clubs, entertainment, art lessons, politics. She no longer said please.

He tried Reno, then Tahoe. His wife loved both, the excitement, the crowds, the color, the gambling. He decided that she was a bum. In New York it had been bridge. In the west it was nickel slots. A take down. A come down. A bust.

And prices were high. Lord, Lord how high were prices. He started bucking for the next grade and thought of a mistress. In shopping he found that even the idea was expensive.

Far past the baler now. Soon there would be a gentle curve. Sunset would find him overlooking the sanitary landfill. Traffic settled into a reluctant five-mile crawl; hesitating, sometimes speeding up, making conforming ripples of start, stop, brakelight and screech.

It was really the traffic that got him. Finally, he had to admit that it was really the traffic. People were about the same. His wife had returned to New York Normal. But he was not the same. Something of him responded to the mountains, looked toward the sea, remembered Minnesota.

And the traffic never ceased. Once, returning home from an ordinary party at 3 AM on a Tuesday he had waited five minutes before daring to cross a street. Traffic. Traffic.

He remembered the truck wistfully. The driver. A hundred thousand miles a year. A hundred thousand. One night with pencil and paper he figured that he would drive to work and home not less than fifteen hours a week, fifty weeks a year. Seven hundred fifty hours. More than thirty days. Twice his vacation. In that time he would cover, well, he would cover almost five thousand miles. There was no question of moving from the high-speed, commute community and expensive house. The office would peg him a loser. He thought about the truck. One day, glancing through the classified, he had seen an ad which explained how he, too, could be a Big Rig Man. The idea was loathsome.

What he needed was a cabin in the forest. Deer playing. A stream. Trees. Maybe a farm. Sunlight. A loving woman. The bit.

His wife was blonde. He thought a lot about brunettes. Thought on thought. Passion unexpended. He clipped the ad and shuddered. It was several days before he understood his motives.

He planned a final gesture. Perverse. The highest violence he could conceive. Then he and his blonde wife could leave forever. There were other ways to live, other places; Australia, Iowa, Manitoba. Maybe she would go with him. There was some money saved. Some. They could cash in the insurance. Maybe she would not go with him. It was the traffic that was the cause, or maybe it was the traffic that was fruition. There is no race when the rat won't run.

On the following Saturday he had gone to the driving school. Monster trucks stood around. The biggest one . . . . "That one," he said to the friendly proprietor who eyed his check with the same cold eye he turned on the nineteen dollar lite-weight casuals. "Call me Art," he explained timidly to the honest proprietor.

"Not that one," the man explained. He pointed to a different truck. "That one's for beginners. You start there if you aim to bust gears."

The truck had been old and small, but homey. It smelled of stale tobacco, sweat, and things discarded from lunches carried in paper bags. In a single lesson he had learned all ten gears and how to shift them. His shift was lumpy. On the following week he returned. His shift improved. In three weeks he could drive but not maneuver. He needed to know how to maneuver.

"You're really serious, fella." The man was even more friendly: the checks were clearing. "What the hell," he grinned. "Take out the big one."

A concession. An advancement. The big one turned out to be easier than the smaller one. When he backed it made a longer lever, easier to judge. There was a great feeling of fascination and satisfaction. His bank statement showed checks to M. Jones for services. His wife began talking of people named Marie and Muriel. He could not explain and was afraid to challenge. She seemed very busy, desperately busy, yet there were some things for which anyone could make time . . . not that he cared. That was the trick. Care only for the drama and a decent exit.

Twice he left work on some pretext, learning how to drive, how to jack the huge van down simulated alleys, against simulated curbs, through simulated mountain passes which were perfectly flat but horribly curved. He was an apt student. He was awarded a degree.

They offered to find him a job. He refused. He did not want to drive a truck. He only wanted to *know how* to drive a truck. The plan. Maybe his wife would not go with him.

He speeded up because traffic speeded up. Now his car was going thirty. Soon he was up to forty. Then he came to the correct ramp and turned for home, the auto lights searching through the early darkness. The new car was a good car but lately it seemed puny. His big rig degree (hidden between leaves of *Games People Play*) was warranty against the smallness of life. It was insurance. It was power.

When he arrived home there was a note. He was to meet his wife for dinner and a party. He had forgotten about that party. To dress was a matter of minutes. To shave was a matter of deliberation, then planned forgetfulness. Hipster, hip . . . he would grow a beard and wear lumberjack shirts. He was tired. He wanted to sit in the sun, wanted to get quietly loaded, wanted, wanted. Instead he allowed himself a quick one before returning to the car and broaching the evening.

Coming from the drive he waited for a car to pass. Then he waited for another car to pass. Then he entered traffic and decided that tomorrow was the day. Tomorrow was Friday. Fridays were excellent days for endings. At the party he would drink with care. A sure hand.

At the party his wife was cool. Maybe the forgotten shave. Maybe the bank statements. His wife danced three times with a chubby man named Vernon. Trucker Art drank. He watched the shapeliness of his wife and refused to worry. There was no affair after all. If she was looking, she had found no one yet.

No affair. Vernon used the same freeway, worked the same hours. No time. Trucker Art fuzzily mulled a vague sorrow for Vernon who was never going to make out, either. Then he felt an absolute sorrow for himself. It felt like New York. It did not feel like Minnesota. He was a little over his limit when they went home and slept.

"Today," he said when he woke up.

"Don't wake me," she told him. "Why today?"

"It's past time."

"I agree. You woke me up. Time for what?" She put her hand against his face.

He checked his watch on the nightstand. He was a little behind schedule. Everything must look normal. Nothing must go wrong. Nothing. "Go back to sleep," he told her.

She went back to sleep. No breakfast. He swilled coffee and orange juice. Smoked cigarettes. He got in his car and drove for an hour and a half; checked into the office; checked out of the office. "Later," he told the receptionist with neat ankles who looked as if she hoped for a double meaning.

"Liar," he told himself and looked at his desk before he left. Wife's picture, she smiling. Pretty when she smiled. Embossed desk set. Monogrammed pen given by former secretary on his promotion. Lucky piece. Clutter. Crap. He slipped the picture into a pocket and went down to his car. "Sentimentalist," he told himself. "Fool. She will throw you out."

He paused to light a cigarette. He squinted over the tilted butt, looking at the executive parking lot through smoke. "I am a desperate man," he told himself, "the next Vernon will be someone without a commute."

He paused again. Surprised. "So that's the reason, after all. Not revenge. The grand gesture and leave? No. The big wake-up and win, or throw and crap-out."

He climbed in the car reading the sign that shimmered from his imagination across the windshield. *One Owner Repo—Take Over Payments.* It was a beautiful car. He thought that he would miss the car. He started the engine and drove aimlessly, across cable car tracks, through the beautiful park, into the chatter of Chinatown and the erotica and pizza of North Beach. The beautiful city. Well, he would miss those parts. But on the other face he had been missing them anyway. At two-thirty he changed to working clothes in a service station. At three o'clock he was at the rental agency to keep his appointment.

It was a huge truck. The instrument of question, after all, and not of revenge. It was a premium instrument. Fully as long as the mover's. Fifty feet. Fifty feet. It stood grumbling on the readyline, huge, snouty. He did not want a tilt cab. Long. A conventional. Long.

The gears came in smoothly and made him proud. He moved into traffic, standing high above traffic. Look down. Cars going by. Girls' knees, fat men's paunches, kids waving from rear windows, yappy dogs. And smooth, those gears. He made the freeway easily and thought that it was not bad at three o'clock. The traffic was heavy like always, but moving. He wheeled the rig like an expert. The traffic was moving too well. It threw him ahead of schedule. He slowed down and a cop tailed him. A speed up and the cop passed. He slowed down again. Cars crackled around him blatting horns. He was afraid one would run under the trailer.

With the speed back up the schedule was shot. He entered the approach to the main bridge that carried traffic for half of the city. The bridge that handled eighty thousand cars a day. The bridge that was a whole five lanes wide. It was a beautiful bridge. A man could buy a postcard . . . .

He paid his toll and continued across the bridge to drive into the hills. The engine roared big against the grades. He downshifted the gears. The hills spilled wild flowers. The speed caused a tiny vibration in his driving mirror that glinted sunshine. He played with the giant and enjoyed the exhaust crack, coasting hills, tapping the brakes to hear them hiss, testing the air horns. He liked it more than any car. Very comfortable. Easier to handle at speed. He confidently turned it around and played all the way back to the bridge where he entered the ramp headed back into the city.

He decided to do it immediately. He slowed.

Traffic boomed around him. He was blocking the curb lane at five miles per hour. He slowed to a stop. Traffic backed up behind him. He cut the wheel hard left and eased the cab across the next lane. Traffic backed up more. Loud honking. He checked and then eased the truck into an oncoming lane. The trailer was huge in his mirrors, swinging across two lanes while the cab blocked the third. Traffic screeching and trying to by-pass. Ease across the fourth lane. Violent yelling. Screeching of brakes. No bumps.

He pulled straight across the bridge to block all five lanes. Pandemonium.

The cops would come. The getaway was important. He had to hurry. He climbed down and locked the cab. Maybe someone would leave a car and attack him. No one did. "Sheep," he told the rapidly lengthening line of cars, "Lemmings." He raised the hood to the accompaniment of crying horns and took the distributor cap. He threw it and the key into the bay. The two miles of bridge were nearly full. Cars turning around, trying to go back. Dinged fenders. Hollering. He looked at the truck. It was a beautiful truck. It was a beautiful bridge. They looked good together.

He checked his watch. Four-thirty. Going home time.

He stepped to the pedestrian walk to stroll from the bridge. A breeze caught his hair and he smiled in the din of horns. Far out on the bay a white glint of afternoon sun came from a billowing sail. The sea. The hills.

He wondered what his wife would do. As he walked beside the magnificent view, in triumphant parade before the salutation of horns, he found himself framing arguments that would persuade her to leave with him.

The Curious Candy Store

CITIES ARE NOT SUPPOSED TO HAVE ALCOVES, BUT PLACID CITY DOES. The Curious Candy Store still stands two blocks from our old grade school, and the school itself stands in what amounts to an alcove. When any of us return we feel that we step across time. Traffic buzzes everywhere, until we cross the centerline of Maple Street and our feet find the inner curb.

In this place it might as well be 1930, or 1910. Victorian houses stand newly painted. Outside one house a bronze deer ornaments a huge lawn behind wrought iron fences. Summer breezes lay light fingers on mown grass, and the breezes touch ornamental stained glass windows as if everything here were kissing cousins.

At the Curious Candy Store the old woman who always ran the place stands still behind the counter. By anybody's reckoning, she must be a hundred and thirty years old by now. That isn't right, but unless time itself is playing games we know it's the truth.

Children still enter, and they emerge with licorice whips, jawbreakers, lemon drops, stick candy, and occasionally a balloon. I remember the magic of childhood, and remotely recall the day I left the candy store with my own balloon. The balloon was red and bouncy in a breeze that danced fancy figures around the grade school. The day was filled with autumn light.

A red balloon. No child was ever given more than one, and for reasons we did not understand red was a little scary. Green was good, and blue might be, sometimes. I think we feared—even if we did not look over our shoulders—the yellow ones and the white ones. We were hopeful with orange. Who, after all, remembers their fears at age six? Older and tougher kids on the playground always yelled about gray and black balloons, but in our day no one ever saw one.

But those days of my childhood, before World War II, were not so complicated as days are now. It was still easy to recognize magic during the long summers and autumns. Many families did not even have radios, and televisions were unknown. Since it was the time of the Great Depression children had few toys. We played 'make believe'. So much of our play came from our own imaginations that it was no surprise if a balloon talked to you in a tinkling voice.

"Dum hiddly dee-dum, play as you grow. Red is so chancy, it's scary, you know?"

I am an old man now, visiting an old neighborhood, and watching children pass. The Curious Candy Store sells bubble gum and baseball cards and malted milk balls.

"It's color, it's color, it's color, you see. Play always with color, oh hum diddle dee."

Most of the balloons popped, of course. A few of them got loose and went tumbling into blue sky. Even fewer made it to home or school, where they either burst or slowly deflated.

I grew and became an artist, never an easy task. Color and light and depth ran through my dreams. There were years and years of struggle, and yes, the color red is chancy. Color itself—or rather playing with color—can lead you through divorces and booze and decades of rejection. At the end lies great success, but one travels a badly cobbled road.

Some led vanilla lives, those who received the white balloons. They grew and married and loved and worked and had children. Nothing really bad ever happened to them, and perhaps they were luckiest of all. Blue was considered good, sometimes, and blue balloons slipped from the fingers of future teachers and politicians. Green showed the way to actors and gardeners. Orange produced musicians, businessmen, interior decorators. We all grew and left the neighborhood, but some return.

I think time freezes in a few small places around the globe. There's nothing cosmic about it, and there's no grand scheme. In spite of what our scientists say, time has a way of doing what it wants.

Sometimes it wants to be fey. This is surely the way that time hoards up memories. Maybe in Egypt, somewhere, scholars still write on scrolls. Perhaps in China one small section of the Great Wall stands newer than new.

And so this neighborhood is a place where time collects memories. The balloons contained our futures. I know that now, because of all the things that have happened. Rather, the balloons carried the spirits of who we might become. A lot depended on us.

However, there is more to it than that. The old woman at the Curious Candy Store still gives balloons. Children pass with grave faces and grave eyes.

When I entered the store after fifty years away, it seemed smaller. The oak counter was the same, and the gleaming candy jars still stood ranked like soldiers. Kites and kite string were arranged in bins. Party favors and tin whistles, and the little tin crickets, lay in careful arrangement on shelves. Pink and blue packages of birthday candles were stacked beside crepe paper streamers of gold and silver. The ceiling was lower than I remembered, and soft sheens of polished oak and glowing glass stirred childish memories. I felt yearning, and a kind of dazzlement before the sight and smells of candy fish and peppermints.

Only one thing had changed. There were different candies. Of course, these are different times, and I suppose children are never horrified by candy. There were other things. What I took to be baseball cards were cards of a different kind, men with red staining their beards. Comic books were different, which surely meant that childhood was different.

"Go away," the old woman said, as she squinted in dim light and finally seemed to recognize me. "You can't come back here. Why would you want to?"

She looked the same. Her white hair was bound in a gypsy scarf, and her long dress was faded purple with carefully ironed pleats. Eyes, brown as the chocolate she sold, were not unkind, only factual. Her hands were nimble, and her face was webbed in wrinkles.

"You were old when my father was a child," I said in bewilderment. I felt in the presence of mystery, but maybe the mystery could be solved. "Is there some eternal game you are forced to play?" I asked.

"Are you trapped here?" Kindness and concern brought layers of gentleness to my voice.

"I will be here when your great-grandchildren are old," she said. Her voice was not angry, only sad. "You should not be here. You grew up and lost your childhood. Will you now insist on losing your childhood memories?"

"I only inquire."

"You inquire in the wrong place," she told me. "There's only one future to a customer, and you've had yours. Be content."

"There are changes here."

"I'm a merchant," she said. "I stock what sells." She turned away, dismissing me.

I should have left then. Only a fool would stay. "You are more than a merchant."

"You should leave," she said, "but since you have not . . . " She rubbed her forehead, just below the line drawn by the scarf. The woman was not unkind, only dispassionate. "I am time incarnate," she told me. "I *am* memory. You deal with powerful forces."

Memories of childhood surrounded me. Reminders of childhood lay on shelves; jump ropes and balsa model kits. I felt overwhelmed by the magic and play that are never far from a child's mind. I felt the hopes and fears of a child—small hopes and fears in adult memory, but they were not small at the time. The memories began to grow.

"You sell memories," I said, and pointed to some of the candy and cards. "These are not good memories."

"They are the best memories still in stock," she said curtly. "I didn't make the world, I only live in it."

Later, I would realize that her very curtness was a denial of memories. It denied gentle fingers of wind caressing grass, of my mother's voice calling me home from play as night fell. Of course, these days, even in this quiet neighborhood, children are no longer allowed to play outside in the gathering dusk.

"If you can work small miracles, if you can give away spirits of the future, I could hope the children would have better futures."

"I give the only futures that are available." She looked through the small front window onto the quiet street, the seemingly quiet neighborhood. "There are no simple futures now. Including what is left of yours." She paused, watching me, and she was neither kind nor unkind. "Although if you leave your own memories here, maybe I can turn them into some child's future."

I went away quickly. When you are old, memories are what you own.

But I did not leave quickly enough. These days I remember that I once had memories, and even what they were. A creaking swing on the front porch. A schoolmate practicing piano, and the notes of the piano on a warm evening breeze. I no longer remember how the memories felt. Hope is gone, as is excitement. Love has disappeared, and when I place paint to canvas no spirit rises from the work. It is only paint and canvas.

And so I sit, an old man, shuddering as I watch children pass. Their balloons carry colors unknown in my time: fluorescents of hot pink, hysteric pastels of beige and turquoise, and not a primary color in the lot.

There are gray balloons, and there are black. Black balloons dance in the breeze.

I wonder what the balloons are whispering, and feel the horror of those futures; the only feeling I have left. I watch because, maybe, fashioned from flimsy and from my own lost memories, perhaps a last brightly dancing balloon will pass.

LAND

"My grandpa, my drinking grandpa, not the preacher, came to these parts just after the Civil War. The land was taken. He married a widow to get land. She had almost two sections. It's a good thing, I guess. He would have killed to get land.

"I like to think of him. Scandalous old rip. He started a little general store down by the crossroads. There's a town there now. Made a living off the store and a fortune off the land.

"Caused scandal too. Use to have a little two-horse rig, surrey painted red and white like a circus and ran a matched tandem that never saw a plow. Ran it into town, the horses stepping high and easy, pocking along the road out there which would have been dust in those days. The horses were white, of course, and the leather was deep worked and beautiful, decorated in red. You can see yourself how it would have been, them horses, head high and pulling that dinky little rig.

"Take it into town, the horses snorting and that rig gleaming like he'd captured the sun. Pull it up in front of the courthouse like an English squire. People flock around. Him blowing and taking on, making like it wasn't nothing. Then, by and by, he'd disappear and you could bet some family had trouble. Awful good man with the girls, my grandpa was. Awful bold. Painted his fence posts white and gave them red caps of barn paint. Caused about as much scandal as his women.

"But my dad was different. Loved the land just as much, kind of hated the store and so after while it went down hill. He never took much after grandpa. Steady man. Use to hitch up a team once a month and drive it into town. He'd bring back the news and supplies to sell in the store. I still remember cracker barrels, tub cheese; still remember.

"And I like to think of my dad, like I like to think of grandpa. But I picture him different, of course. Like to think of that old, old man as a young man, getting up on a clear morning, the taste of morning on his tongue and going out to the barn. Chilly morning maybe, frost hanging out across the fields like fallen fog. Him harnessing his work team to a spring wagon and heading into town.

"Sun coming up, burning off the frost, and my dad would sit behind that team, maybe not even driving because he owned good horses. Sitting there watching birds rise off a field where somebody had put in wheat. A quiet time. You know, he never questioned. Married, maybe happy, but never had to ask. There was only one thing he could be.

"Well, I ramble. You want to farm. Get your land and you'll still need twenty thousand dollars. Don't believe a man can do with less just starting from scratch. But, it needs more than that. More than that. There's the feel of things.

"I kind of see the land sometimes. Like in my head. And I've been on this land sixty-seven years. See it. Especially times like now. Crops worked, land lying healthy but resting, and you know it's healthy because you've worked and schemed it all out, what you'll do.

". . . like a crop I had in the early forties. Corn so high in the rich places that you walked through it like a forest. Twelve, fourteen feet tall. No corn like that now. Better yield but not so tall.

"No, you wait. I'll get there. You come here with money and a hunger in your eyes. I've seen it. Seen it, and men do get impatient. I'm tryin' to tell you.

"You go look at your fields. I know mine. Some land works easier than others. You get a kind of gentle, easy strip down a field, or maybe a whole field that's like it wants to be turned. Field right beside can be a bastard. Work it up, fertilize, refertilize . . . nothing you do will make that field match the one across the road. Nothing but a road between. Before the road it was all the same.

"Yes, I know them. Wander through them like my dad used to when he worked the land. Sometimes it's like he lingered, you know. Old. Old when he died.

"And my grandpa. He built the barn with my dad helping after the first one burned. Lost most of their feed that year. Animals slaughtered against waste because grandpa wasn't going to neighbors for feed. Stiff-necked. Proud. I don't remember him too well.

"Well, you want to buy and I'm old now. Yes, I admit. You drove all this way to talk. Give an old man a minute more.

"I see him, you know. Sometimes on the land it's like I see him, bending down maybe to clear something from a fencerow, or walking past the grove. Remember him young, like when he was teaching me. Full of interest. Full of plans. Coming in tired of a night. Not like later when he was sick . . . he got sick. Kind of took the starch out. Lingered awhile and then he died.

"I'm kind of sorry you came. I thought . . . well, don't keep many animals now. When the boys were here. But, there's no sense in that. Two good boys and both of them gone. One in Bridgeport, the other in Sarasota. Educated boys, but good ones too.

"I don't know. I'm sorry you came. I thought I could sell. Thought it all out and said, 'Yes, you must,' but I guess I can't. I'll give you the name of a fella I know. Hard up. Place run down a little. Maybe he'll deal. Mister, I'm sorry, I just can't sell this land."

Resurrection

Take the path behind the Kingdom Hall, the path circling back into blackberry bushes and scrub and trees—where on most mornings gray mist hangs in the tops of young fir and old madrona—and there is a clearing where most evenings a solitary man talks with dead neighbors. His name is Em, he is sixty. He always has a white dog with him. Some folks say he has two.

Lona-Anne-Marie is the only one who knows all Em's movements. Lona-Anne-Marie is stove up with eighty years, and with thirty years of doorbelling, and tracts, and waiting the awful coming of a resurrecting God. She lives in a wonderland of faith. The waiting makes her beautiful. She is wrinkled and tiny and clothed in repaired things bought for a quarter at thrift shops. She can walk a little, but mostly she sits in her kitchen and watches the neighborhood. When summer sun is vague in this Pacific Northwest mist, it falls in silverish-yellow pebbles across the roof of Kingdom Hall. It isn't hard to imagine the Angel Gabriel standing astride the roof. Even we who have our doubts can think him there.

"The world is getting old and Em is aging," Lona-AnneMarie explains. "The world is holding up pretty well, all things considered."

Behind the Kingdom Hall, and dug in beneath sheltering blackberries, lies a private cemetery. Somebody's people were buried in vague and unremembered graves: John, another John, Sarah, Esther, Timothy. The whole business sits on a bluff; and, off to the left, deer and raccoon and a black bear inhabit a deep ravine that angles down to the salt water of Puget Sound. Before young trees grew, before blackberries covered them over, those five graves looked eastward at the Sound, like planted sailors pointing boots toward the sea. A homestead once stood where now stands a broken chimney. The people died of illness. Madrona trees seeded. Some of the madrona are seventy or eighty years; hard to tell. Madrona doesn't grow like other trees. You can't count the rings.

Our neighborhood is small. A little block of apartments anchors the head of the street. People move in, then move out. Clunkity cars with mattresses strapped to roofs arrive and leave like aging gypsies. The cars are many-colored, like Joseph's coat frayed after years in one or another desert. Each time the paper mill hires or fires, people reshuffle. Faces of school children are exchanged for other schoolish faces. Beside the apartments sits Nancy's prim and puffy house with yellow shutters. The children call her 'the mean lady', and children know.

"Nancy has such a pretty name," Lona-Anne-Marie ponders, sometimes to Nancy. "A body has to wonder what went wrong."

Across from Nancy's sits the ramshackle house of Jim and Lois, although Jim now lives at Odd Fellows Cemetery; he's dead these three years. Winter, summer, every week, Lois carries flowers to his grave. The ramshackle is crowded with junk on three floors. Jim collected stuff. Beside Nancy's house is the smallest house in the neighborhood, which is Lona-Anne-Marie's, and beside that, a vacant lot where a poetic lady from the apartments in years past strowed some seed. The lot is all grass and weeds and the lady's poppies, purple and red and orange and white.

Em's house sits across from Lona-Anne-Marie. Beside Em sits the nice little place with Pete and Mona. They're retired. Then comes two more vacant lots. Kingdom Hall comes at the end of the street. Beyond the Hall's parking lot there is nothing but trees, and the private cemetery; and, when the wind is wrong, the mill's smell.

"Em is learning something about graves," Lona-Anne-Marie explains, sometimes to Em. Em visits her when he's not working. "Em is learning that between the living and the dead there ain't no difference." Lona-Anne-Marie chuckles, like she was the only snapdragon in a bed of asparagus. We figure Lona-Anne-Marie can be so sure because she has eternity locked. She likes patched blue housedresses, red sweaters, the coming rebirth of the world, and garage sales. She likes children from the apartments, and she likes the overweight and worried mothers who come looking for kids. Lona-Anne-Marie's hair is whiter than Em's dog. That's white.

"Are we old and wise," Pete says, "or only old?"

"Ask me stuff like that, I'm gonna Witness." For Lona-AnneMarie wisdom belongs somewhere in the heavens. It may descend to earth on Sunday mornings.

Through the neighborhood conversation flows. What's said to Em is later heard by Pete. Lois talks to Lona-Anne-Marie, then Nancy hears. Lona-Anne-Marie tells Nancy to stop acting mulish. About that, Mona hears. We don't talk behind the others' backs. Talk circulates like a family.

When his first dog died Em supposed himself in many ways a fool. Nancy agreed. Lona-Anne-Marie said things would mend. Pete was sympathetic. Mona worried. Lois is youngest, being fifty-eight. She baked pies.

It was not a dog that should have been in business. He was happy-go-sloppy, a dog that rode in Em's old truck. Em peddles. He sells and trades: chainsaw parts and magazines. Rope and tack and tools and books and notions. The truck sags with wants and needs and used up dreams. It carries useful stuff and other people's junk. Before Jim died, a lot of trading went on between Jim and Em.

That dog, and Em, and truck made quite a picture. The truck is more-or-less a Ford, but improved. Used to be a milk truck painted green. Funny color for a milk truck. Em is skinny and hawk-nosed, frowzy like the truck. He wears work clothes. The dog was shiny white, a curly tail. They held conversations, people heard. Em never even sings in church, but in that truck he sang a monotone. The dog would whine and woof. Em is modest. He never bragged except about the dog. He claimed he traded out a five-buck Chevy carb. "Best five-dollar dog I ever owned," he'd say, and he was lying.

It was the *only* dog he'd ever owned. Like a fool, he guessed it to live forever. Inexperience can hurt.

"How can people live when they lose children," Em asked Lona-Anne-Marie. "Because this was just my dog and I can't stand it."

"Depends on who does the losing," Lona-Anne-Marie told him. "Creation's perfect, people ain't."

"I don't know what that means."

"Let's hope you never do," Lona-Anne-Marie told him. "I never met a man so like a child."

After burying the dog beneath an apple tree, Em took up playing pool. He hung around the bars.

"He'll bring a floozy home. Expect that next." Nancy is ironhaired and skinny, but chesty. Claims nobody sees her nicest parts. This shocks Mona, tickles Lois. Lois kind of slid while Jim was dying. Got overweight. A florid smile with painful eyes. She drinks a little. Mona dyes her long hair brown. It looks nice. Tiny women don't much show their age.

"It's like he's still around," Em said to Lona-Anne-Marie. "Like he don't want to leave . . . all in my mind, of course."

"Don't count on it. You think the world's that simple?"

"It always was before," Em said. "I may retire. I'll get myself a cat and settle down. Learn to fly a rocking chair."

"Don't do it," Pete told Em when word got round. "It only *sounds* like fun." Pete is tall and sixty-eight, skinny and baldheaded. He fished for a living. Now he fixes and refixes on his house. The way that man can go through paint. Gallons.

Em went through a phase. Talking to his dog. With morning mist above the Kingdom Hall, Em walked the path that leads down to the graves. The dog went with him. Invisible, of course. "C'mon, mutt-dog," Em would say, and off the two walked among the trees.

"He wants a padded cell." Nancy claimed that Em was going nuts.

"He wants a woman," Lois said.

"And that's the man who says he'll get a cat? He wants another dog." The paper comes out once a week. Mona started reading classifieds.

"He's got a dog," Lona-Anne-Marie told Mona. "Tarry awhile on those puppy ads."

"He wants to give up pool and get to work." Pete figured Nancy was close to being right. He figured Em's brains were moon-scuffed. "I've seen ten-year-olds with better sense."

"I've lost people who I didn't miss as much," Em confided to Lona-Anne-Marie. "Pretending makes it better though." Em went back to work. Each morning when he climbed into his truck, he held the door until the dog jumped in. The whole thing looked natural. Lois claimed she nearly saw the dog.

"If that's the way to handle grief I'm going to try," Lois told Lona-Anne-Marie. "I'll walk through all my rooms and talk to Jim."

"There goes the neighborhood," Pete said when he was told. "This place is gonna be a loony bin."

"The preacher says that dogs don't have a soul," Em told Lona-Anne-Marie. "I think of changing churches."

"It's what you get for being Methodist."

Lois' health improved. She cut back on wine. She no longer carried flowers to Jim's grave. Autumn came with autumn rains. The path behind the Kingdom Hall became a swamp. Fat blackberries of August turned to September blue and purple pulp, while mist ran rivers through the stand of trees. We fed our woodstoves, looked toward the rain; salvation. Boot and slicker weather. Folks who love the sun don't like it here. We get a lot of wet. We get a lot of winter.

Em still walked his dog along the path. Then Jim and Lois joined them. Three people and a dancing dog, the living and the dead.

"It's getting out of hand," Pete said to Nancy.

"Maybe so," said Lona-Anne-Marie, "but Lois has quit drinkin."

Lona-Anne-Marie is rarely puzzled. When resurrection's certain, not much else is going to fool you. Still, Lona-Anne-Marie was thinking. The rebirth of the world seemed out of kilter.

Em bought a female pup with pedigree. "Because males fight," he said to Lois. "I want them to be friends."

"For what that mutt cost," Pete said, "he could of paid the taxes on his house."

The rains swept in across the western range, rains bred in Russia, the Gulf of Alaska; sou'westers coming from Japan. The roof on Kingdom Hall sat glazed and black. Em turned to motherhood and so did we.

"We're acting silly." Lona-Anne-Marie was gratified. "A man of sixty ain't too old to learn." She watched Em's patience as he trained the pup. She boiled soup bones and watched as Em, and Jim, took walks with the two dogs.

"She'll get pneumonia," Nancy said, "that's sure. They come in cold and wet." She searched her attic, found a blanket. She and Lois made the pup a bed.

Pete built a doghouse. "Big enough for *one*," he pointed out.

"I look to the redemption of the world. Not this. Right now I've got a mare's nest." Lona-Anne-Marie was always sure a resurrecting God would sweep the sky and make things new. For thirty years since her conversion she's passed out tracts.

"Jim don't explain why he's returned. Might be he can't. And I don't care." Lois started working on her weight. "I used to be nice looking."

"He really likes her." Em told everyone about his dogs. "It's going to work out fine."

"I think Em did just right, and so does Jim." Lois' eyes were nowhere near as painful. "I know you think it's crazy," she told Mona.

"I don't know what to think. There's something to it." Mona started greeting Jim, when Jim and Lois took their morning walk. It like to drove Pete wild.

"I almost, just about, can see him," Mona said. "Maybe they're not crazy."

"I don't care much for kids. I do like dogs." Nancy got maternal. She swore that Em was going to ruin the pup.

"She seems to pee a lot," Em said.

"She's got a baby bladder." Nancy went downtown, and bought a book on how to train your dog.

"How to *ruin* your dog," Pete said. "They've got that little girl downright confused."

"Maybe so," said Lona-Anne-Marie, "and maybe not. Watch where she *doesn't* jump, watch where she does."

"There's no predictin' what a pup will do." Pete watched close. The pup seemed romping with another dog. When Jim and Lois went along with Em, the pup seemed with three people. She danced in front of Jim; like he took space. She didn't run across his space.

"It's mass delusion," Pete explained. "The neighborhood is nuts, and so's my wife. I've lived beside that woman forty years. I think I've lost my mind."

"Folks get lonesome," Nancy said. "We're old. If everybody's happy why complain? The world don't care for old folks anyway. We get to act as silly as we please." Nancy didn't give a thought for Jim. She only walked along to bother Pete.

=

On Sunday mornings at the Kingdom Hall folks come and go like businessmen at lunch. They chomp an hour's message, then leave. Used to be, when church was over folks would stand around. They'd talk and gas and gossip, swap the news. Girls would flirt with boys, and boys would blush. There was no helter skelter.

On Sunday mornings Lona-Anne-Marie can almost always walk to Kingdom Hall. Unless the weather's awful, or unless her rheumatism bends her. On such days, Em or Pete walks with her. They don't stay. They pick her up when services are done.

One day she walked with Jim. People took no notice. Except the people in the neighborhood. Lona-Anne-Marie leaned on Jim's arm. Her white hair puffed beneath a mended scarf. Her red coat was a thrift store hand-me-down.

"That tears it," Pete said. "I must be missin' something."

"My dog has caused the resurrection of the world." Em spoke to Lois. "Don't tell nobody yet. He died and didn't want to leave. I take no credit."

Used to be that things weren't lonesome. When church let out the old folks stood around, and counted blessings. They had families, they had friends. They knew about each other back to Adam. Some were even feuding.

"It don't pay to fret about the past. I've nary chick nor child to plague me. I think about the future." Lona-Anne-Marie was optimistic. If resurrection's certain, folks can plan. "It's just," said Lona-Anne-Marie, "redemption should be fancy. I thought the skies would open."

The pup grew winter fur. Along the path behind the Kingdom Hall, and on the bluff where the old chimney rose, someone cut young trees. We heard the axe-chunks carried by the wind. Winter brings us freezing rain. Our world is covered with transparent glaze.

"John's resurrected," Em explained. "His whole family. Those five graves behind the Kingdom Hall. John's putting up a cabin. John Jr.'s helping; nice young man. Esther's just a little girl, and Tim is ten. Sarah can't be more than thirty-five. Folks married younger eighty years ago." Em told all this to Pete and Jim while rummaging his truck. "I've got some stuff they're going to need. Cooking pots and such. They gotta have a stove." He turned to Jim. "I'll bet you've got a couple in your shed."

"I must be gettin' old," Pete said, "I'm tired. This disbelieving wears a fella down." The sound of axe-chunks carried from the bluff. "It won't be up to code," Pete said. "There's no permit. The sheriff's gonna come and raise some hell."

"We're past the time of sheriffs, I expect." Jim seemed certain-sure. "Woodstoves weigh a lot. We'll have to pack it down in parts. Bolt it back together on the site."

"Oh, Lord," Pete said, "I just now heard Jim's voice. Now *everybody's* crazy."

Used to be, miracles abounded. Every family had at least one tale, of someone on the far side of death's door that death tossed back. Or maybe angels cruised the neighborhoods. There was a time when faith moved mountains. Pete was old enough to recollect.

"I'd ought to call the sheriff. Get this done." Nancy can be mulish. The minute Pete began to talk to Jim, Nancy balked. Her iron-gray hair looked like a puff of mist as she peered from her windows. When Em and Jim and Lois and the dogs went walking down behind the Kingdom Hall, Nancy stayed at home. "I've been playing this just like a game. Never took it serious."

"Pipe dreams come from smoke. I see no smoke." LonaAnne-Marie cleaned house. She washed her windows, polished up her stove. "I ain't seen Pete so lively in awhile. He's finally taking interest. It's making Mona happy."

Lona-Anne-Marie washed curtains. The rebirth of the world would find her tidy. She had few words about the resurrection. "It had to happen sometime. Why not now? I've been predictin' it."

When woodsmoke rose behind the Kingdom Hall the sheriff came. Webster Smith ("Call me Web") is sheriff. He's friendly when election comes around. "There's law and folks," he says, and what he means is comfort lies in balancing the two. Web does like comfort.

"I'm not so young myself," Web said to Pete. He stood beside his car and watched the trees. Dead poppies straggled in the vacant lot, while off a-ways, two playing children looked like bouncing toys.

"Old folks imagine things. I ought to know. Try sittin' in a car night after night. Looking out for drunks." Web had walked the path, looked at the site. Nancy got so bothered she'd joined Pete. They'd waited side by side until Web got back. Web is not badlooking, tall and built in chunky squares.

"What did you see?" Nancy frets at things, won't let them go. She's not above some flirting. Web has always been a ladies' man.

"A cabin built by axe. It's some poor duffer. Riding out the winter. Don't own a chainsaw, even."

"I'd just as leave this didn't get around. I think there's something to it." Pete winked at Jim, who only Pete could see. From up the path behind the Kingdom Hall Em walked with his two dogs.

"The folks at Kingdom Hall made no complaint. The land belongs to them. Come spring the guy will move along. Meanwhile, I won't roust him." Web had got distracted. Nancy'd pulled her shoulders back. It made her front stick out.

"None of us has got that many years." Web looked at Kingdom Hall like he was tired. "We mix up fact and memory. These days I spend a lot of time remembering my folks." Web looked where Em was coming from the trees. "I heard he bought a highprice pup. Why's he need two dogs?"

"Sweet loving God," said Nancy. Then she drooped her shoulders.

The sum of it is John and Sarah stayed, together with their kids. They feared hard times. It isn't easy, after eighty years, to make a living. They were raised with horses, not with cars; but everybody helped.

On Sundays, going to the Kingdom Hall, folks drove past and sort of looked confused. They'd wave to Pete and Em, and Em's two dogs, or maybe one. When spring rains came, a few of them began to wave at Jim.

"I got to guess," said Lona-Anne-Marie, "the skies will open soon."

In spring the rain is constant. It walks across the mountains and the Sound. It floods our gardens and the vacant lots. Hard to work the ground, the earth gets soggy. The roof of Kingdom Hall grows moss. The moss is softly green. It burns away come summer.

The pup grew to a dog and Em was thinking. "It's old folks make this happen," he told Jim. "Lona-Anne-Marie knew all along. The living and the dead are all the same. I'll get it studied out."

"Faith don't amount to squat," Pete said to Em. "Unless you're stuck with facts. Then there's something to it."

"Maybe we all died," said Em, "and none of us took notice."

In May the rains turn warm and start to thin. Our world is green. New growth tips the firs. The pines grow whitish candles. The roof of Kingdom Hall looks like a lake, reflecting trees.

"It comes from being lonesome," Em told Jim. "I'd guess it's more than that, but there's a start."

"It's getting ticklish down at Kingdom Hall." Lona-AnneMarie still went to church. "Some folks say 'yes', and some say 'no'. Can't blame 'em much. A quiet resurrection's real surprising." Lona-Anne-Marie was feeling spry. When kids from the apartments came around, she gave them little parties.

"It's kind of cute," said Nancy. "Folks from Kingdom Hall talk resurrection. Then it comes and they don't see it. I guess it don't amount to much."

"It's having *everything*, plus lonesome." Em told Nancy, then told Pete. "Youngsters couldn't do it. Been listening to the preachers sixty years. It took my dog to teach me."

When John and Sarah took their kids to church, the congregation put its cares aside. Redemption maybe—maybe not—but here were folks who had to make a crop. The elders took a vote. They had a man come in. Tractored up the vacant lots. They bought hand tools and seed.

"I know now how it works," Em said to Pete. "Dead folks are all around."

Young folks have needs, Em claims. When they get lonesome they just chase their tails. They do those things young people have to do. Em says the resurrection always was, has always been. It just takes folks who have no wants, but feel the pain of lonesome. Em claims the skies won't open.

Lona-Anne-Marie believes they will. She waits and watches. In the vacant lots, the poppies have give way to scarlet runner beans. John and Sarah seem to have the touch. Their crop is thrifty.

John thinks Em is right; Jim isn't sure. The rest of us are waiting. When summer dawns throw silver light in patches through the trees, we watch the sky. The roof of Kingdom Hall is pebbled gold, not much has changed. On Sunday mornings folks pass to and fro. They wave and go their ways when services are done. The neighborhood falls quiet, save for children's play, while in the parking lot of Kingdom Hall two white dogs dance, or sniff at oil spots where the cars were parked.

Daddy Dearest

IT BEGAN IN A TEAROOM IN SEATTLE, ONE WITH ROSE-COLORED tablecloths and stained glass lamps. A tearoom, I ask you. A tearoom with pictures of bunnies and duckies quilted on the napkins, the whole show run by a granny-lady named Mrs. Perkins.

In addition to bunnies the tearoom sported furniture like riff-raff from an antique store, you know the kind; a late Victorian breakfront, 19th century reproductions of 17th century chairs, and kitschy washboards, trivets, and unwarranted junk from rural America of seventy years past.

Into this tearoom, on one of those rainy northwest days specifically designed for funerals, slipped two quiet people who murmured to each other while touching hands. One, the man, carried a jar. The man (who looked like someone named Harold but who was actually named Aubrey) seemed nondescript in spite of grooming. His slender frame stood topped by brown hair, and he gazed about with brown eyes, a man eminently suited to brown; a man, one assumed, accustomed to brown thoughts, and it looked like he'd been thinking them for about thirty years. He dressed not in brown, but elegant tan cashmere and wool, most expensive.

The woman, smashingly beautiful, tended to the green of springtime. If the man seemed sad, the woman seemed only mildly serious. A touch of girlishness chased away rain and wind and gloom of streets where cars ran wet and umbrellas turned inside out. Whereas the man looked like a shirt advertisement, albeit a depressed one, the woman looked like an artist, which in fact, was the case. A bit bohemian, perhaps, but an artist who knew her business. Her piled hair looked Norwegian, her features classic Greek. She stood taller than Aubrey, not so elegantly dressed, but a green wool skirt fell just far enough to display trim ankles, and her green wool jacket snugged tidily around narrow shoulders. Name of Patsy.

The jar was one of those funerary things crematoriums give the bereaved, and which hold ashes. This cream-colored jar carried a gold leaf inscription reading: "Blessed is he who don't dip his finger into this jug-a-trouble 'cause he'll sure-God get it bit."

"I wanted a really nice inscription," the man murmured sadly. "Something from the Bible. But, Pop had to be snotty 'til the end. The whole memorial ceremony was compromised."

"It's been your problem all your life," the jar said. "Making compromises. Cutting deals where you come out on the short end of the stick. I tried to pay attention when you was growin'." The voice spilled from beneath the lid of the jar, no more than a whisper, but steady as wind across Montana. Aubrey looked at the jar, looked mournful, but not a bit surprised. He looked like he had been expecting something like this all along.

"Being dead doesn't seem to shut him up." Patsy suppressed a giggle.

"I had many a doxie in my day," the jar whispered proudly, "but nobody prettier than you." The jar chuckled, its voice not a little horny.

"I wish I'd known him better," Patsy said. "He's the sort of rascal who seduces entire convents."

"He had that reputation," Aubrey admitted in a brownish voice. He held a chair for Patsy, then seated himself. "This is a nice place," he hissed to the jar. "Just this one time try not to embarrass me."

"I thought the memorial was actually very nice." Patsy looked around the room, at prints of kitties, piggies, and sunny children. She wrinkled her nose.

"My father's friends," said Aubrey, "were various."

"Apple knockers," the jar whispered, "and lonesome cowboys, railroad station agents, bar girls, torch singers, lady truck drivers, plus bozos, battleaxes . . . I'm talking here about ex-wives . . . lumberjacks, used car salesmen . . . ."

"She gets the picture," Aubrey muttered. He also looked around the tearoom, looking at nicely dressed women at lunch. The women chatted about dreams and plans of husbands, sons, grandsons, daughters, nieces; chatted of piano lessons, while making distressed noises about Democrats and orthodontists. A few women cast cautious glances at the jar. They pretended nonchalance. The jar chuckled, the chuckle lascivious.

"I suppose one never gets completely away from his father," Patsy said. "But yours is a special case." She glanced through a menu. Her hair held just a touch of russet. She smiled generously and reached to touch Aubrey's wrist. "I'm not sure why or what you need . . . ."

"For openers," Aubrey said quietly, "what do I do with him? I can't park him on the mantel at home. He'll just hit on the cleaning lady. I can't dump him. He'll turn into dust, and the dust will have a million teeney-weeney little voices. I'll be surrounded."

"We'll think of something," Patsy said, her voice a trifle cool. "You should look at your menu."

"There was a time when I dreamed you and I would become much closer." Aubrey blushed while Patsy brightened. He started to speak, blushed a deeper red, then waffled. "I feel uneasy with decisions unless we've talked."

The jar expressed a disgusted sniff. Patsy smiled. The owner of the tearoom, Mrs. Perkins, arrived to take orders. She hovered above the table like a beneficent deity of doilies, a lacy, gray-haired lady capable of expressing cupcakes with the wave of a hand, capable of cookies.

"Sadie," the jar whispered mournfully in the direction of Mrs. Perkins. "You must-of sold the brothel. You and the girls must-of retired." The jar sounded appalled. Then it began to hum, the hum sounding suspiciously like "Long Ago and Far Away."

"Did someone say something?" Mrs. Perkins sounded puzzled. "Is someone humming?" She gave a grandmotherly chirp. "At my age one gets to hearing things."

". . . got a birthmark on her right leg, well above the knee . . . ."

"Excuse me." Aubrey stood, removed his jacket, and placed it over the jar.

"Cucumber sandwiches, Darjeeling tea, and a pair of your lovely lady fingers," Patsy told Mrs. Perkins. Patsy smiled happily at the thought of lady fingers, certainly not at the thought of cucumbers.

"That one's gonna cost." A muffled whisper came from beneath the jacket. "I'll keep you up nights singing, 'cause I ain't sleeping, I'm only dead."

"A period of mourning is appropriate," Aubrey said after Mrs. Perkins left. "I can even get leave from the office. One does not lose a father lightly, even that father." He pointed to the lump beneath the jacket. His eyes shone a little misty, a man with more to say, a man about to stutter. Then he sat quietly.

"I'm not at all sure you've lost him." Patsy could not suppress a chuckle. "When you stop to think of the power of fathers, and how they live in your life and your dreams, I'm not sure any of them are truly lost." She sat quietly, perhaps remembering her own father; or perhaps wondering when Aubrey would get to the point, if there was a point. "In your case," she said, "I'm sure you've not lost him. Have you wondered why this is happening?"

"Solar flares?" Aubrey asked. "Radiant energy from the center of the earth? Spaceships? Malicious gods? Time warps, bad luck, karma . . . do you believe in karma?" He reached to touch her hand, his touch tentative. "At first I hoped it a simple case of madness. Hearing things, you understand? I hoped it an aberration of grief. But, you're hearing him as well."

"And so is Mrs. Perkins." Patsy giggled. "You may be crazy. I may be crazy. But I double-guarantee you that a sweet old bat like Mrs. Perkins is not crazy."

"It's an out of body experience," the jar whispered from beneath the jacket. "I kid you not."

Tea arrived ahead of the sandwiches. Patsy poured two cups, raised hers in a toast. "To fathers."

"To fathers and to lonely nights," Aubrey replied. Another blush began, although his first blush had not yet finished. "Was there ever a chance for us?" Beyond the windows, in the gray light of autumn, traffic reflected in the polished surface of a store's large front window. Images passed back and forth as people mirrored in the glass. A teenage boy wearing a red baseball cap strolled past, hands in pockets and with a faraway look. He did not whistle.

A policeman waited at a traffic light while three other people jaywalked.

"I love autumn," Patsy told him. "The world is just a little gusty before it goes to sleep for winter." She smiled, but her hand trembled slightly as she rearranged a napkin. "There still *is* a chance for us. Still is, but with alterations."

Aubrey stared brownly into his teacup as if reading leaves or searching for ultimate wisdom. "You're talking about my melancholy."

"You can do better," the jar advised Patsy. "With a bod like yours a girl could get to Vegas."

Patsy stood, took off her jacket, and piled it on top of Aubrey's jacket. Whispers of indignation barely sounded through the folds of cloth.

And it is true, without the jacket, Patsy displayed a delicate combination of features which would turn the head of any statue, if the statue were male. She touched her shirt front, realized she drew attention to some assets, blushed . . . then leaned back in her chair as cucumber sandwiches arrived.

Mrs. Perkins glanced at the pile of jackets as she set plates on the table. "We can't allow pets." Her mouth formed an unhappy line. "You cannot believe the strictness of the health department. If you have a little one there, he'll have to wait outside."

"It's not a pet nor ever was," Patsy assured her. "It's not alive." Patsy looked beyond the window and into the day of rain and wet leaves. She smiled at Mrs. Perkins. "A lovely day."

"I count myself lucky," Mrs. Perkins murmured. "So many friends have gone before me, yet here I am healthy and cozy in my little shoppe." Her voice trembled. "One does miss friends, though. Rather badly, in fact."

Unintelligible whispers rose from beneath the pile of jackets as Mrs. Perkins returned to her kitchen.

"Melancholy," Aubrey said. "It's all around us."

"A brown study," Patsy told him. "That's what old-time poets would have said. You're always in a brown study. Your mind must look like a piece of English tweed." Her voice, though critical, sounded tender. "My dear, dear man, with one life to live why must you choose only gloom and sorrow?"

Aubrey mutely pointed to the pile of jackets. He seemed near tears. Even his tan cashmere sweater appeared affected.

"Because a girl can't live with gloom," Patsy told him. "At least this girl can't. I'm basically a happy person."

"I think an evil jinn causes this." Aubrey pointed to the pile of jackets. "When I was child that . . ." his finger shook as it pointed ". . . that man denied my childhood. He made me clean out a chicken house. Worst day of my life."

"A chicken house?"

"Among other indignities." Aubrey sighed, but did not sound particularly sad.

"I'm looking at you in disbelief," Patsy told him, "because I don't believe a word of this." She stood, carefully removed jackets from the jar, and hung them over the backs of chairs. To Aubrey she said, "It's the restroom for you, my man. Get in there for at least ten minutes." Her tones were those with which one did not trifle.

Aubrey, bewildered, passed toward the restroom and beyond hearing. Patsy turned to the jar, her voice changing to tones most raspy. "Crap me around one time," she said, "and we head for the ladies' can. A royal flush will be dealt. Only one of us will return."

"Even if you can't do better, you can do different." The jar's whisper sounded impressed.

"I can't do either," she told the jar. "Even if I can, I don't want to. Artists are surrounded by people with weird egos. You can guess how a quiet and attractive guy . . . ." She shrugged. "So, explain love? Go ahead."

"I have the time," the jar whispered sadly, "but you don't. You still have some livin' to do."

"What's this chicken house business?"

"The whole family had chores during a time when we went broke farmin'. He's not feeling sorry for himself, he's protecting his mama's good name. She pretended we weren't broke. Put on a few airs." The jar paused, the pause thoughtful, or almost. "He's his daddy's boy. He's got a sense of humor. He just never learned how to laugh."

"When he returns," Patsy said, her voice grim as graves, "I'll head for the can. You have ten minutes. Teach him to laugh."

"You two kids are gonna get along just fine," the jar murmured. "You are soundin' exactly like his momma."

"Ten minutes. He's on his way back here right now." Patsy grabbed her purse and left.

"One advantage in bein' dead is bein' able to tell the future," the jar whispered to Aubrey, after Aubrey returned looking unsettled. ". . . . Or rather, futures, because everybody's got a lot of them, depending on their choices."

"Give it a rest, Pop." Aubrey stood, looking like a man who did not know whether to stay or flee. He looked a little lost, and plenty lonesome.

"So I'm gonna tell you about a boy who could be you, a good boy 'til he married the wrong woman. He may hook up with the right one later on, or maybe not."

Aubrey sat, elbows on table, looking into the wet street. He pretended not to listen. He pretended he did not feel befuddled.

"This boy's daddy was a famous buffalo-rider of the old school," the whisper continued. "Won loving cups and stuff. When the buffalo-rider's wife had a little kid, he named the kid Spike; only the wife didn't like it and named him after some artsy-fartsy guy who moped a lot and died young. The kid grew and turned into the boy who married the wrong woman."

"Spike?" whispered Aubrey, and he seemed interested. His mouth twitched in a way that said it would be hanged if it was going to smile. "All my life you flipped b.s. Aren't you ever ashamed?"

"Did I ever lie?"

Aubrey considered, looked at wet streets, wet leaves, slicky sidewalks. ". . . told some pretty wild stories."

"Every one true," the jar whispered. "This boy I'm tellin' about married this gal . . . she sold his furniture . . . rearranged his place . . . bought a goldfish named Clarence and a hamster named Rasputin. She donated his suits, all brown and tan, to a home for delinquent Arabs, and she decked him out in stuff that would get him shot in Milwaukee. He had to grow a mustache. The mustache shed down his shirtfront. Hair worked under his belt and tickled his crotch . . . caused a case of the hots . . . he goes home in a hurry . . . she's not home . . . he takes his case of the hots to a cowboy bar. Boy gets a snootful, ends up with a bargirl famous for card tricks, sharpshooting, bareback riding, and occasional hustles . . . they run off . . . live . . . you're chuckling, what'n'the hell's so funny?"

"You're trying to con me out of something. What?" Aubrey tried to make his voice brownish, and only managed something close to dark ivory.

"I got it on the line here, boy. Listen up, 'cause this is what happens with the second choice.

"Boy still marries the wrong girl. Boy still goes home with the hots. Goldfish intact . . . hamster happy . . . girl is home, copulation certain. Lots of hollering, rolling around, and in nine months out pops a kid. Name of Aloysius. Boy secretly names him Studs. Goddammit boy, there's a third choice, quit giggling . . . ."

"Can't help it," Aubrey said. "You're running a con, and I'm seeing through it, and for once your b.s. isn't . . . hush, here comes Mrs. Perkins."

"Is everything all right?" Mrs. Perkins sounded the way a woman might, if a young man sat in her teashop talking to himself.

"Sadie," the jar whispered loudly as it could. "Long time . . . ."

Mrs. Perkins stopped, paused, looked around her tearoom. She checked out tea-drinking ladies, pictures of duckies, doilies, and lace. She quickly took a seat. "One of the boys from better days," she whispered to Aubrey, and looked fondly at the jar. ". . . give you fifty bucks for him . . . ."

"He's my father."

"Forty bucks," Mrs. Perkins said. "I thought he might be someone else."

"Don't let her shove you around," the jar whispered. "A dozen times I've seen her run that number. You can easy get a hundred."

Aubrey laughed, practically helpless. Patsy, returning from the ladies' can, heard the laugh. Aubrey tried not to laugh, messed up royal, and laughed some more. Patsy took his arm, smiled happily, murmured something unintelligible, and Aubrey blushed. In the street, watched over by gods and flying saucers, by radiant energy and plain-dumb-luck, rain paused as if pondering a spot of sunshine; a new beginning, a blessed dawn. Then rain seemed to shrug its shoulders, puffed a gust or two, and decided to drizzle.

"I'm staying here with Sadie," the jar said to Aubrey. "You'll know where to find me." To Mrs. Perkins the jar said, "It's you and me, kid. You gonna display me on that sorry breakfront?"

"On my nightstand." Mrs. Perkins whispered so low Aubrey could not hear. Of course, by then, Aubrey had already helped Patsy with her coat and the two were nearly to the doorway, doubtless headed toward intimacy.

"On your nightstand?" the jar whispered, a whisper between awe and mild excitement. "You always was creative."

"We'll figure something out," Mrs. Perkins said, her voice throaty and bright as she watched Aubrey and Patsy step into the wet street. Aubrey raised an umbrella. He looked ready to tsk.

"I expect they'll be all right," Mrs. Perkins said. "But it's just going to be Hail Columbia for the first few years."

"It surely ain't a match made in heaven, plus he had another option. He could of learned to be a buffalo rider."

"It's a match made in a teashop," Mrs. Perkins said. "You'd be surprised how often it happens these days . . . no, nope, you wouldn't be surprised."

"I tried to be a good daddy," the jar whispered. "Take it easy, Spike."

"You have to cut them loose sometime," Mrs. Perkins said. "Let them make their own mistakes."

"She's too pushy," the jar whispered, "and he's a natural worrywart. A' course they're both good kids."

And Mrs. Perkins and the jar stood looking onto the busy street, a street of sales and traffic where it may be that a beneficent eye hovers godlike in the sky, directing the affairs of men, the affairs of women, and of women and men who have affairs; and then Mrs. Perkins picked up the jar and stashed it beside her umbrella where it would be handy when she closed shop and went home. She heard a slight sound as she turned to attend to customers, but missed seeing the jar nearly tip from the shelf as it gave a small hop and a jiggle, while weeping only a little.

The Sounds of Silence

DONIZETTI IS DEAD. LOUIS ARMSTRONG IS DEAD. VANCOUVER IS another rainy city.

Velma Middleton is dead. Mozart. J. B. Arban. Stravinsky. The ranks form in my mind. Composers, performers, all of them teachers. I stare into the rainy streets at a store front which advertises cheap boots. Galli-Curci is dead. The water pounds like nails. Jim is walking around out there someplace.

The theme does not leave my mind and I do not try to dislodge it. The Firebird. The horns and trumpets have it on open bell and the music is wild and triumphant. We came to this motel a half hour ago, a fifty-year-old man with thinning hair and his nineteen-year-old son. How many journeys? How many miles? It has only been a few hours.

Jim's guitar is in the corner and his trumpet is by the bed. On my next visit I'll bring the cello. For the last hour all of my memories have seemed less than one morning old.

Because it is not yet noon. We left Seattle early. Jim slowed toward the end of the packing. He was discarding books and folding things that did not need to be folded. Always before the room was cluttered, the evidence of rebellious sloppiness never quite hidden. His mother and I have tried for order in our lives and have been successful. Jim will use those learned patterns later.

He is a tall kid. This morning he was learning to become a man and he slumped under his decision. We had talked it out on an evening last week. After the defensiveness and flamboyance and third-world metaphor, his decision (stated quietly and almost with surprise) was a relief. He would refuse the draft. He would go to Canada.

I hope I did well. Finally, even between husband and wife, father and son, there is a vacuum that cannot be bridged and I believe it is the first part of maturity to recognize this. I also believe it is the first part of wisdom to continually struggle against it.

Jim's new haircut is too short. He looked like a Marine home from boot camp. Last summer's tan ran halfway up his forehead to a demarcation where the hair had thickened and curled, sometimes falling nearly to his eyes. His eyes are blue, touching toward green like his mother's. He had been proud of his hair. I felt sentimental and then did not feel that way. What are these symbols? He could grow his hair down his back once we got into Canada.

"I'll bring those," I said. He stood with a half dozen phonograph records and a puzzled look.

"Now?"

"When I come up next time." His walls were covered with posters. It would be necessary for me to come back and clean the room. "Will you want these?" I motioned to them.

"No." He laid the recordings on the single bed and stared from a window. Short answers were all he had on tap. Over the past years the posters had changed. When he was a freshman he surrounded himself with hatred. Clenched fists, gutter words, lampooning and sarcastic statements. Now the hatred seemed temporarily stilled, either by mental fatigue or a change of perspective. I hoped for change. Of all things I feared, the hatred was the worst.

In a way he was already a veteran. He has been beaten twice, once by a policeman and once by a carload of drunks who caught him on the street late at night. The posters were of trees and beaches and birds. I wondered if he really watched those things. I did not at nineteen, and now I doubted that Jim did either.

"About ready?" It is hard to make your voice kind. Your intention clouds the natural kindness.

"You go ahead. I'll be right down." His voice was harsh.

It was good-bye to a particular place and it seemed strange to me that he was learning this. Both my wife and I are musicians.

We've said good-bye to a lot of places and felt sad; and some of those places were not as good as this. I turned from the small room in the off-campus house and descended the old stairs. The station wagon, which I trade every three years and which has become a symbol of suburban America, had the seats kicked down and was loaded with suitcases and paraphernalia. It is an expensive car and an indulgence. For so many years I had to own junk, nurse it along, be grateful to a piece of machinery because it did not break down when I could not afford to fix it. Jim scoffs, but I remember. Money went for other things. From the very first lesson he played on instruments of concert quality. You build with good tools.

Already the fog was lifting and commuter traffic was in the streets, taillights popping above the mist-slickened pavement with short darts of brilliance. Traffic lights shifted and clicked, the one at the corner buzzing and staccato like a small computer. The sky was lowered by the fog and the buildings of Seattle's university district were sharply halved as they disappeared into the overcast. This gloomy place. We have lived here for five years and it suddenly seemed time to go. Perpetually clouded beauty is as difficult to live with as ugliness.

Two girls walked past chattering. Their hair was long and casually tied. Jeans, light jackets, notebooks held carelessly. They were headed for restaurant coffee and an early morning class. Was Jim saying good-bye to his bed? He is respectful of most other people. Even with little experience he will care for his women. I started the car and in a couple of minutes he joined me. His face was set like cast metal. The anger and hatred that I had not seen for a while was back. His sneer was so tight that his teeth showed. It was a wrong way to say good-bye. He climbed in the car.

"Is there anything else?"

"Nope." His voice was telling me that he hated me, the university, the chauvinistic super-establishment; and that, child-like, he was asking for help and getting none. He did not realize that for this there was no help.

Sometimes you talk. Sometimes you listen. Sometimes you shut up. I pulled into traffic, waited for a light, and in five minutes we were on interstate and headed north. If there is pain in living there are also lessons. One does not file as a Conscientious Objector and believe that indignation and good intent are sufficient. During the last part of the interview he was pushed so hard that he yelled manifestos at the draft board.

During the second war the decisions were different but I do not think the men were essentially different. How to explain? I turned the radio on for the noise. There was a lot of it. Pop clanged like untuned cow bells.

Then news. We were still at war.

Then rock, with a perennially breathless, thrust-throated D.J. Jim turned the radio off, perhaps as a concession to me, perhaps for himself.

I looked at him and thought of his mother who does not need to be told that evil exists. She, who reaches beyond the usual perceptions to particularly translate her genius and the genius of others. I have seen two thousand people hang breathless on the spaces between the perfecting and visual strokes of her interpreting bow. She, tall and auburn haired. Happily laughing. A master who teaches a discipline of music so strict that it is transcendental.

"About two hours," I said. "We'll take it easy."

No answer. I think he will begin work now. It has been sporadic. Like poetry, music makes nothing happen. His legs are so long that he propped them against the dash. It dents the padding and makes it crack. I've told him before. This time I did not tell him.

I remembered and must remember. His mother comes from a small town in Wisconsin. The town had no standard of excellence but her teachers did. We met in Baltimore in forty-six at the conservatory. I had just lost four years with the Army. There was a choice for me. My own father's business had leap-frogged during the war. My embouchure was gone, my ear no longer trained, and the manual dexterity was imprecise. A French horn operates in four octaves. At first I worked mostly in two of them for six, eight, sometimes more than that hours a day. She was impressed and did not ask why, although from someone else it would have been a good question.

It is a good question now. I could answer it now.

But what would the answer mean to Jim, this passionate American who is committed to a nebulous notion of change in a world that is changing so fast that the young cannot keep up while still believing that they must. After the war there were greater decisions. I do not want to explain. Only this, that in the middle of chaos a man may still concern himself with beauty.

I drove and the speed kept easing upward. That also is an American pattern. Jim rushes everywhere.

After a half hour of driving a thin rain started. It rarely rains very hard in the Northwest. The interstate runs through a variety of land forms and the expressions of towns. Lumber processing plants, knobs, pasture land, high countryside not even good for grazing. To the east are mountains. West lies the sea. It is always green and the interstate runs black and gray between great trees, smokestacks, small businesses whose owners are living out of the till. More fish are dying. More people are dying.

More people are also living.

"You heard nothing this week?" I referred to his inquiry at a Canadian university.

"They hate Americans."

"The university is under-enrolled. I think it will be okay."

"I think so too." He wanted to be friendly and did not do well. "I guess they'll wait until the last minute just to sweat me."

"Paperwork takes time." I thought not of Canada but of this country and sent an imaginary note to a mythical heaven. Dear Sir, when you instituted the New Deal did you realize how dangerous a bureaucracy could become?

The most horrible vision that my mind ever conceived was of my son holding a brick and screaming, his open mouth a fury of hate, his eyes blind with ignorance.

Hey Jude, Hey Jude . . . . I am critical of one thing with these kids. They do not listen to their own music, really listen. Try asking any of them to write down all the lyrics to any popular song'.

How can you explain? There are so many great moments. *Universal Judgment*. The bass rumbles in my mind. Would Jim understand if I told him that I once saw Krupa run a syncopation with both feet, tight roll with the right hand, and flipping the stick in the left high over his head to come down with rim shots; in blue light and cigarette smoke, to a lounge filled with sophisticates who were not listening. When I was Jim's age I also played a trumpet.

There was nothing to say. I wondered if my insistence had been too great. In the beginning the practice. Later, the discipline. After an hour of driving I wanted coffee. The road is wide and too straight. It lulls the mind with a false tranquility. Jim was terribly tense. He was startled when I eased down for an exit.

"Trouble," he asked.

"I just want to take a break."

"I can drive."

"If you want." He would not be driving for a long time. He would be studying, if the school accepted him, and also working at a job. Political theory and pumping gasoline, probably. Pumping gas in a world where there is Aaron Copland.

It is hard to think of Jim walking washed-gray Vancouver streets; sleet in winter, automobiles firing through French and English marked intersections like corks popped from bottles. He is correct in some respects. He will not always be welcome, not if he is only another displaced American. He will have to work hard.

I found a restaurant and parked. The place seemed a monument to plastic and luminescent paintings on black velvet. A construction crew sat in one booth, the men with strong shoulders and weather-beaten faces. Eloquent hands and eyes. I have seen workmen in this country hit the fine line on a grade using little more than a bulldozer. In Europe they would use grading rakes and take a week. The crew did not know that they were improbable people, only that their competence was assumed. Jim almost certainly filed them in the category "hard hat" and took a seat at the opposite end of the room. He sat facing them. It was not easy to watch him finding strength in hatred. With the fresh haircut he seemed nearly hatchet-faced. His youth dissolved the impression while his intolerance increased it.

"You're going to have to do better than that," I told him.

"What?"

"You don't know their politics."

"Coke," he told the waitress. I ordered coffee. Jim watched her move away. Young girl.

"It's not the politics, it's a whole rotten value system." He stopped, apparently resolved not to end in dialectics. His face worked to control his hate. Then he was sanctimonious. "They're victims." He tried to smile.

Outside a truckload of new automobiles roared into the parking lot. Plastic ferns in a plastic pot sat by the doorway. The waitress returned with our order. A cash register purred and spit electrically.

"It's not the end of the world," he told me, telling himself.

I agreed and said nothing more. It was the end of one of his worlds. He will never be the same. The flame of his own country's hatred may follow him for the rest of his life. The possibility of being better is the only one he can afford to consider. The coffee was tasteless. I handed him the car keys.

He drove. Jim has always told me what he thinks. He has never asked what I think.

I think that I once carried a rifle and that the business of an army is to take and hold ground.

I am proud of my son and I know that he wants to know that, but he does not know how to ask and I do not know how to tell him. He is both theoretical and ignorant. To one without historical sense explanation means excuse. It increases hatred.

My generation had few philosophers. It came from small towns and cold beds, hell-shouting preachers, petrified morality and depression. After a global war it was a generation concerned with never having to live that way again. My short-haired revolutionary is not a revolutionary at all. We were. He is an exponent of the new Reformation.

"Half an hour," he said, and I was surprised. Thinking. Time was lost, but time to say what?

"You'll do well," I told him. "In a few years the C.O.'s will be repatriated."

"To this God-damned place?" His lips were white and thin.

I stepped on my anger, the anger which he has never asked about. It is a question not of government but of morality in transition. The old is gone, the new not yet arrived, and the average man finds himself more immoral than usual. There are many people who will harm my son. He harms himself.

"A government is not a nation." He is going to find that out, but does not know it now. If there are illusions perhaps it is best that they be kept until he gains strength.

"It all stinks." The tension was so great that his temples were bloodless.

"Have it your way." I wanted to remind him of the many hours of his own practice, remind him of the magic time when the instrument is no longer a problem but an extension. This kid has an instrumental voice that sings, one that needs only authority, and there is no authority in hatred.

His great grandfather was a bugler who played the cornet in the evenings to his troop's horses.

"I just want to get out. I can handle it all, but I just want to get out."

He was defending with hate. Argument was wrong. When we reached the border I leaned back in the seat and stayed silent. There are no guards. It is an open road to Canada, a road easy to plug but I do not think the government wants it plugged. A way to alleviate dissent is to allow it to leave. In less than a mile, past the monument to friendship between two nations, Canadian customs lay in a low-sprawling building with roofs like wings over the road lanes. Jim parked the car. We entered. It was there that inquiries had to be made.

Jim was nervous to the point of trembling. Behind counters men in the uniform of another country were busy. The one who approached us was muscular with a florid face, washed blue eyes, and a conservative and untrained smile. He looked at me, carefully looked at Jim, and guessed the obvious.

"Political asylum?"

It sounded like a spy movie. It sounded unreal.

There were forms. There were questions, places to apply, procedures. It took a long time. Jim was allowed in on a point basis and my function was past. Finally, I did not even function as one who reassures. When I became unnecessary I sat on a bench and waited. Jim talked. The officer talked, called questions to another officer, turned again to speak to Jim. I thought of a ten-year-old awkwardly wrapped around a cello and knew that it was a specifically wrong and stupid thing to do.

The interview ended. Jim turned. We were free to go. Free to find a room, make applications, plot directions toward a continual and, at this time, provisional standard of success.

Jim turned back. His shoulders were hunched with tension. Thin, like a tall child. The officer pointed and Jim walked to an alcove where there were restrooms.

I stood automatically, took one step, waved pointlessly and like a fool to the officers, then reversed my direction and walked outside to the car. His guitar was on top of the load. I pulled it out, the music already beginning like a thin, strong exclamation in my mind.

It's to his credit that there was no sound. Even outside, waiting, I know that there was no sound. He took his time because he had to, and I wondered, holding the guitar and not chording it, if he thought of my unfair anger at some of his practice, at his reasonable foibles. It is certain he thought of his mother, and because of her he thought of the music.

Later, when the control was back, he joined me with swollen eyes that he desperately tried to hide. His mouth was firm, his face and body set in determined lines, and I searched with the certainty of a man who feels the discovery of truth just beneath his fingertips. It was then that the theme burst like a flood in my mind, the sound growing and growing. The brass was walking full. It was strong and proud and victorious.

Jeremiah

AT THE MEETING OF TWO SECONDARY ROADS, HELL-FER-CERTAIN
Church stands like faded rag-tags left over from a cosmic yard sale.
This once quiet country church, with a single bell in the steeple, has
virginal white paint decorated with psychedelic shades of pink and
orange and green; those colors mixing with hard yellows and blues
positive as bullhorns. For a short time in the past this abandoned
church was used by a commune.

In the tower beside the cracked bell dangles a loudspeaker that
once broadcast rock music, or called faithful flower-folk to seek
renunciation of a world too weird for young imaginings. Then
the speaker died, insulation burned away, the whole business one
gigantic short circuit as sea wind wailed across the wires.

And the vivid paint, itself, faded before the wind and eternal
rain that washes this northwest Washington coast. Those of us who
once congregated at the church have dispersed, some to cemeteries
to doze among worms, some to board rooms of corporations. And
some, of course, have stayed in the neighborhood, too inept, or
stoned, or unimaginative to leave; although in dark and mist-
ridden hours we sometimes recall young dreams.

Then, lately, the church added one more perturbed voice to its
long history. A new preacher drifted here from dingy urban streets.
In the uncut grass of the front yard a reader-board began carrying
messages. It advised passersby to atone, although around here folks
show little in the way of serious transgression. They cheat at cards,

sometimes, or drive drunk, or sleep with their neighbors' wives or husbands; and most shoot deer out of season. On the grand scale of things worth atoning, they don't have much to offer.

But the reader-board insisted that, without atonement, the wages of sin are one-way tickets to a medieval hell, ghastly, complete, and decorated with every anguish imagined by demonic zeal; seas of endless fire, the howl of demons, sacramental violence in the hands of an angry God.

And fire, we find—be it sacramental or not—has become part of our story.

On Sundays the new preacher stood in the doorway. Jeremiah is as faded as the faded paint on his church. His black suit and string tie are frayed, his white shirts are the only white shirts left in the county, and his sod-busting shoe tops are barely brushed by frayed cuffs of pants a bit too short, having been 'taken up' a time or two. He needed no loudspeaker or bullhorn as he stood preaching in the wind. When it comes to messages like "Woe Betide" Jeremiah had the appearance, vision, and voice of an old time prophet predicting celestial flames and wails of lost souls—no amplification needed.

=

There are, in this valley, some who view Jeremiah and sneer. A few others value Sunday morning services. Many are too busy or drunk to care. Some are outright displeased. Rather than tell all opinions about Jeremiah, or lack of them, a cross-section of comments by some of the valley's main players seems appropriate:

Mac, skinny, balding, and fiftyish, runs Mac's Bar and was first to see Jeremiah arrive: "As long as he stays on his side of the road I treasure the jerk. There's a certain amusement factor."

Debbie, who is an artist, a barfly, a fading beauty, and thoughtful: "I've tried a lot of this-and-that in my time, but I never molested a preacher. Have I been missing something?"

Pop, gray and wiry and always sober, is a small-time pool and poker hustler: "Seems like he works purty hard for blamed little in the collection plate."

Sarah's religious beliefs, like her tie-dyed clothes, have followed currents of popular style. Through the years she has embraced Hari

Krishna, the Pope, Buddha, Siddhartha, Mohammed, and Karl Jung, while mostly wearing Mother Hubbard styles. "It's the Lord's blessing has sent Jeremiah to us. Praise the Lord. Praise him!"

=

Not many people live here anymore. One of the secondary roads that meet at the church corner leads up from the sea. At the harbor are abandoned docks and fishing sheds where ghosts drift through fog-ridden afternoons. The buildings are huge, like a town abandoned by giants. Ghosts glide through mist, whisper like voices of mist, fade into mist when approached. We've gotten used to them. The ghosts threaten no one, except they seem so sad, the sadness of ghosts.

The other road leads through a flat valley where empty farmhouses lean into sea winds that rumble from the western coast. The houses are ramshackle. Shakes on roofs have blown away, and broken windows welcome the scouring wind. They are, themselves, ghosts; ghost houses that daily remind us of mournful matters; symbols of abandonment and failed plans.

What was once a valley of small dairy farms has been purchased farm-by-farm, and built into one huge corporation farm worked by only a few men. Our farms once had names: River View, Heather Hill, and a dozen others.

Now, cattle are bred, no longer for milk, but as blocks of meat. The valley has become a source of supply for a hamburger kingdom, a franchise that ships product to fast food joints in Seattle, Yokohama, and maybe, even, Beirut. The cattle, well adapted to wind that roughs their heavy coats, grow thick on hormones and valley grass. Then they are trucked to slaughter.

Across the road from Hell-Fer-Certain stands an old post office little larger than a postage stamp. Weathered benches in front of the post office serve loafers, or people waiting for a bus to Seattle. A country store stands next to the post office. Mac's Bar stands next the store. If you visit the bar on a Saturday or Sunday night you'll swear this valley holds every old pickup truck in the world. People congregate at the bar to forget they are survivors of a failed place. No one farms anymore. No one fishes.

One important thing happens on Sunday night, and it draws the Sunday crowd. Cattle get restless as headlights and marker lights of trucks appear on two-lane macadam. The trucks, twenty or more, arrive in groups of two or three. They pull possum-belly trailers built like double-deckers so as to haul more beef. The truckers will not load live cattle until Monday morning, but by Sunday night the cattle already know something stinks. The beasts become uneasy. The cattle, bred for meat and not for brains, still have survival instincts. The herds cluster together, each beast jostling toward the middle of the herd where there is an illusion of safety. Bawling carries on the winds. The entire valley fills with sounds of terror.

Folks swear it's Jeremiah's preaching riles the cattle, but we know it isn't so. As trucks roll in, Sunday nights turn into Jeremiah's busy time. He stands before Hell-Fer-Certain and preaches above the wind. His string tie flutters like a banner, and his white and uncut hair is whirled by wind that carries the bawling of bovine fear.

With no place to go, and a twelve-hour layover, truck drivers drift to the bar and buy rounds. They're good enough lads, but they have steady employment and that gets resented. They generally come through the doorway of Mac's bent like fishhooks beneath the flood of prophecy coming from across the road. Jeremiah puts the fear of God in them. Plus, truck driving builds a mighty thirst in a man. It's that combination causes them to stand so many drinks.

=

This, then, is the place we live. It is not the best place, not the worst, but it's ours; a small and slightly drunken spot on the Lord's green earth. It was never, until Jeremiah and Mac got into it, a place where anything titanic seemed likely. Then Jeremiah confounded Mac's hopes. He crossed the road.

=

It began on one of those rare August afternoons when mist blows away, sun covers the valley grass, and hides of cattle turn glossy with light. The macadam road dries from wet black to luminous gray. A few early drinkers stay away from Mac's, vowing not to get fuzzy until the return of ugly weather.

Mac busied himself stocking beer cases behind his polished oak bar. Polished mirrors behind the bar reflected a clutter of chairs and tables around a small dance floor. The mirrors pictured colorful beer signs, brushed pool tables, dart boards, and restroom doors that in early afternoons stand open to air out the stench of disinfectant. Either a reflection in the mirrors, or a silhouette in the sun-brightened doorway caused Mac to look up.

"Praise the Lord," said the silhouette. Then Jeremiah moved out of sunlight and into the shadow of the bar.

"All I needed," Mac said as if talking to himself, "was . . ." and he squinted at Jeremiah, "this," and he squinted harder. Mac's balding dome shone like a small light in the shadowed bar. Although he's thin, he's muscular. At the time most of the working muscles were in his jaw. "You're a bad dream," Mac told Jeremiah. "You're the butt end of a bad joke. You're turnip pie. You're first cousin to a used-car salesman, and what's worse, you're in my bar."

Jeremiah looked around the joint which stood empty except for Debbie, the artist-barfly. Debbie looked Jeremiah over with her blue and smiling eyes, brushed long hair back with one hand, and gave a practiced and seductive smile that went nowhere; although it would have worked on a truck driver.

"A customer is a customer," Jeremiah said, and he did not sound particularly righteous. "And it appears that you could use one." He stepped to the bar like a man with experience. "Soft drink," he said. "Water chaser." Seen beneath bar light, Jeremiah turned from a cartoon preacher into a real person. His face looked older than his body. His hair, not silver but white, hung beside wrinkled cheeks, pouchy eyelids, and a mouth that sagged a little on the right side; a mouth that had preached too many adjectives, or else the mouth of a man who had suffered a slight stroke. He looked at Debbie. "A woman as well found as yourself could make a success if she cleaned up her act." Jeremiah commandeered a barstool, pushed a dollar onto the bar, and sat.

"You want something," Mac told him. "What?"

"We'll get to it," Jeremiah said, "and for your own good I will shortly get to you." He slowly turned to look over the bar. "It will be a quiet afternoon." Beyond the windows a beat-up pickup pulled away from the post office. Across the road Hell-Fer-Certain Church stood in faded psychedelic colors.

"I believe in evolution," Debbie said, her interest suddenly piqued.

"Who doesn't," Jeremiah told her, "except that it didn't produce humans. It only produced Charles Darwin. You may wish to think about that."

Debbie, thoroughly confused, now found herself thoroughly fascinated. She tried to think.

Mac, on the other hand, was not confused. After all, Mac is a bartender. "You talk like a man who is sane," he told Jeremiah, "so what's your hustle?" Mac looked through the front windows at the church. He seemed remembering the loud prophecy, the dogmatic hollering, the Sunday nights of wind and truck engines and sermons. "You don't talk the way you should." Mac's voice sounded lame.

"It's a problem preachers have," Jeremiah told him. "The words we use are old, timeworn, water-smooth, and even, sometimes, decapitated. Our traditions are ancient, as are the symbols; crosses and lambs and towers of wrath. Plus, in today's world the volume on everything has been cranked higher. Would you pay attention to a quietly delivered message?"

Mac hesitated, wiped the counter with a bar rag, and seemed to remember younger days, days when people actually thought that they were thinking. "You just busted your own argument," Mac said. "I never paid attention before, but I'm hearing you now."

"In that case," Jeremiah told him, "we may proceed with your salvation, and possibly my own." His voice sounded firm, advisory, nearly scolding.

Medieval hells of fire and brimstone, according to Jeremiah, were problematic ("I honor the tradition.") but Hell, itself, was certain, either in this world or the next. "All versions of hell get boring, because even anguish wears out sooner or later. I care nothing for it."

Debbie looked at her small glass of chablis, pushed it two or three inches away from her, and sat more sad than confused. Debbie is not a bad artist, and she might have been great. These days she paints cute pictures for sale to tourists. Things happen. Life happens.

"Don't get me started talkin.'" Mac's tone of voice said the opposite of his words. Mac used to be a thinker, but few abstractions ever make it to a bar. Bartending causes rust on the brain.

"Which is why my main interest is atonement, thus redemption." Jeremiah sipped at his soft drink, looked at the label on the can, and gave an honest but crooked grin from his sagging mouth. "This stuff is not exactly sacramental."

"It's such a pretty day," Debbie said, "it's such a pretty day." She retrieved her small purse from the bar, walked to the doorway and stood framed in sunlight. Then she stepped into sunlight. She walked away, not briskly, but like one enchanted by a stroll in the sun.

"Handsome woman," said Jeremiah.

"Lost customer," said Mac.

"We'll speak again, and soon," Jeremiah promised. "Between then and now you may wish to ponder a question. How many differences, if any, are there between a preacher and a bartender." He stood, gave a backward wave as he walked to the doorway, and stepped into sunlight. His shabby suit and clodhopper shoes made him look like a distinguished bum, or an itinerant living on the bare edge of respectability.

=

The fabulous weather did not last. Mist rolled in from the coast. It was followed by rain. Hides of cattle turned glossy, and rain puddled in the churchyard of Hell-Fer-Certain. On next Sunday night, as trucks rolled in, Jeremiah performed like a champion, but with a different message. Anyone who paid the least attention understood that new images entered his calls for atonement. Instead of talking about lambs, he spoke of cattle. When speaking of heaven he no longer pictured streets of gold, but streets of opportunity. The image of the cross gave way to an image of the morning star. Hardly anyone gave two snips about images, but later on we would figure Jeremiah made changes in order to get Mac's attention.

And through the week, and through the next, it was Mac who changed the most, because (though no one knew it at the time) Mac tried to answer Jeremiah's question.

=

A good bartender is a precious sight, and Mac was always good. His instincts were quick, accurate, nearly catlike. He knew when to be smart-mouthed, when to be glib, and when to be thoughtful. He never lost control of the bar, but now he went beyond control and even directed entertainment.

If bar talk slowed, or the pool tables stood empty, Mac resembled a school teacher introducing new subjects. Instead of baseball, used truck parts, and cattle, we found ourselves cussing and discussing local Indian legends. We talked about the fall of empires, Roman and American. We quibbled over histories of Franklin Roosevelt and Henry Ford. In only two little weeks Mac's Bar turned into an interesting place to congregate, and not simply a place to get stewed.

Conversation improved but beer-drinking slowed. Mac ran a highly enhanced bar, but made less money. For those who know him well, Mac seemed slightly confused but almost happy. Since no one around here has been really happy for a long, long time, we were confused as well.

Meanwhile, gray day followed gray day and life went on as usual. On the coast, mist cloaked the broken wharves, warehouses, and abandoned fish cannery. Ghosts whispered through mist, nearly indistinguishable from mist; we thought them ghosts of fishermen lost at sea, ghosts of fishing boats long drowned. Thus, from the coast to the fields, memories of work and order and dreams lay as sprawled as wreckage.

Those ghosts of the land, the abandoned houses, leaned before wind and seemed ready not to shriek, but groan. Cattle lined the fences beside the road. As they appeared through mist, the cattle looked ghostly; silvered black hides, pale white faces, bovine stares toward us, and toward the road that would shortly carry them to slaughter.

Then, on a Saturday afternoon when baseball should have been the topic, Mac looked across the bar, across to Hell-Fer-Certain, and said "What does he mean by atonement?"

"It's being sorry for screw-ups." Pop, our local hustler, leaned against the end of the bar nearest the pool tables. As afternoon progressed, and as beer built confidence among customers, one or another booze-hound would challenge Pop to dollar-a-game. Pop would clean the guy's clock, and his wallet. For the moment, though, Pop was free to talk. He is a short, graying man, usually taciturn.

"It's more than that," Debbie said. "I can feel sorry for screw-ups any old time I want." She sipped at her wine. Her eyes squinched a little, and sorrow entered her voice. "Come to think of it, I usually want. Sorry most days . . . ." She realized she was saying too much. She saw her reflection in the bar mirror, smoothed her hair with one hand, smoothed wrinkles on the sleeve of her blouse with the other.

"It's recognizing that you're out of sync with the universe." Sarah, granny-skirts and all, attends Mac's Bar on Saturday afternoons. She would be happier in a sewing circle or a book discussion group, but she doesn't own a sewing machine and we don't have a library.

"Ninety days for drunk-and-disorderly. That's atonement." Pop looked down the bar where sat at least three customers who knew all about doing ninety days. "I rest my case."

"That's only punishment," Debbie whispered. Almost no one heard her.

=

Jeremiah next appeared at ten a.m. on a rainy Monday. Truck engines roared as truckers slowed for the intersection of roads, then caught a gear and started building revs. The possum-belly trailers were crowded with living beef standing silent as ghosts, the animals packed together and intimidated; the trucks rolling purgatories for beasts.

Mac and Sarah and Debbie opened the bar. Or rather, Mac opened the bar while Sarah made morning coffee and Debbie loafed. Mac brushed pool tables and cleaned rest rooms. Sarah drank coffee and watched the road. Sarah, who is nobody's mother, looks like she would do for the sainted mother of us all. Her face is sweet, her hair hangs in long braids, her figure is slightly dumpy. Her hands are workworn because she lives by cleaning houses of corporation people. If Sarah has a problem, and Sarah does, it's because she's a sucker for any new trend. She keeps ideas the way other people keep goldfish. Like goldfish, the ideas swim in all directions.

When Jeremiah entered the bar, rain glistened on his black suit and dripped from ends of his white hair. Wrinkles in his face looked like channels for rain. He sniffed the morning smells of the bar, stale tobacco, the stench of disinfectant. The smell of fresh coffee seemed to draw Jeremiah. He sat beside Sarah who was, at least for the moment, one of his parishioners.

"Praise the Lord," said Sarah.

"You got that right." Jeremiah gave a couple of sniffs and asked for coffee. He hunched above his coffee cup. His black suit made him look like a raven regarding road-kill. "Although," he said to Sarah, "if we must unceasingly praise the Lord, does that mean the Lord has an inferiority complex? If the Lord needs constant praise we may be dealing with a major case of insecurity."

Mac used a narrow broom to sweep between bar and barstools. Jeremiah's question stopped him. He shook his head. "I got to wonder whose side you're on?"

"I like you more positive." Sarah's voice did not tremble, but she seemed alarmed. "The Lord is supposed to let people feel safe, and stuff . . . like, no mystery stuff."

"Thank God for mysteries." Jeremiah's voice sounded nebulous as mist, although his words did not. "Life without mystery would be life without dreams. The universe would be dull indeed." Outside, at the intersection of roads, a truck engine roared as its driver revved, then caught a higher gear.

"For instance," and Jeremiah looked at Mac, not Sarah or Debbie, "do cattle dream? Does a young heifer or steer muse beyond that next mouthful of grass? Are there great cattle-questions? Better yet, are there herd dreams? Does the herd graze according to music tuned only to bovine ears?" Jeremiah's voice seemed not exactly sad, but he certainly was not joking.

"And do ghosts dream?" Jeremiah looked into mist, at the road that leads down to the sea. "A ghost may actually be a dream. After someone dies, maybe a leftover dream stands up and walks."

"Quit scaring me," Sarah whispered. She raised work-worn hands to cover her ears.

"I hope to scare you, because faith may not be as productive as doubt. Doubt asks questions and faith does not." Jeremiah's voice was not kind. He paused. "Is there some dread realm where human dreams and the dreams of cattle are appreciably the same?" He looked across the road at Hell-Fer-Certain. "If so, what does that say about all of us?"

At the time Sarah didn't get it, and Mac didn't either. Knowing Mac, though, it was a lead-pipe cinch he'd catch on sooner or later. He leaned against the bar. "Bartenders and preachers have a lot going," he told Jeremiah. "Both have something to sell, both exercise control over others, both serve as handy ears for the confessions of sinners." Mac grinned like a naughty three-year-old. "Both flip a certain amount of bull, and what they sell wears off after a good night's sleep."

"I'd fault your logic if it was worth my time." Jeremiah pushed his coffee away. "Also, I asked about difference, not similarity."

"My mistake." Mac sounded like a ten-year-old kid caught stealing nickels.

"Meanwhile, suppose a ghost really is a leftover dream?" Jeremiah stood, stretched, looked through the windows at mist and rain. Then he looked at Mac with distaste, like a man regarding a favorite nephew arrested on a burglary rap. "You can think more clearly than you have."

"You know it," Mac said, "and I know it."

"When I was young," Jeremiah told him, "I wanted to change the world . . . wanted to make things better . . . figured to find a cure for common hatreds, ignorance, wanted to defeat war . . . prejudice . . . ." He seemed as puzzled as Mac. He looked across the road at the fading colors of Hell-Fer-Certain. When he left the bar he walked slower than usual.

=

Atonement became the name of our game. Redemption became more than a word in a sermon. Our problem came because we didn't know what needed atoning. If anybody needed redemption it couldn't happen until we figured out our original foul-up.

But anyone with brains could see that Jeremiah made a bold if harsh play for the heart and soul of one man, Mac. Jeremiah seemed old as King Solomon, at least in experience, and maybe as wise. Being old, he knew he had little time left. What he'd said about wanting to change the world told us he wasn't fooling when he talked about dreams. We supposed if he couldn't change the world, he figured to change one man.

And, if Mac made less money, our local hustler, Pop, made more. As the bar became a place for interesting topics, guys stayed sober, longer. Pop enjoyed a surge of prosperity because a good hustle depends on the full attention of the guy being hustled. Sober guys have longer attention spans. It was during a lull in sober conversation that an awful thing happened.

On a fog-bound afternoon when headlights on the road appeared as silver discs, and as fog muffled the sound of engines, Mac absent-mindedly drew a beer. He set it before a customer, and muttered to himself, "He's trying to figure out what happens when dreams fizzle . . . the death of dreams . . . ."

Only Pop and Debbie heard. Debbie touched her wine glass, gave a dry little sob, and sat silent. Pop looked at Debbie, then at Mac. "You'd better not lay that one on the table," he whispered. "It will empty out the joint."

Mac emptied the bar, anyway. During the next hour he grew completely silent, then surly. If he was angry at himself and taking it out on customers, or his bar, or the universe, or on Jeremiah, no one could say. All we knew is that Mac was not jolly. As afternoon misted toward evening, customers stepped through the doorway into mist. By happy hour only Pop and Debbie remained. Bar neon glowed through mist like a token of sorrow, or like the subdued symbol of a small and unimportant corner of Hell.

"Everybody had big plans at one time or other." Pop murmured this, more to himself than to Debbie or Mac. "Time was when I didn't make a living with a pool cue." He looked at Mac in a kindly way, a way no one expects to see in a pool hustler. "We're gettin' old," Pop told Mac. "I guess we expected more . . . ." He looked around the bar, at twirly beer lights and the green felt of pool tables. ". . . didn't expect more of the world, maybe. Expected more of ourselves."

"I'm headed home," Debbie whispered. "Art is not an illusion. I used to know that." She shrugged into her jacket and looked at the men. "Pay no attention. I don't understand it, either."

=

Fire struck our land during early morning hours. It drank deeply of wind, flared and flamed through mist like a maddened imp squalling in the middle of fields. It blasted the farmhouse of Indian Hill Farm.

Indian Hill's house stood ramshackle and wrecked a thousand yards from the road. As the first touch of dawn moved grayly above fields, fire towered and blew sideways, tongues of flame lapping at mist. Mist blew into the flames, mixed with flames, and steam exhaled from the very mouth of fire. Wind carried the fire, and fire flamed ascendent above wet fields. By full dawn, Indian Hill farmhouse lay as embers beneath a steady morning rain.

That first fire saddened us. Bar talk remembered people who once owned Indian Hill, their sons, daughters, cousins; even the name of their collie-shepherd mix, once known as the best cattle-herding dog in the valley. Bar talk remembered August days of cutting or baling hay, or of trucks pulling silver-colored tank trailers, making milk pick-ups at each valley farm. A drunk wrote "I miss you so goodam much," on the wall of the men's can, but Mac painted it over right away.

The cattle corporation uses the old barns to store equipment, even though the farmhouses are abandoned. The corporation brought in a bulldozer, cleaned up the burn site, and seeded it with grass. The bulldozer knocked down outbuildings. The old barn stood solitary in the middle of fields. It seemed a testament to memories.

The second fire took the house of Valley View Farm which stood behind a stubby lane, and up a little rise. That house had become a fearful thing. Because of the short lane, and the rise, the house brooded above the road like a specter. It was larger than most farmhouses, and two fanlights had once looked toward the road like colorful eyes. With abandonment the glass had been broken. The eyes stared toward the road, hollow as eyes of the blind.

This second fire was hard for us to talk away, think away, or drink away. It continued to flame in the minds of those who saw it (and most everyone did) long after rain washed ashes down the rise. The fire began just after nightfall on a Tuesday when the valley stood empty of tractor-trailers, of truckers, and reduced by some few hundred cattle. As fire towered above the road, pickups pulled to the side, parked, and people talked or stared. Mist once more blew into flames, turned to steam, and steam blew across the road and into our faces. The stench of burning carried in the mist, but something worse walked to us.

Cattle were in the fields. Against all nature, the cattle drifted toward the fire. The herd formed a semi-circle in the wind-blown mist. White faces of cattle stared through mist, were reddened by reflections from the fire. The cattle stared not at fire, but stared in ghostly illumination at the road where we stood helpless to affect events, and watched; where we spoke excitedly, or with sadness, or, with but a murmur. The cattle seemed to stand as witness to our lives, their eyes blank as the blind eyes of the dying house.

=

The corporation bulldozed, seeded, and called the sheriff. One fire might be accidental. Two fires spelled arson. The sheriff went through motions, but couldn't see the point. After all, the houses were worthless.

=

"It's a trick question," Mac confided to Debbie on one of those afternoons when wind drops and fog gathers thick enough to hinder traffic. Across the road Hell-Fer-Certain stood in the fog like a ghost. "The difference between a bartender and a preacher is no difference at all."

"Because?"

"Because jobs have nothing to do with the basic guy." Mac looked around his bar like he saw it for the first time. "That preacher is not a beat-up church, and this bartender is not a bar. You got it?"

"If you came to that smart an answer," Debbie told him, "then it wasn't a trick question."

If Mac had changed, and if Jeremiah was using different images, Debbie changed as well. Although she told no one, images of fire occupied her, as did sadness. "There's a word called 'expiation,'" she said in a low voice. "I think we'll learn about it."

The third fire took Heather Hill Farm, and the fourth took River View. By then August was long past, September waning, as fall rains began in earnest. The valley filled with flame and steam. Cattle now grazed nearer the road, stood looking across fences in that dumb, animal manner that seems asking for explanation.

Then, on a night when the sky seemed to seep absolute darkness, as well as seeping rain, Debbie trudged toward the bar. Throughout the valley, as fires continued, sadness had become not only ordinary but a custom. We did not understand that it was not simply a few old houses being burned away. Symbolically, flame engulfed our history. People headed to the bar where night could not be defeated, but could be allayed. Neon signs colored our night world. Cone-lights above pool tables suggested focus and illumination. As Debbie passed the reader-board in front of Hell-Fer-Certain she sensed movement in the darkness. She gave a small, involuntary gasp.

"It's only me." Mac's voice sounded controlled, but fearful. "Pop is running the joint for an hour or two."

"You're standing in rain before a church that drives you nuts. Plus you've been acting spooky. Are you the arsonist?" Debbie hesitated, thought about fires and Mac's whereabouts. "You couldn't be unless you're setting them with a timer. You were behind the bar for two fires out of four."

Mac made a vague motion toward the church. "He is," Mac said.

"For the love of God." Jeremiah's voice came from darkness before the church. "For other loves as well."

"You're helping him?" Debbie asked Mac. She felt for a moment that she should flee. "What are you doing out here if you're not helping him?"

"Because I thought I liked the guy. Because I'm sick-a selling beer. Because it isn't raining inside . . . how the hell do I know . . . ." Mac's voice turned apologetic. ". . . sorry . . . I'm not sure why I'm here, but I am sure that hell is about to start popping. Look west."

Debbie turned. "You guys are scaring me. You are." In the west, like beginning sunset, a slight glow of orange showed at docks and cannery. "Mass fire, massive," Debbie whispered to herself. "If any of that goes, all of it goes."

"No water down there except what's in the ocean." Mac turned to where Jeremiah stood in darkness. "I reckon this is supposed to mean something?"

"I reckon it does." Jeremiah's voice did not sound preacherly, but grim. "Or maybe it's just a reckoning."

"Why are you doing this?" Debbie sensed Jeremiah's presence but could not find him in the darkness. Rain patted on her hooded parka. It puddled at her feet. "Everybody was getting by," she said. "Things aren't great but we were making it." She watched as the orange glow increased. "I won't cop on you," she whispered to Jeremiah, "or at least I guess I won't. But, you'd do well to have an explanation." She turned to Mac. "Everybody will be going down there pretty quick. Drive me."

Mac stood quiet, a man afraid, or maybe only indecisive. Debbie took his arm. She turned toward the darkness before the church. "Go ahead and tell me this is the will of the Lord," Debbie said to Jeremiah. "Then I'll know you're nuts." She walked toward Mac's pickup.

"Redemption by fire." Jeremiah's harsh whisper came from shadows before the church. "I don't think the Lord has much to do with it. You're an artist. Figure it out."

=

Immense fires, fires as big as cities burning, cast heat so huge they must warm the toes of heaven. Lesser fires, like the burning of a way of life, are localized, thus more spectacular.

By the time Mac and Debbie arrived, fire already covered docks and rose into the night through the roofs of warehouses. Sounds of burning, the crash of timbers, the roar of volcanic updrafts silenced the sounds of seawind and surf. Fire moved toward the enormous cannery as heat melted asphalt on the road between warehouses. When the road began to burn, a stench of petroleum mixed with dry smells of woodsmoke from flaming walls and floors; this while rain wept and blew across the scene, sizzled, pattered through mist.

Mac and Debbie stood halfway down a hill leading to the cannery. Heat coasted up the side of the hill and stopped their advance. Behind them, cresting the hill, headlights of old pickups pointed toward the fire as people arrived, the beams of light swallowed by fire. Firelight rose toward the scud of low-flying clouds, and black smoke crisscrossed through the light as heat mixed and churned the winds. As more and more people arrived headlights were switched off. People milled, clustered together, sought an illusion of unity, of safety. Fire swept into the broken doors of the cannery. Fire illuminated faces in the crowd. Firelight glowed orange on cheeks and hands. It glossed clothing with a sheen of red. Fire caused shadows, made eyes seem like hollows of night.

"Is this expiation?" Debbie whispered beneath the roar of fire. She watched as flame burst through the high roof of the cannery. Then, because it seemed nothing so awful could be focus for good, she looked away, then gasped. She tried to turn, tried to look back up the hill, or at the wet and weeping heavens, or anywhere except where her gaze finally was forced to focus.

On the periphery of the fire vague movement began in blowing mist. At first the movement seemed only swirls of mist, then shapes began to coalesce. Shapes drifted like unimportant murmurs. Mist blew among them, seemed to offer substance, and the shapes became human figures drifting toward fire, unhesitating, herd-like and passive; not, after all, only the ghosts of fishermen drowned, but the ghosts of dreams summoned to the burning; dreams that like threatened beasts gave final screams, then fell into mute acceptance.

. . . and Debbie saw a young Mac bouncing a basketball while coaching kids, and a young Jeremiah standing before a mission school. Mostly, though, she saw a young woman sitting before canvas, saw the turn of a young wrist properly pointing a brush, sensing the depth of colors in the palette, saw a young woman alive with the high dreams of art; then watched the diminishing form of that young and lovely woman, a woman aspiring to creation, drift slowly, inexorably, to disappear into the roar of flames.

"I think," said Mac in a voice too husky to come from anything but tears, "that it's time to get the hell out."

"And I think," said Debbie, "that your expression is apt. But I'm not sure I like you anymore. Go back without me. I'll catch a ride." She managed to control her voice.

=

Climax and anti-climax. Fire swept across the scene in fountains and waves. When the cannery roof fell machinery glowed red. Water pipes and steam pipes twisted, boilers stood like the crimson cauldrons of medieval hell, and people gradually stopped exclaiming, because nothing, it seems, can be remarkable forever. People climbed in their trucks, turned around, and told themselves and each other that what they really needed was a drink. The show was over, the festivities ended, a way of life had passed and no one even knew it.

Debbie, riding four-to-a-cab in a rickety pickup, looked beyond headlights and into mist. She felt slugged in the stomach. A glow stood in the sky.

=

To those who arrived from the destruction of the cannery, Hell-Fer-Certain Church burned as an afterthought. Flame lighted the inside of the church, and stained glass windows pictured scenes from Bible stories. Stained glass gradually fell away as heat melted lead, turned glass to powder when fire burst through to rise along the outside of the building. Psychedelic colors of pink and orange and green twisted beneath flame, turned brown, turned gray, and fell to ash. Fire roared to the top of the steeple where wind caused it to wave as a hellish flag. When the cracked bell and the broken loudspeaker fell from the steeple, only Debbie gave it more than passing thought.

As emotionally exhausted people drifted toward the bar, Debbie found she did not want a drink, did not want company, but did want to wring an explanation out of Jeremiah. And, Jeremiah, it turned out, was not to be found.

Debbie looked toward Mac's bar, saw the glow of barlight, heard the loud voices of people with little information and large opinions.

She turned back to the church and watched the last flames die to yellow flickers above coals. The flames licked feebly at mist, and Debbie became conscious that in the fields beyond Hell-Fer-Certain, herds lined the fences; cattle white-faced, ghostly in the illumination from dying flames, and mute.

=

We woke, next day, bewildered. Dullness spread across the valley. It invaded our lives, or rather, seeped into our lives. We lived in a place where dreams had died, a world of rain and cattle and embers. It was a world stripped of sense, stripped even of ghosts, and we began to understand that hell need not be spectacular, only dull. At least that seemed true.

Debbie watched, wept, thought, and recorded in her journal this history of our destroyed world. With the eyes of an artist she watched herself in mirrors, saw drawn features, the high and accented cheekbones of age, the ravages, not of time, but of loss; and she despised Jeremiah. She listened as hatred flared among us, hot hatred because people wanted someone to blame. As guesses turned to rumor, then to conviction, it became obvious that it was Jeremiah who dealt in flame. People cursed his name. Men sought for him throughout the valley, and swore vengeance.

Our destroyed world, what had it been? Abandoned farms, abandoned fishery, and dregs of memory that recalled honest lives and loves. Many of us had come to this place in search of spiritual amity, of community; but all of that died long before the fires.

"But," Debbie said to Mac on a gray morning before the bar opened, "how much of this sits on our own shoulders?"

Mac, who since the fires had remained largely silent, did not answer. Debbie turned from him and watched Sarah, because Sarah's shock seemed deepest, bone-breaking deep. Sarah made coffee and muttered Bible-text about king Nebuchadnezzar who God changed to a beast ". . . *that you shall be driven from among men, and your dwelling shall be with beasts of the field; you shall be made to eat grass like an ox, and you shall be wet with the dew of heaven . . . .*" and then Sarah's voice whispered gabble, as though she spoke in tongues.

"The sumbitch rubbed our noses in our own lives." Mac moved like a tired man after a twelve-hour shift. Gray light crowded against windows of the bar in the same way that, beyond the burned church, cattle crowded fences. Mac picked up a broom, looked at it like he could not understand its use, then leaned it against the bar. He sat on a barstool and waited for coffee.

"*. . . and he was driven from among men, and did eat grass as oxen, and his body was wet with the dew of heaven, till his hairs were grown like eagles' feathers, and his nails like birds' claws . . . .*" Sarah's voice trembled with fear or ecstasy, and Debbie could not say which.

"That preacher drove himself," Mac said to Sarah, as if they were holding a normal conversation, "and he's driving us right now because he was serious, and we only think we are." He turned back to Debbie. "He's not in the fields. He's ashes. He's across the road right now, ashes in his burned church. I watched him set the fire. I walked away. He didn't." Mac turned back to Sarah. "He's preaching right now, if you listen you can hear . . . what do you hear? . . . or, maybe it's the voice out of the whirlwind . . . like in the Book of Job."

It seemed to Debbie that, if Mac were not exhausted, he would be nearly as hysteric as Sarah. "I hear nothing from across the road," she said, "and if he chose to burn it's his expiation, not ours." Even though she detested Jeremiah, her mind filled with sorrow. Then she felt guilty without knowing why. And then, she felt something she could not at first understand. She had not felt joy in many-a-year.

She began to understand a little. Her first understanding was that she no longer despised Jeremiah. She fell silent. Listening. It seemed to her that from the fields came a sense of movement, the herd movement of cattle; and from the coast, echoes of screams.

"You're right about one thing," she told Mac. "He rubbed our noses in our own lives. Even if he's ashes, he's still doing it because nobody's leaving town. We're all still standing here, and we're unreal. We're staring over fences."

"The dreams were real," Mac whispered. "We're the husks of dreams." He looked across the road where white-faced cattle stood in mist. At the intersection of roads trucks slowed. An engine roared as a tractor-trailer driver caught a higher gear. Another engine roared. "Why did the guy do his own atonement and leave us holding the bag?"

"That's a cop-out," Debbie told him. "Dream new dreams and quit blaming the other guy." Debbie paused, alive in the knowledge that Jeremiah had failed with Mac but had succeeded with her. Jeremiah had forced them to hate him, had sickened them, so that they must rebel against their lives or die. He had fought that they might once more learn to love. There were many arts, and many roads to them. Maybe Jeremiah had been traveling a road of art, and not religion.

Debbie yearned to comfort Mac and Sarah, and yet she knew that would be wrong. She felt, in some harsh way, ordained. She watched Mac and saw that her words were going nowhere. But, Mac, being Mac, would think about them, so maybe later . . . and then Debbie made her voice stern, nearly punishing, and hoped it would not break with compassion.

"The world is full of gurus," she told Sarah above the roar of truck engines. "Find another one. Lacking that, you may want to consider a question."

Wintering

"... the housemates sit
Around the radiant fireplace, enclosed
In a tumultuous privacy of storm ..."
    —Ralph Waldo Emerson, "The Snowstorm"

BEYOND THE HUNDRED-YEAR-OLD STAINED GLASS WINDOWS OF OUR house, the branches of a hundred year old pear tree reach into the winter wind. Here and there a few dead leaves cling to the branches. The sky is gray. Spits of wind and rain wash against the stained glass, and the Strait of Juan de Fuca tumbles against beaches. Winter, it seems, should not mean much in this house that has seen a hundred of them.

I have seen fewer winters, and to me winter is always a new and hopeful time. The reason, no doubt, is that I am a man of gardens and trees; have spent so many seasons with trees. In few words, I want to trace the cycle of seasons that have finally brought us to this winter.

That old pear tree is my familiar in every season, although I have known many trees. I've planted thousands, cut a few hundred, and climbed hundreds more during the years when I supported myself as a gardener while learning to be a writer. I have worked beside men who spent their working lives in trees, and they had the gardener's wisdom in their old eyes, eyes which also seemed young. My mind finally came to understand what they knew. They were

168

men not of years but of seasons. They spoke, when pruning a tree, of how the tree would look in three springs. They were men who welcomed winter. The sap in the trees was down, and they could prune trees, or even move them. Each winter they gave new forms to their worlds.

This year took so long to arrive at winter. Last spring came early. My housemate and I planned our half-acre of garden, and wondered, as gardeners do, what the summer and fall would bring. I watched her dark-haired head bent over lists, watched her fingers sorting seed packages; and I wondered how many thousands of people around us were doing the same. The cold March rains were proof against frost, and the wet soil clogged the tines of the rototiller as it turned a thick layer of compost into the soil.

I wondered how many thousands of people around us were laying aside the winter's work and entertainment because of the advance of spring. At my place we were readers and writers. Our books are shelved in spring and the typewriters sit quiet for weeks. We are serious gardeners because we love gardening. We always grow more than we need, more than we can store. The over-supply is pressed on neighbors or given to food banks. Two summers ago we had too many peas, and this spring mistakenly planted fewer. Two summers ago we had few beans, so we planted more; then urged pecks of them onto neighbors. In this cold spring our hands and feet were wet and raw as usual during the early planning.

Then summer arrived and lingered. The first crop of spinach made but indifferently. It looked like it would be a dry summer. We shot water from rainbird sprinklers. The first crop of onions stood like thin green wands. The broccoli was full leaved, and it was soon clear that the cauliflower was in trouble. We transplanted plants. The root systems were healthy, but the summer progressed and the cauliflower languished and died. We were too busy with too many raspberries.

The summer continued to linger. In early August there was one full autumn day. Then summer returned. It seemed proof against the pumpkins which developed wide orange streaks on their green hides. The second set of onions, and the corn, looked like old men and old women who were honorably bound to stand upright beneath the sun. We braided garlic, and we continued to shoot water; the arcing splashes from the rainbirds sometimes feathering into spume blown sideways by the wind.

The cherry trees had produced abundantly, as had the plums. The pears and apples were heavy with fruit. We propped the sagging branches. Already it was the middle of September. Would summer never end? The quince were yellow beneath the sun, and the chrysanthemum leaves silvered beneath still tightly closed buds.

Then the swing of the seasons finally began. Autumn was in the air, although some of the trees seemed not to know it. The mimosa put out new, pale green growth.

I love the seasons, but I love more the swing of the seasons; like the rush of autumn and the rituals of autumn. We ran the gasoline out of the rototiller before it was stored, thus protecting it from gummed fuel lines. We mowed the grass short before storing the mower. On our wet northwest coast, grass obeys a different doctrine. In cold weather areas it should be long, but on this coast it should winter closely cut. Long grass here is an invitation to mold, fungus and rust.

Autumn progressed and we moved comfortably with the ritual swing. We sealed the handles of the garden tools with varnish, sharpened the chain saw and put a new handle in the axe. We listened to soft jazz on the radio, and put primer over the sanded-off rust spots on the pickup. The primer had a sharp, chemical smell that did not seem unhealthy. We watched the weather signs, and went to the slash piles for firewood. The stoves, which had set like forgotten pot bellied Gods, now came alive with fire behind the glowing isinglass.

Then winter finally arrived with its own demands and ritual. The cold rains swept in and we unpacked sweaters, hooded jackets, and boots. The book-lined shelves seemed suddenly alive with as much promise as the promise of spring. We turned the wheelbarrow upside down and put it in storage. Other tools came out; the long handled and short handled pruners, the ladders, and the dark tar for sealing pruning cuts. We planted tulip and crocus bulb in the wet, cold soil. Winter is so short. We wanted as much winter experience as we could get. All too soon we will again be in the swing of the seasons, the swing in to spring.

Now even the conifers are slowed toward dormancy as they discard needles in the slow process that continues all year round. The only broad leaf conifer, the gingko, dropped all its leaves at once after the first hard frost.

I watch the bare, reaching branches of that wintering pear and know exactly what is happening in that hundred-year-old tree. It is expressing a variety of strength.

In summer that tree will move as many as 400 pounds of water each day through transpiration and the making of fruit. The as yet not fully explained process of photosynthesis is an active, manufacturing force. Life and water channel up and down the cambian layer. There is a road inside that tree, and in winter the road leads to the roots where energy is stored in the form of sugar. That tree is dormant, but it is expressing power. When spring comes the sugar will be transformed, and the tree will express a great burst of energy. Were such energy transferred into heat it would consume this old house in one enormous blaze.

I split balks of wood; the salmon colored fir, the clean lined cedar, the white alder that falls in two so easily beneath the axe, and the red coated madrona with its ringless white interior that carries occasional small streaks like rust. The rains wash, the winds crash, and I privately hope for snow. The trees restore themselves and so do we.

There are books to be read and books to be written. She, my wintering housemate, silhouetted against gray sky and stained glass windows, sits reading. She worked so hard during spring and summer and fall. We have earned this time of restoration. It is a time of books, of walks on the cold and windy beach, of pages written, puzzled over, rewritten. We are in the swing of our own season, and winter will be far too short.

Some Remarks on the Literature of War

When you drive inside the gate at Quantico writing in very big letters there says the mission of the Marine Corps is to take and hold ground. I like that because it is honest. It does not talk about learning a trade, wearing a woman-getting uniform, or traveling the world. What it plainly says is the business of the Marines is the infliction and receiving of death. It is left, perhaps, to the Army, the Navy, and sociologists/philosophers/political theorists/politicians/educators and fiction writers to throw crap about patriotism, manifest destiny, and historical necessity. I am a fiction writer and I do not intend to discuss truth and illusion beyond my own trade, but I will note that both exist.

Moreover, as a fiction writer I am not exactly sure what the term 'literature' means. When General Motors passes out slick brochures praising the engineering that has gone into its latest death trap; well, General Motors calls that brochure literature. I do know something about why I write fiction and what fiction intends. It is well to get our thoughts straight on that before talking about war stories by various writers.

It may be that different writers have different approaches to fiction, but I believe the serious writer will be in agreement when I say that fiction deals only with the truth. The literature of war is mostly fiction; which is to say that it is one area of human experience that has been greatly explored for the truth.

This is a relativistic world that likes to take care of cracks at the word: truth. There is no question that attack and defense can be made for the proposition that truth is relative, not eternal. There are those who will claim that truth changes every time a research psychologist gets a different result from running rats through a maze. Fiction writers could hardly care less about such arguments, and fiction writers have written the most books concerned with truth.

The great truth seems to be the truth of facts. The sun rises and sets. Men are born, reproduce and die. The female of the species bears the children. Grass grows in nearly every kind of soil. These are true because they are predictable as the grass, running a coefficient of correlation to nine point nine of the millionth decimal.

The truth discovered in fiction relies partly on these facts. They are known as context. Into this context is shoved individual knowledge and emotion, experience, the need to discover what is the meaning of all the diverse parts that are brought to a story. More of this in a minute.

You see, it is not enough that a writer writes in such a way that his audience believes. It may be that many readers believed Booth Tarkington at his worst, or Bret Harte—the most maudlin of sentimentalizers. It is necessary that the writer works with such intensity that he discovers truth.

How do you do this? First of all, you have to have respect for your characters; a respect that Joseph Conrad called sympathy. Conrad did not define the term, but after you have read everything Conrad wrote a couple of times then it is possible to define that term for yourself. Sympathy is empathy for the character, plus the total respect that allows the character to do what he must in a harrowing situation. If the character must make a fool of the writer, then the writer may not interfere.

What all this means is that the fiction writer knows that for a given person in a given situation there can be only one truth, and that truth is discoverable—usually. That is fiction at its simple best. Add more characters in more situations and the problems compound; yet, for each of those characters there is only the situation as he may perceive it. There is a truth for each of those people, and it may be that collectively they have a truth that will speak independently of their individual situations.

Write it hard enough and it may be that the specific situation examined will also contain a general truth. My favorite example of this is Hemingway's *Old Man and the Sea*. As a general statement it is a hymn of praise, of hope, of sanctification that endorses the condition of being human. This from Hemingway. It seems a great contradiction, but what it really is is a great endorsement of a writer courageous enough to write truly a story that on the face seems to contradict all of his other work.

Hemingway wrote honestly and intensely about the old man. You may be sure that he was uninterested in symbol, allegory, denouement, plot or any other terms in the current literary sweepstakes. He was interested only in following Santiago through a culminating situation: what would happen, what must Santiago do, what is the luck and the forces that aid or hinder him? When the sharks arrive they are real sharks. If there is greater meaning to them, then that meaning comes from the reader's emotional and intellectual state—or lack of it. Hemingway was only interested in the sharkiness of sharkiness. No two truths are articulated quite the same because they are individual truths. We do not feel the same amount of horror over the same things. Our thresholds for pain are not exactly alike. We perceive, feel, learn as individuals, not as committees or peer groups (although we may learn from groups). If we read well, we experience revelation in the same way. Revelation is an antique word, but it is a good word and it has use beyond the religious connotation.

The writer has no message when he is at his best. He tries only to discover the individual truth of an individual in a situation. If the reader reads well enough, and if the writer has worked hard enough and also has some luck, then the reader will discover his own truth. He will experience some degree of revelation; and the quality of the revelation depends on his own openness, tenacity, determination to understand . . . and on his ability to be humane. A good reader is almost more rare than a good writer, and he is as creative.

Now I think we can turn to talking about war stories.

The best that deal with the military aspect of war are *The Thin Red Line* by James Jones, *One to Court Cadence* by James Crumley, and *Guadalcanal Diary* by Richard Tregaskis.

The best that deal with the civilian population are The *Dollmaker* by Harriette Arnow and *The Painted Bird* by Jerzy Kosinski. To these, may be added *The Diary of Anne Frank*. A good reader will want to read that one in dedication to the glory and pathos possible for his own soul . . . and because good readers like ultimates. I call these six books the best because they are all written in the same severe honesty that one reads on that sign inside the gates at Quantico.

Beyond these lie a great welter of writing that ranges from very fine to potboilers. There is plenty of causeserving tripe available. There is a lot of sentimentality. There are even a few by very great writers that are just terrible, because they are so clouded with young experience that the writer has been unable to rid himself of romance before hitting into his material. I'm not going to name any particular people, because I respect some of them and they are still alive. Yet, I will say that the Second World War produced stuff that was published before the writer got sufficient distance. If you're interested, browse the five-cent racks in a used bookstore and look for famous names. War mostly attracts midgets, but a few giants almost always attend and some of them are going to stumble.

Still, there are more than six good books on war. And it is a good thing to read some of them, because writers learn from one another. Jones could probably not, for example, have done *Thin Red Line* had he only had military experience. He also had the experience of reading a whole batch of other writers. So before discussing the six I've mentioned, I will mention some others and examine one that kind of sets the scene and the possibilities for at least four of the six.

War books I like are: *Stella* by Jan DeHartog, *The Cruel Sea* by Nicholas Monsarret, *The Red Badge of Courage* by Crane, *For Whom the Bell Tolls* by and *Men at War* (anthology edited by Hemingway), *All Quiet on the Western Front*, and *U.S.A.* which I want to discuss. There are a lot of others I like, but those will do for a start. If you read them you will find traces of heroics (unexplained), sentiment (uncontained), and preaching (as in the case of *Red Badge*) that maybe war ain't good for everybody, but if it is an ill wind, etc. I like these books because they show what had to be done before the writers of *Line*, *Dollmaker* and *Cadence* could really get in and show what could be done. At least I think this is true.

One more aside before getting into *U.S.A.* Sometimes a completely effective piece of writing comes from very average motives, and I especially like *The Officer's Guide*, so beloved by graduates of The Point. I like it because of the bland regulation type chapter about making wills and preburial arrangements. The chapter is suitably titled, Death. I like the official U.S. Army recommended attitude to cultivate toward eternity; and the carefully committed and therefore obvious remark that once he is dead, gone and rotten, the officer corps's ex-wife will be screwing someone else. The chapter is a small masterpiece.

For it is true that one of the great victories of war is death. It is not the greatest victory, but it will do for openers.

When you are dead you heart stops beating and your flesh gets very cold and you do not think or talk or love anymore. You need no space to move around in, and indeed, you need very little space anyway, no more than a hanging side of pork—which, if you are dead in a war you will probably resemble. Moreover, there is not real further use to be gotten from you, unless there are hogs rooting around on that battlefield (as there were in the Civil War, World War I & II, the Korean handslap and the Viet Nam fiasco.) If there are hogs then maybe the hogs will get hoggier and maybe someone will eventually get a slice of them. You can only see further use or creation by way of osmosis.

Now we can talk about *U.S.A.*

In my opinion the book is a demarcation point in the literature of war. Up to the time of its writing it still seems possible that a serious writer might have seriously considered writing a book in a war context where there was a winner. After the publication of *U.S.A.* it seems unlikely that any writer could be so deceived.

It is a book peopled by losers, not simply by people who lose. The characters are juiceless, banal, willful and tepid. A principal character, J. Ward Moorehouse, kind of sets the stage and gives contrast to another character named Yossarian who would show up about thirty-five years later. J. Ward Moorehouse is a loser because he is able to rationalize something that Yossarian calls by its right name. Fear. Moorehouse spouts persuasions of honor and necessity and patriotism to himself. Yossarian plainly states that if he is killed no one wins as far as he is concerned. This isn't exactly a winner mentality, either; but at least it is not the loser mentality of J. Ward Moorehouse . . . who is not even combatant. His fears are on the level of status, getting ahead, money and influence.

U.S.A. is a grand, three-book portrayal of a bunch of losers who can hardly wait to lose, and who do lose, and all because they live on one of the greatest loser nations on earth and call it good. The nation that brought the European import notion of "The War to End All Wars." The nation of sanctimony and good advice. The nation which at this very time has the capacity to kill everyone in the world seven times . . . and continues to record the biggest military arms budget in its history . . . but, I editorialize.

What I meant to say is that Dos Passos was doing pretty good considering that the romantic and naturalistic traditions in our literature were all around him. In *U.S.A.* even the winners are losers, probably the biggest losers. The intercalary writing on people like J.P. Morgan is some of the most powerful writing in the book.

Dos Passos was angry, sometimes bitter, and sure was cynical. It is an occupational hazard of writers, for generally writers love their land and history and the vision they get from the other voices of their literature. Damned few writers have really loved the notion of killing, however.

What war and killing does is shock a man's innocence. It shocked Dos Passos, it shocks me, and if it does not shock you then I must remark you are much older than I.

U.S.A. was the book that put the literary sanction on the end of American innocence. It would set the stage for the revulsion of the '30s and the realities of the '40s. I think I could talk for a century about that period. It was when I was born and grew up. Instead, I'll just make a few remarks.

Innocence was pretty well gone in the '30s, but there was plenty of ignorance to make up for it. There was sociological reasons, of course, and if we had time they could be accurately traced. Sufficient to say that the depression finally required a scapegoat mild enough to attack, but luminous enough to make the attack feel valid and heroic. In the '40s the American people would be led to hate the 'dirty little Japs' and the 'Nazi murderers' with some claim to validity. In the '30s the most visible people to hate were the Jews; and the 'International Cartel of Jewish Bankers.' There were a hell of a lot of citizens who backed the Hitler-Mussolini team in '38 and '39. The depression was a hard time . . . surely the understatement of the year. It saw disillusion, guilt, self-hatred and boredom and fear. There is no reason to romanticize the depression. American innocence was at a low ebb, and even World War II would not supply the patriotic revival that had occurred during World War I.

From the years 1939 to 1945 the world was steeped in blood. From Murmansk to New Zealand, across the Burma Road, through the tolling waters of the South Pacific, and the torpedo wakes that were like a network of curses on the Atlantic. Combatants, civilians, natives of islands, jews and gypsies, and the workers on African rubber plantations. The rivers fed blood to the bloody oceans. In the industrial cities of big nations the workers were casualties of juryrigged equipment, blasted by unsafe conditions, sacrificed up to keep the various Victory E's of the various killers waving from factory smokestacks. The victims of cost-plus-six. Death walked the world, but money was in the wind.

Now I can quickly mention a couple of the books and you can read them and then everyone will understand each other.

The Diary of Anne Frank and *Guadalcanal Diary* are very important because it is hard to make a tragedy out of statistics like six million Jews exterminated. If I tell you that a good low guess for casualties in World War II would run to a hundred fifty million people if would not impress you. The problem is that no one can imagine that much meat, leave alone the death of that much spirit.

The mind stumbles before such figures, cannot comprehend that kind of fury.

The Diary of Anne Frank is a diary kept by a young girl who happened to be a Jew and who happened to be in the wrong place at the same time. It records hopes, dreams, aspirations, the beauty that is implied in the growing notion of touching one another . . . and it ends when Nazis discover the hiding place and lead everyone off to extermination. I think you will cry a lot when you read it, and if you don't cry don't tell me about it. Instead of six million, the figure is one. Take that figure and abstract it one at a time six million times and you have about three percent of the violence and grief of World War II.

Guadalcanal Diary is effective in another way. Tregaskis lets you know what is happening by objective reporting. He was dealing with twenty-six thousand deaths in three weeks, of which four thousand were American and the rest Japanese. At its best the book is flat as a camera, as reflective as a mirror. The constant beat through the book is death, death, death. It ticks and tocks and ticks with popping skulls under tank treads, flaming bodies, fearful men filled with bravado . . . and recounts that "We lost twenty people at that place," and then goes ticking and tocking and death, death, death . . . "And we lost seventy people . . ."

After you get done with it you might want to read a book by a Japanese writer called *Fires on the Plain*. The writer is Ooka Shohi.

And now I can speak about the greatest war novels.

James Jones is one of our great American writers, although no one in your English department will ever tell you that. One reason, I think, is that Jones does not write his books for English departments. Perhaps I am a tad bit biased here, but I must remark that professional readers often feel themselves so smart that they only end up reading about their own egos. To illustrate, here is a little story.

In a book that Jones wrote titled *Some Came Running* the character Dave Hirsh is working on a combat novel in which death is a comic hero. I'd been reading Jones for a good many years and liking him a lot. One day I sat down and wrote to him and happened to mention that *Thin Red Line* was the book that his character David Hirsh had been working with. Jones wrote back in a slight state of shock. He told me that not one reviewer had ever caught that, and no one else had understood it except for one editor. It made me wonder how much critics miss, or if they read the books at all . . . for I have had students who loved to read and they caught the connection without help. It is very obvious.

Anyway, Jones does not write for English departments. He writes to get at the truth of the matter, and in *Thin Red Line* he got all of the truth that will ever be needed about the fact of death in war.

When *Line* was published the fairly standard reaction by reviewers was that it was another combat potboiler written in the very conventional form of a company going to battle. If one reads it with even ten percent of the seriousness that it was written, then it is quickly seen death is the only hero in the book. Death gets all the funny lines, and the straight men get death. The funny lines are not funny but absurd; as for example, when a man accidentally grabs a grenade on his belt by the pin. The grenade blows, and the dying man says something like, "what a stupid, recroot stunt." No one is likely to crack any ribs laughing, but any reader will quickly understand that one of war's great victories is death. He will also understand a bit more about the comic, and the human pain that often composes the comic element. I think it is especially important that we pay attention to such things in a world largely dominated by the president, the congress, the F.B.I. and Donald Duck.

The other victory of war, and war's greatest victory, is dehumanization. There is plenty of this shown in *Line,* and in *Dollmaker,* but it really is the main subject of *One to Count Cadence.* The ironies, the bitterness, the comic and the absurd all combine in the figure of The Warrior.

In *Cadence* the profession of giving and receiving death is brought to a strong emotional sense, a way of becoming. It is very strictly moral, and it will remain moral for just as long as bankers and tank manufacturers and tinhorn patriots and flag waving mothers insist on honorably killing everybody who offends them. The emotional becoming is a very warm sense, finally. It is an intelligent business. In fact, it is the only intelligent business . . . given the world in which the D.A.R., and C.I.A. and the V.F.W. function well and happily. The fury of the book is in complete and perfect control. It is like Crumley has muzzled the toughest tiger that ever lived and then taught that tiger to beg for bowls of whipped cream.

It is a great book and *Line* is a great book. I use the word 'great' advisedly.

Let me distinguish. I would not, for example, describe the U.S.A. as a great nation. It is a damned big nation, and it makes monumental successes and mistakes, but it does not at present have the quality of greatness. Too many lies and violences have been happening for too long.

Yet, I am easily persuaded that the American people are or can be great. During the turbulence of the '60s I thought this. Divided they may have been, but the greatness was pulsing. They were certainly great through the Second World War when they were killed, lied to, conned spiritually and fed the same old warmed over pap about God, Country, and Destiny. In fact, any people who through seventy years of the 20th century have been able to prevail in spite of the U.S. government almost have to be great by definition. In my opinion our last great nation dissolved when Andrew Jackson allowed the railroading of the Cherokees, and when Chief Joseph laid down his arms.

This illustration is to give the feel of what I mean about a book. It is not to draw tight guidelines. I judge a book by asking three things. It is about somebody? It is about something? Does the writer search and truly say the truth of the material? When these things are all present the book is likely to be great. It can even be that way when some part is missing. *U.S.A.* would by this definition be a loser, if the something it was about was not so important and the characters who volunteered spoke to that importance . . . and if Dos Passos had not worked so hard.

The greatest books are those that handle all three at their highest pitch, and the best book I know of that does this is *The Dollmaker*. I consider it to be of the best novels of this century, or any century; for it handles completely the aspect of dehumanization and realizes a victory over what seems totally crushing dehumanizing force. It denies in its truth that the original state of man is depravity. It affirms with its truth the creative capacity of human, and in spite of every hell that can be wrought by an industrialized, greed-filled society, it ends in beauty.

Briefly, *The Dollmaker* is about Gertie Nevels, who, with her husband and family, moves to Detroit during the Second War. Her husband works in a war plant and the family begins to die while everything is dying around them. To call it simply a war book is to miscall it badly. It is a great book, and that is speaking exactly to the point. Read it. It is good for the heart. It evokes compassion beyond all fact or statistic or fundamentalist social science argument. It is heaven and hell, and finally it is the transcending spirit of mankind . . . and it is also the best book on war about a civilian population.

The last book I want to talk about also deals with dehuman-ization. It is *The Painted Bird*. It makes the writings of DeSade look like an adolescent hiding in the john and masturbating. Do not read the book if you are totally convinced that evil exists for there is no reason to bludgeon your mind. Instead, give it to your friendly neighborhood preacher, politician or English professor. Tell them it is a story about a small, refugee boy being shuttled around through the peasantry of Europe during World War II; after all the men of God, the Gods of politics, and the tweed-bottomed professors have proved that their freedom really was an academic question after all.

One note before conclusion. I will say that the degradation and insanity of war does not preclude the valiant gesture, the loving heart, or even the courageous act. These are however, not expressions of war but expressions of people who happen to be trapped by war. The incidents are countless. I suppose that symbolically they are best summed by two of the most heroic battles in history: the battle of Thermopylae and the battle of Britain. Churchill's remark, "That never have so many owed so much to so few," is apt for both occasions.

Finally, there is only one thing more to say about all this. That is to apologize for the lack of stage props. To properly evoke what I've been trying to say here, it would really have only been necessary to have brought along in my arms a human being killed by violence. You would not have liked it very much, but perhaps it would not be disliked as much as you will individually dislike the results . . . if some personal insecurity ever prompts you to indulge in, or advocate the violence of war.

Play Like I'm Sheriff

SUNSET LAY BEHIND THE TALL BUILDINGS LIKE RED AND YELLOW SMOKE. The cloud cover was high. Shadows of the buildings fell across the circle that was the business center of downtown Indianapolis. The towering monument to war dead was bizarre against the darkening horizon. On it figures writhed in frozen agony, except when they caught the corner of his eye. Then they seemed to move, reflecting his own pain.

About the circle a thousand people hurried. The winter cold was nondirectional as the circle enclosed the wind and channeled it here and there. The temperature was nearly freezing. Lights in store windows began to glow with attraction and importance. Everywhere there was movement.

He stood before a store window, a young man of slight build with uncut black hair, looking at coats. There was tension about his eyes. Occasionally his mouth moved. Muttering. Then his face would tense under a surge of mental pressure.

The mannequins in the window smiled; tiny female smiles dubbed on faces above plaster breasts and too-narrow legs. Some of the coats were gaily colored. Others were black with fur collars. Some were fur. The wind hailed against his thin work jacket but he was not cold. He was accustomed to weather much harder than the kind blowing.

There was no question in his mind that he was a little insane. He sobbed. Not because he was insane, but because his wife had not ever had a nice coat. Only a few times had she had really nice dresses. He felt a deep and very personal shame. She had come so far with him. He sobbed, trying to divert his thoughts and remembering that he had read that madness was never admitted. He wondered if anyone else had ever admitted it to themselves. He thought of the man who would be his wife's new husband and wondered if he would buy her fine clothes.

Farther down the street he believed there might be another store. He walked slowly, looking. Unhappiness depressed his body so that he walked with a slight stoop. Before he found another store a girl idled along beside him, walking slowly, just fast enough.

"Hello," she said, and smiled a little cleaver of a smile. He was taken by the look of her, but in his mind there was no inventory. He was conscious only of a female image. It was very general. Light and dark hair mixed. A slim girl with a pretty face. He was fooled at first, vaguely wondering if she were lost and wanted direction. The word direction sang in his head and caused him to smile.

"Hello," he told her. He walked at the same pace. She fell in beside him. It seemed almost as if they were going somewhere. As if there was a place to go and something that must be done when they arrived.

She was silent for a little while. "Do you know," she said finally, "I've come from home with practically no money. I could stand a drink. Or a sandwich." Her voice had started softly. It ended strained.

He looked at her. "Come on. It's cold here."

In the half light of the bar she seemed younger and more unhappy. He took time to look, surveying her across the table while he felt in his pocket for the fifteen dollars that must buy restaurant food and bus fare to work for the next four days. He found himself wanting to go home, reacting familiarly with despair as he realized for some thousandth time that it was impossible.

As always with women he was shy. Now he did not know how to tell her. He did not want to miscall her and edged around it. "I'm pretty broke, myself," he told her. "Will be all this week."

She did not leave. She did not seem disturbed about the money. "I'll pay for the drinks. The money part wasn't true. I have some."

"I don't understand."

She suddenly seemed smaller. Almost like a child. "Talk," she said. Her voice was also smaller. She looked at him as if she were lost. "Talking to. There's lonesome in the wind. I walked to the bus station, and there was lonesome in the crowd. Like something evil hovering . . . I haven't talked to anyone for more than a week."

Her voice, as much as what she said, told him. He looked directly at her. "You're crazy, too. You've found a good ear. A good voice."

"Yes, crazy. I just want to know that someone cares. Cares just something. Want you to know. Want me to know." She hesitated. "You are so unhappy. Look so unhappy. I wouldn't have been able to speak otherwise."

"Maybe no one does care. You said it. There's lonesome all over."

She watched him. Her coat hanging beside the booth was new.

"Norma," he said. "Norma Marie."

"It isn't, but I know what you mean."

A crowd of couples came through the doorway. They were laughing. He watched them then looked at her. "What do they know?" he asked.

"How to pretend," she said. "I don't really like to drink. Let's go."

They walked a long way off the circle to a parking lot. The wind pressed at the back of his legs. The girl wore no hat. Her hair was blowing.

The car was good but not new. She drove it for a long time out of the center of town. He wondered if he was supposed to make love to her, then wondered if he could. Instead of touching her he lit a cigarette and passed it. His hand was trembling.

"No," she said, taking the cigarette. "I don't think so. At least not now." She smiled at him and he felt ashamed, felt himself withdrawing into recollections of another time which held more shame. "I'll do better," he told his wife under his breath. The girl touched his hand.

"Talk," she told him. "Talk away at the lonesome first. Maybe that's all it will be."

"Do you tell me or do I tell you?"

"I don't know." She drove slowly for several minutes. He watched the streets and then the sky where the clouds seemed to be lowering. There was no light except along the streets.

She turned a corner. He realized suddenly that she was also nervous, more than she had been. "My house is down this block," she told him. "I have a whole house."

"You don't even know my name."

"I think it's Johnnie. If it isn't, lie to me."

"You guessed right," he lied. "But I haven't been called that in years." He thought it sounded authentic.

"You lie good," she told him.

"Only to myself."

The house was a tall white frame. The driveway and porch were dark. She parked the car at the back of the drive.

"My grandmother's house," she told him. "Then mother's. Then mine. Any sound will be grandma trying to get out of the attic." She laughed faintly.

"You mean haunted?" He watched her, wondering at her nervousness and at himself. The pressure of his hurt, the tension in his mind, was not relaxed but was relaxing. He quickly pulled the hurt to him because it was his and familiar. "Haunted?" He wondered if she were not worse than himself.

"Sure. Ghosts get as lonesome as people." She tried to smile and it did not work. "At least, I think they must." She stared through the windshield at the sky. "I think it will snow."

She turned to him, the tension seeming to break a little with controlled excitement. "I pretend a lot. Since I was little . . . . Well, for a while I didn't pretend. Yes, I did. But now I pretend a lot. Like when you were little you know, and you said 'Let's play like I'm the sheriff and you don't know I'm here and you come around that corner.' . . ."

"I remember."

"All right. Now, I'll play like Norma and you play like Johnnie and we'll go into our house and I'll fix dinner. And while I fix dinner you can sit in the kitchen and talk. And be friendly. And good, and tell me how well I'm doing, because . . . ." She turned to him. Her eyes held tears that she would not allow to come. "Because he never did, you know."

"But, you pretended." He could not help interest.

"Of course. Didn't you?"

The question alarmed him. He sat watching the sky through the windshield and was quiet for a long time. Finally he turned toward her. "Yes, but I called it lying to myself."

"It is. Do you like the real way better?"

"No." The longing for something that could not be came back hard. He felt it, then fought it, surprising himself. "All right. Pretend." He opened the door on his side and she watched him. He got out, walked in front of the car and around to open the door for her. When she got out it was with a smile that he believed, and not a muscular gesture. "You never did that before," she whispered.

"I will now," he told her. "I will show you more care now, but I'm sorry for before."

"Don't be sorry." She took his hand and they walked around the old house. "People should use their front doors," she told him, "it makes them more important."

The house looked like a museum. The furniture was of mixed periods. He recognized some as old and valuable. There was antique glassware sitting about. The rooms were ordered and neat.

"We are the fourth generation in this house," she said. "It's always good to think that."

"I don't know much about my family," he said truthfully.

"I know," she told him, "but that's not important. As long as we're proud of us."

He took her coat, holding it and looking about.

"Thank you," she said. "The closet under the front stairway will do." She moved from him, through a series of rooms to the back of the house. He hung the coat and his jacket in the closet, which was empty except for an old trench coat. He looked at the coat, thinking it long enough to fit him but made for a heavier man. Then he walked through the rooms where she had gone. He found her working at the counter in the kitchen. The kitchen was modern, contradicting the rest of the house. He stood, not quite knowing what was expected of him. "Can I help you?"

"No," she smiled. "Just sit with me." Her movements at the counter seemed natural and nearly familiar. She looked at him seriously, then hesitated. "I'm glad to have you home." Her voice was faint, but it seemed clearly determined.

He was surprised, then remembered. "I'm glad to be home."

There was a different kind of worry on her face. "I was afraid. Well, you like Charlotte too well. I wish she were married."

He looked at her. "Not that well. A friend."

"Too well, and she's awfully crude."

"Yes," he said. "I wish she would move. Tough. Very hard."

"She's been gone since you left, and I thought."

"Of course. But, here I am."

"Sometimes. Oh, I'm sorry. Sometimes you're hard and I don't understand."

He was startled and then defensive about being charged with something he could never be. "I'll not be that, not anymore. I'm different now, you know. I've stopped losing my temper." He wondered if he were saying right. The girl had her back turned, working rapidly. Then she turned to face him. Her face held shame.

"I'm sorry about something, too. I was going to kill myself if I didn't find you tonight. You'd been gone so long."

He was startled. "How long has it been?"

"Nearly five months. Your mother called last night and said you were on the coast. She wanted the rings back. She wasn't kind." She turned back to work. "How did you get home so soon?"

"I flew." He did not understand his action, but he rose and walked to her. He touched her shoulder.

"Sometimes," she said, "you used to touch me here." She placed his hand in her hair. "It'd be all right if you muss it." He touched gently under and about her hair.

"Thank you," she said, then turned to him with a pretended smile because the hurt was deep in her eyes. "Now go," she told him, "or go hungry."

"I'd rather go hungry."

Her hands shook over the bowl. "Thank you again," she said. He returned to his chair. "Kill yourself?" He wondered, thinking that she was even more troubled than himself. Then he denied it out of an obscure loyalty to his own trouble. He wondered if there were not more complications than he could handle, and he wondered that he cared.

"My grandmother was so happy," she said. "This fine house, fine husband and nice children. But my mother was not. So I locked her in the attic."

"Your mother?"

"No. You know when we buried her. But grandma died when I was little. I helped carry her things to the attic. They told me . . . . I don't know. Whatever you tell children. But she has lived in the attic ever since. But I locked the door. Against losing her, you know."

"But, kill yourself?"

"By going to sleep. In a special way. Someday, and that day was tonight, I think, it would have come on so very lonesome. With you gone. With you gone. And only people to talk to who wanted to buzz at you. Friends, you know." Her back was still turned. He watched her tense, then clench her hands and he heard the bitterness in her voice. Then her hands relaxed a bit. Her voice was low and strained. Worse, he thought, than it had been.

"When no one cares. What to do?"

"What were you going to do?" He was surprised at the softness of his voice.

"Get the key and unlock the door. Then I was going up the steps. Very narrow. Very straight. And I'd go quietly and catch her asleep. And I'd say 'Grandma, grandma,' and she would come, like when I was little . . . . I had a dog once, remember I told you, but he died. That dog loved me. I played with him when I was a little girl. And grandma loved me—and, she'd touch me and hold me and make me like a little girl again, because, because . . . ." Her speech stumbled and the tensions moved to tears and heavy weeping. "Because I'm so damn lousy—at being a woman."

He moved to her quickly around the counter and held her while she wept. She was tense in his arms. Her body seemed slim nearly to thinness. He was confused. Wondering who. Wondering what was her name.

"Norma," he said, and held her closer.

She raised her head to look at him while still weeping. "Do you want me? Will you want me? I'll do so very badly." She lowered her head. "But I'll try. Because I'm crazy now. I'll be lots better crazy."

"Wait," he told her. "Come now, calm down." He felt nearly afraid. "Come, sit down." He moved to try to lead her to a chair.

"No," she told him. "It's all right. It will be all right." She moved back toward him. He smoothed her hair as he held her. They stood for several minutes until her weeping subsided. Then she turned and left, to come back with a handkerchief. She was trying to smile.

"I took my vacation to find you. The whole two weeks."

The continued pretense made him angry. He reacted in a way familiar to him and became very quiet. It occurred to him that she needed him more than he needed her. It was a strange and warm feeling to be needed. Then it occurred to him that he might be lying to himself again.

"I changed jobs." He paused. "The other wasn't that good anyway." A rush of misgiving overcame him. He had surprised himself by having been taken by the pretense. "I wanted to do better."

"Better?"

"Not right away." He heard shame in his voice. "In a little while you get raised."

"Don't worry about money. Oh, please, not now. Don't worry." She turned to the window then turned back with a tiny laugh.

"See," she told him, "I was right. It's snowing."

He stood and went to the window. The snow was light and carried by the wind. "A light fall," he said.

"It will get heavier." She was placing silver and dishes on the table. "I just have wine." Her voice was apologetic.

"Just a little," he told her. She looked up quickly.

"The table looks so pretty," he said.

"Thank you."

"And the house looks nice."

"I kept it for when you came. Now we'll eat before it's cold."

The meal went well. They ate quickly. She seemed more at ease to him. Once or twice the unfamiliarity of his surroundings surprised him. Or he looked at the girl and recoiled at the pretense. When that happened memories of his wife and memories of his loss and aimlessness came back. His mind would try to recede each time into the trouble. Instead, he would speak.

"When I was little," he told her, "we'd watch a snow like this. Kid hungry, you know. If it were early in the year, like tonight, Dad would watch for a while. If it got heavy he'd get the sleds out of the barn. We'd polish the runners."

190

"Great Grandfather died on a night like this," she told him. "When I was very little. I mostly remembered the snow. I've always loved it. Like a fresh beginning in the morning."

"You've always lived here?"

"Always here." She looked at him reproachfully, maintaining the pretense. "I didn't know you ever lived on a farm. You should have known about Great Grandfather."

"Yes."

She smiled, then stood to clear the table. "But I'll tell you something the cousins never told you. He didn't come to Indiana because of the oil wells. He left Philadelphia in front of a shotgun."

"Girl?"

"The family skeleton. No, that's not kind to say. Because the girl died soon after. I don't know how."

He helped to clear the table while she placed dishes in the sink. "He was an old rip, I guess. But I've always loved the snow."

While she ran water in the sink he moved to help her. She turned, surprised, but said nothing. They worked together quietly. He stacked the dry dishes on the counter. When the work was done she began putting them away.

"Do you know," she said, "I'm so tired. I seem to get tired quicker, lately."

He watched her. Unsure. "I figured it out because I'm the same way. Every minute you're awake you're tensed up, burning energy. I sleep a lot."

"Good," she said. "Come with me." She took his hand and they walked slowly through the house to ascend the front stairway. At the top of the stairs she hesitated. He stood beside her, moving away a short distance. He did not hold her hand.

"No," she said. "That way is the door to the attic." There was some quality of determination in her voice. She took his hand and led him down a hall to the front bedroom. The room was very dark until she pulled the shades at the front window. Tall trees stood bare before the house, partially obstructing a streetlight. The snowfall was getting heavier. It was still being pushed by the wind.

"Please stand here," she said and squeezed his hand. He stood, watching through the window and listening to her movement about the room.

When she spoke her voice was faint. "You used to like to watch me but I was shy. I still am but not so much."

He stood watching the snow. The onetime familiar feeling of excitement filled him as the snow swirled about the streetlight. When she stepped beside him she was naked to the waist.

"I love you," she said, "I was so stupid to doubt." Her breasts were lighted by the faintness of the snow-shrouded streetlight. They were shadowed underneath. The light fell across her face and hair so that he saw that she was beautiful with the prettiness. Her face seemed even more sensitive than before. Then across her face there seemed a small realization of fear.

"We stood this way once," she murmured.

He nodded, saying nothing, but knowing that with the fear and the pretense he could not make love to her.

"Would you like to sleep now?" he asked.

"Yes." She smiled. The fear vanished as she saw his understanding. "But, first. Hold me, please." He put his arm about her waist then moved to touch her.

"Thank you," he said, and he did not know why.

"Come." She led him to the bed which was on a darkened side of the room. She lay down and he removed his shoes then lay beside her. He did not touch her. They were quiet. He listened to her breathing. It seemed to him that the darkened room was filled with questions and the questions were mostly about himself.

"Norma?"

"Yes."

"Are you still pretending?"

"I'm not sure. In parts, I think."

He paused. "I always blamed myself, you know. Never figured anyone was wrong but me."

He touched her hand. It was relaxed and did not respond. Her breathing was quiet. For a moment he felt badly. "Maybe I was right," he said. "Nobody does care. Maybe nobody cares for anybody."

"Don't," she said. "You're feeling wrong. Not for you they don't care that way. Maybe they don't care. Not for me. But each cares that no one cares for the other."

"That isn't enough, is it?"

"No. That isn't enough. But it's enough to keep yourself from dying. And, thank you."

"My mind gets so full of the other . . . ." He realized what she had said. He tried to draw back a small feeling of pride.

"And mine," she told him. "But can you pretend a thing until it's real?"

"I think it's what we haven't learned." He touched her hand again. This time she held his. "In the morning when we get up I'll say hello to you. I'll say, 'I love you, Norma' and you'll say . . ."

"I'll say, 'I love you, Johnnie.'"

"And I'll go to work."

"If the streets aren't impossible I'll drive you. Then I'll go back to work. And when work is over . . . ." She stopped. He wanted badly to tell her that at least he was really wondering about tomorrow.

"You don't know," he told her instead.

"That's the truth. Yes. That's the truth. I don't. Maybe it's how hard you pretend, Johnnie." She turned to him and whispered her shyness. "Before we sleep, will you pretend something if it doesn't hurt? Will you kiss me and say good night and call me Catherine? Not Cathy, but Catherine. Then I'll pretend for you and call you . . . ."

He held her and kissed her. He was surprised at her response in the short kiss. Her body against his seemed in some way familiar. He did not know if it was the familiarity of the form of Norma who was not there or the familiarity of the stranger who was. There was a rush of pressure in his mind. He had lived with it for so long. Now he fought it back.

"Thank you, Catherine," he told her. "And, something that just occurred. Maybe you have to love yourself a little first, Catherine."

She touched his hair. His hand felt necessary to him against her back. He wondered what his hand meant to her.

"Pretend, Catherine," he whispered gently. "Good night, Catherine," he said.

Fog

The moving finger having writ moves on
Nor all your piety and wit
Will call it back to cancel half a line

I

THESE MISTS ONLY HAPPEN IN THE RIVER-SOUTH WHERE FOGS HANG thick as soiled fleece; and where, in that nigh-solid cloak, the dead are not exactly dead; the alive not quite alive. All an outsider can say is that movement trudges, dashes, or slides like luminescent streamers through the fog.

Folks who live here understand movement, or some parts. It happens from listening to old people tell tales:

"Yass," they say about movement now going on in the fog, "that there tall fellow is the preacher, still a-huntin', still callin' for his datter, still searchin' for a man to send to hell. Now, that preacher is blacker 'n Old Nick's backside."

Or, they say, ". . . Perfesser is back, the sonovabitch. Old perfesser is payin' his tab for sin . . . old Perfesser is gonna meet the preacher one-a these days . . . 'cause Preacher ain't gonna be much longer fooled about the Hand . . ."and they let it go at that. They sit on porches, or around coal fires in worn parlors, or in the galleys of riverboats . . . tugs, workboats, even motor barges.

194

=

I came to the fogs these twenty-seven years past, in days of driving truck along the Cumberland River. I flogged a 600-series Ford with an eighteen-foot van, always running like tiptoe on slickly asphalt because night roads along southern rivers are hardly ever dry. Back then, they called me Slim, or sometimes only "hey, you."

Today they call me Joe, or sometimes Mr. Joe, and I have become "old folks." My bald spot is surrounded by a silver circle of hair, but my eyes are clear behind thick glasses. My head bobs between rounded shoulders as I stock shelves in my small store. (I live in rooms in the back.) The store—groceries and gas and a little hardware—doesn't make much of a living, but it's just across the road from the river.

The river is the mother of fogs, and it is motherly to we who live along its banks. It isn't big and show-off like the Ohio or Mississippi. It carries no floating palaces; restored steamboats, sternwheelers and sidewheelers, nor even many motor yachts. It's a utilitarian river of workmen, work boats, tall tales, yarns, and a few stories that are way too true.

To the left of my store sits the tidy cottage where Annie lives, and beside that a shack where Pete goes to brood, or sleep, or read musty old books . . . he spends most of the time, day and night, fishing; or sitting around the store, jawing. He tells godawful tales about who, or what, walks, or storms, through the fog. We usually believe him. When the low roar of mobs pulse in the fog, we know we believe him.

To the right of my store sits concrete block apartments, rundown and housing tired wives and tired husbands; people wrenching some kind of living from the river. And, of course, there are children.

"'Tis the children, over and over. We need take best care with the children." Annie has sometimes been beset thinking of children. She is a great favorite of kids from the apartments. She tells them stories, or plays games.

Annie used to command a sixty-four-foot oak-hulled tug, *Louise* (known around here as *Stinky Lou* because it mostly towed and carried raft-like barges of oil drums). Annie is lean as a willow leaf, tough as hawser, but now walks a little bent over with age. She has one blue eye, one gray, and she's a little wrinkly, sometimes wise. She still wears work shirts and dungarees. In chilly afternoons she sits beside the stove in the store.

Stinky Lou lies aground, butted against a rotting finger pier. She looks dead, but life lingers. On nights when fogs roll thin instead of thick, small light glows in her cabin.

Sometimes, when fog is thick, I imagine the river rises and *Stinky Lou* goes a-traveling; looking for a tow.

Annie, who should care, claims she doesn't. "What's done," says she, "is done. I put that old girl to bed with 'airy a sob.'" She's probably lying, mostly to herself.

Pete's story is different, and more like mine. I got sick of the road and settled. Pete got sick of lay-doctoring up-and-down river; traveling to desperate folk choking, or bleeding, or staring in disbelief at broken legs or arms. Pete is a man of nostrums: old Indian recipes, since he's Indian himself. He can deliver a colt or calf, purge a pneumonia, or sew up wounds . . . not many lay doctors left anymore. Not since medicare happened. These days, if sick folk want help, they generally come to Pete, not Pete to them.

And so we live, living with just enough problems to keep us occupied and somewhat happy. Or rather, that's the way it was for years, but is no more. Since the preacher returned, and the professor started his old foolishness, our lives have darkened. The story started many years ago:

=

When all of us were younger, a preacher named Rev. Rufus Middling drifted this way from hill country. He wore a dandy suit and polished shoes, and his minstrel voice could wrap around your soul and make it sing.

Even white folk started church, even white riverfolk; even rivermen, although that voice mostly drew the ladies. Reverend Rufus caused dismay to a stump Baptist preacher, Millard Dee Grubbs. Millard Dee figured coins were dropping in the wrong collection plate.

Looking backward, I thought Rufus Middling honest, but short of judgment. In a day when being black could get a man killed in these parts, Rufus forgot where he was. Or, maybe he'd been too long missionarying in coal camps, where black men were scarce as walnuts on a plum tree. Men in coal camps didn't kill over color back then, but over slights, or when drunk, or when sick with work weeks of twelve-hour days, underground and between rocks.

The long and short of it: one day Rufus showed up with a baby, and that baby was cream-color. In that musical voice he claimed it an orphan, left at his door. Hellfire lighted slowly from Millard Dee's pulpit, and from a man called "the professor." A whispering campaign started.

Whispers said Rev. Rufus Middling had planted his seed where it did not belong. The baby, a girl, Sally, could not possibly have a black or Indian mama. The kid's mama had to have been white.

Whispers grew to shouts because Millard Dee kept nagging the professor. The professor began talking rope. A manifestation started drifting in the fog. For want of a better name we called it Hand, and some people claimed it was real. Talk of a rope would have died if not for the manifestation (some claimed it nothing but swirling fog writing messages to itself. Others whispered "Ku Klux").

Professor was a scraggly-haired piece of white trash who taught one-room school in coal camps, put there by the coal company because no one else would go. He left the camps when beat to an inch of his life, because he whipped a child and broke its arm. The professor got off easy, because he did not die. The kid's daddy took an axe handle and broke both of Professor's arms. Professor came down to the river, mad and hurting.

When Millard Dee Grubbs started running his mouth, Professor found a place to put his hate. He was seen in the mist, following the manifestation as it seemed talking to itself; drifting along the riverbank, or crossing the road. Whatever the thing was, it seemed to us ugly as the wants of Satan, awful as the hard thoughts of God.

It drifted like black mist that had been wrapped in a white mist—a robe—or burial shroud—a ghostly gown to carry foul visions. Riverfolk shivered and wondered and talked together. Riverfolk may be clannish, but they move up and down the river. Because they get around, and see other sights, they do not incline to get picky over who beds who.

Any hell that breaks loose will come from country folk who claim to know everything, while not going anywhere. And, of course, hell comes from preachers like Millard Dee who could do without God, but not without the Devil.

Folks met the apparition only in the fog, and met it at random. It drifted here, there, everywhere; hovering at the end of piers, like a half-formed thought throwing dark charms at the waters. It emerged from fogs to stand along the roadside where headlights appeared as mist-smoking discs, and where drivers crept at low speed fearing to move ahead, fearing to pull over and stop. It floated, a mystery in mist.

=

The sum of it was that talk prompted fear, and fear prompted more talk. Then the talk turned to yells. Millard Dee preached that the hand of Satan had pushed Rev. Middling among us. The professor cursed, and nursed his arms which were healing crooked. He drank red whiskey when he could get it.

On an extra-drunken Saturday night he finally hollered up a mob and there was a lynching. Torches flamed in the fog as a gang of hard-yelling drunks (and some not so drunk) pulled Middling from his storefront church. A few rivermen tried to stop it and got beat into the ground for their pains. Yells, hollers, laughter echoed in the fog as Middling, strung up, hung gap-mouthed and silent. The mob poured whiskey on the corpse, but could not get it to burn. While the mob danced and went crazy before the corpse, a riverman sneaked in and saved the baby. He took it down river and gave it to a family of Indians.

Professor went crazy at the loss of the child. Millard Dee Grubbs hollered that the seed of Satan was loose in the world. They called for finding the baby. Then Millard Dee's church burned; fire set by the less-than-loving hand of a riverman. Then another riverman obliged Professor by once more breaking both of Professor's arms. Lots of hate flowing in every direction.

We got through it, though with looks of shame. We partly got through because Pete managed to disappear for a while into the hills, so as not to treat Professor. Professor was all crooked-armed by the time he died of gangrene. Pete came back after the burying.

I now know the name of the mama. It is Annie, and I know why she clings to the river, and why light sometimes shows aboard *Stinky Lou*. Annie goes to meet Rufus Middling.

I'm not the only one who knows, because Pete is no fool. Maybe others know, but it's history. Rufus Middling and Professor are long dead. Riverfolk attended a closed-casket burying of Rufus, and also lots of farm-folk attended; satisfied smirks as preachers hovered on the sidelines. Rufus drew a better crowd than showed up for Professor's burying, which no riverfolk attended. Riverfolk didn't give a rap.

Millard Dee is still alive and causing grief. That's part of our problem, but only part. "The child is out there," Pete tells me. "Sally wanders her way home, but growed up now."

Pete told me, and, as it turns out, told Annie. He did it on a fog-ridden night when the river had yielded only two small channel cat, and a couple of throw-back trash-fish. Pete slumped on a stool beside the iron stove where an oak fire glimmered behind an isinglass window. Oak makes a good-smelling fire, and it mixed with store smells of leaf tobacco, smoked hams hanging, and the worked leather of tool belts.

Pete once stood over six foot and muscular. Today he's more like five-nine and ropy. He still has a hook nose that's either Creek or Choctaw. He was about to be called away to treat a wound, but neither of us knew that.

". . . she's a daisy," Pete said, talking of Sally. "Tall like her daddy, and sings quiet as the night-river running. Looking for her daddy, I expect. She never knew her ma . . ." and then Pete was interrupted as a scared dockhand came to my door to say that a cable had snapped off a winch. The cable had caught a man across the face: Pete called on to save the eye, which, of course, he did.

I sat in the store when he left, restless, not wanting to work, yet not wanting to close.

Sure as the world, if I closed, someone would call me forth again because of needs for beer or bread.

Pete had been about to tell something more, or suggest something. The more I thought, the more I understood.

Annie could not have kept Sally. A white woman with a black baby might not have been killed back in those days, but the baby would.

At best, it would have been taken to an orphanage, whether orphan or not. It came to me that Rufus Middling had been courageous. He had to know that he walked a thin and dangerous line. What finally killed him was the sin of pride; the pride of the professor, or maybe the presence of the cloak; not the ego of Rufus.

Annie came in just after Pete left, and as nighttime fogs rolled off the river, causing a heavy sheen of moisture on trees, road, and worn cars parked before the apartments. Annie sort of nestled. She hugged up to the wood stove, looking into the isinglass like it was a crystal ball telling futures. Orange fire cut with streaks of blue lighted the front of the stove.

Her eyes, one blue, one gray, seemed even brighter than usual; tears withheld, perhaps.

"Let's go a-walkin'," she said. "I have fears." For the moment she seemed helpless, withdrawn, smaller than her usual small self. It was the first time I had ever seen her that way.

". . . I don't feel needy about walking in the fog," I told her. It was true. When fog hangs this thick, people live close to hearth and home. Too many apparitions appear; folks who have run their calendars and are dead. Living men, who have buried their fathers, sometimes meet those fathers. Anything can walk toward you from the fog.

"You have fears?"

"My girl is out there somewhere. Pete says . . ." Annie generally keeps her feelings to herself. Now she did not. "I fear for her. I long to meet her."

We have been friends for many years. As friends, we have become old together. One may deny oneself at this age, but one cannot deny a friend. "I'll get my slicker," I told her, "and bank the fire."

Walking in the fog is not like walking under water. It's more like movement through showers of wet and muffled sounds. Six paces into the fog, lights from my store disappeared. From the river a boat's whistle sounded a thin, muted line, barely heard; and the river not fifty yards away. Fog ran off the sleeves of our slickers; and though it sounds silly (but is not) I touched my face to make sure it was still there. Nothing much is certain in the fog.

Small movement came at our feet. A collie dog lay curled, panting, distorted, in throes of dying. I stepped aside and around. These sorts of visions are why folk stay close to home.

Our worst memories stalk the fog, take shape. It has been forty years or better since I struck that dog while driving in the fog, an animal surprised by silver discs of headlights as it crossed the road. I had climbed from the truck, could not find a rock or knife to kill it. It was almost dead anyway. On the return trip I saw the body in a field. The animal had dragged itself, and I had caused it hours of unneeded suffering.

How do we reckon with this river? Like any river, it can get dangerous. Like any river, it will threaten to flood you out in spring-times. And not all parts of it fog up. It's here and there that fog rises, which is true of most rivers.

But it sings to us, sometimes, and it makes our livings. And we somehow love it while knowing that it doesn't give a damn. It's just a river. If only the thing didn't sometimes take from us . . .

Whispers sounded through the rain of fog, and a whisper sounded beside me. "I needed to keep my girl." Annie stopped and waited, listening to what started as an echo, became a murmur, then grew to a low roar like animals snarling over kill . . . the sound of a distant mob. The sound rose, wavered, was swallowed by mist. Annie's voice rose. "Keep my girl, I summon . . . summon."

And, as if attentive to her voice, the apparition drifted to us; spectral hands seemed clasped in prayer. It shimmered out of the mist, and its prayerful hands were only satiny-smooth fog. They steepled, and from within an echo lived just above a whisper. The echo sounded like the gabble of a mob.

Then, somewhere in the fog a child cried for its mother. Distant weeping and a woman's sorrow changed to hope, midsentence . . ."Don't move, Jennie. Keep talking and Mommie will come to you," sounded near to hand. I remembered how the river had taken a woman not yet a year ago, a woman looking for a child named Jennie, the child later found wandering the center of the fog-bound road.

The apparition paused for the length of a long second, gave a stiff little bow, then drifted in the direction of the river. From far off, the mob-sound still rolled, then went quiet. We heard nothing but the soft fall of fog.

"There's some who ain't happy except when they're takin'." Annie's voice, a touch hysterical, followed the apparition. "So don't be happy. I got what you took, 'cause your 'took' didn't hold up."

"It didn't have crooked arms." I whispered as much to myself as to Annie. "Professor had crooked arms."

"It's not the professor." Pete's voice sounded soft as the fall of fog. He appeared from the fog to stand beside Annie, protective. "How you ever," he said to Annie, "skippered that boat for all those years is more than this child can figure. You lather up too easy." He touched her shoulder, friend to friend. "If Sally looks for her daddy she'll stay close. She's got to sleep. She's got to eat. She'll show up."

To me he said, "Might be a mistake, bein' out here. I reckon I know what that thing is, and it ain't the professor."

"What?"

"It ain't Klan. It only sorta looks like Klan because of here and now. In times past it's looked like sumthin' else." And for the moment, that's all Pete would say.

II

For three mornings Annie waited in my store, but walked and watched for Sally when fog burned off in afternoons. One night, when fog ran thin, she made her way to *Stinky Lou*. Light burned greenish in the cabin and her shadow could be seen moving, reaching, touching, perhaps. There was no other shadow.

"Sometimes he's there, but ain't," she told me about Rufus Middling. "Seems like it depends on thickness of fog. Sometimes he's but a whisper. Other times, we can talk. There be times when I can see him."

Annie changed, and not a little. She laid dungarees aside and wore neatly pressed house dresses. She arranged her hair, even scrubbed her fingernails. I remembered her as a girl and how she had been beautiful. "When Sally shows," she said, "she's not be ashamed of her ma."

Sally showed up on the fourth afternoon. It was a day of mixed signs, because word from the river said that Professor was back. A riverman saw him stooped over. In dense fog he showed as a bent and crooked figure, and the apparition only just visible beside him. The riverman also said that through mist he heard Millard Dee Grubs, now old, and sounding like the croak of a frog.

Sally hesitated in the doorway, slowly looked around, then drew a long breath of store smells that seemed a comfort. I recalled that she had been raised by Indians, and how she would have learned to use her nose as well as eyes and ears.

Sally stood lean and tall like Rufus, and lean as Annie. Cream-color skin glowed warm in muted store light. Dark hair fell nearly to her waist, tied loose, and she could almost be mistaken for a gypsy. When she spoke, her voice was warm.

"Mr. Joe?" She remained in the doorway.

"You've come for your daddy," I told her. "Come in. Chair by the stove."

"I've heard stories," she said. "Stories called me here . . . can't figure if anything is true."

"In these parts," I told her, "truth sort of comes and goes. But I can tell you what was, and what now seems to be. Your daddy's here. So is your ma."

The story took time to tell, and Sally sat unmoving as silence. She listened, weighed, pursed her lips, and, by turn, looked happy or sad. I watched her and remember thinking that, if I had ever had a daughter, I would wish her to be this beautiful, this smart.

"Your ma and daddy thought to leave the country," I told her. "Go abroad."

"Not north?"

"North was just as ugly."

"'Twas never a matter of forgiveness," she murmured. "Folks do what they must. I just needed to know." She stood, thanked me most kindly, and went to find Annie. I heard nothing more from either of them that day. That night, light appeared in the cabin of *Stinky Lou*.

That night also saw talk of the professor. Frightened women from the apartments kept their children close. The store's phone rang, as men who worked the river called and left messages for their families. The community clustered toward each other. Most folks here had only heard stories, and not believed them. Now one of the stories had grown legs. It walked in the fog.

"Seems like Professor's come for Sally," Pete told me. "After all this time. Can't write it off. Can't let go."

"How? He's dead as he'll ever be."

Pete looked at me like he couldn't believe what he'd just heard. "Professor will have help." His voice sounded grim as a tomb. He looked resigned, almost defeated. "We'll watch it grow," he told me, "and we'll cuss it. And we'll even wrestle it, maybe, and it'll just keep growin'."

"What's *it*?"

"I expect," Pete told me, "that *it* has a name, but ain't to be named. Wait, watch, and grieve." He studied what he was going to say next, hesitated, then told me, "Gangrene stinks. We'll smell it before we touch it."

On days when fog glowed thin, people moved about, came to the store, chatted. The store has always been a neighborhood meeting place; news, gossip, weather, and talk of the river.

Frightened women claimed Sally ought to leave. They forbade their children to go anywhere near Annie. "'Twas Sally," they said, "who brought trouble to the river." The women stopped pushing strollers and held their toddlers in arms.

Men claimed Rufus Middling was out there raising hell, and they called him "Reverend Meddling." Anxiousness filled the store, and people bought food for a week, not for a day.

"They blame who they can see," Pete told me about the women. "Professor's naught but a nightmare. Sally's real to them. They're like a pike hitting a lure. Jump at what they think they know."

On days of heavy fog I closed the store for an hour at lunch. The road lay deserted. Side roads sat silent. From the river, fog horns honked, screeched, moaned. No one moved in the fog, and from the fog came distant yells, murmurs, whispers, sounds of sorrow.

On such days I would take my ease beside the stove and watch fog lean against my windows. On one noon the apparition drifted to the glass, oval eyes staring empty into the store, hands clasped together in some sort of prayer. This time it seemed to live independent of fog. It did not shimmer. Instead, it drew all light from the store. Light flowed into it and turned to darkness; and darkness fell across the inside of the store. The form of a hood took the shape of a hook, changed back to hood, became Fylfot cross—a swastika, thence took full-throated breaths of light into glowing robes, then exhaled darkness and the chill of fog. Luminescence fled into the fog and changed the world milky white.

Twice, Professor appeared, paused, as if about to enter. His eyes were hollow as the eyes of the Hand, his mouth twisted. Fog, or drool, ran from his lips. Scraggly hair hung wet and straight, and he seemed to holler, though I heard no sound. Then Professor limped away, crooked-armed.

And once, Millard Dee showed up to rattle the doorknob and send curses. He stood at the window, face twisted in rage. He still wore his clerical collar, which was soiled, and a dirty tie. His white hair melted into the grayness of fog, so that mostly what I saw were eyes filled with hate. When I moved to unlock the door, he moved even more quickly. I am old, but so is he, and I can take him. "Run, Reverend Bunny," I hollered after him. "Next time bring a weapon. We'll play."

The professor and Millard Dee never appeared on days of sun, but Annie always did. So did Pete. They both showed up on a sunny Saturday. It was the last happy day before sorrow descended. Children played before the apartments while mothers took the sun and relaxed. Tendrils of fog still floated low on the river.

"My man has his head set," Annie told us. She perched beside a cold stove. Habit. We get no chill on sunny afternoons. Pete leaned against my front counter. He smelled fishy and riverish. Through the windows of the store I could see the small bow of *Stinky Lou* rise from the mud bank. Cars whizzed along the road. Shouts of playing children put a happy feel into the afternoon.

"Rufus wasn't gonna do a thing," Annie told us. "He figured Professor made his own hell, so to hell with Professor. But talk says Professor has come for Sally. I tell him 'leave it be,' but my man is out there hunting."

"A ghost hunts down a ghost?" I didn't smile, but thought of it.

"It ain't ghosts." Pete sounded a little too quiet. "This is about spirits." To Annie, he said, "You and Sally go down river for a time. What happens next makes Hell look like a vacation."

"Sally won't leave her pa. I won't."

Pete shrugged. "Before you get your back up, check with your man. He'll know to run you out of here."

Three things happened that night after fog closed road and river, but we first learned about only two of them. While shrieks and whistles and moans of fog horns dwelt in the fog, a light odor of rot drifted in eddies and swirls. As night deepened, the smell turned to the smell of open and rotting graves. We looked at each other, wondered, shivered.

Men came to the store, bought beer, stepped outside to drink, and drew shallow breaths. They stood in small clusters and whispered. Sometimes a man moved from one cluster to another. They muttered and swore that somewhere nearby the Hand floated. They figured it a curse. They whispered about weapons, action, fighting back . . . when I caught the drift of what was happening, I closed the store.

"I know you gents," I told them. "You're good men. Take care of your own hearths. Quit talking trouble."

Some of them listened, then drifted toward their homes. One cluster, though, stuck together and disappeared into fog. Nearby I heard the rough and gaspy voice of Millard Dee, still preaching. "Seed of Satan . . . woman of evil . . ."

I had endured enough of Millard Dee. "If you are the one that brings this stench," I said into the fog, "you're running shoal water."

Explosion blew the back half of Annie's cottage to pieces just after midnight. The crack of explosive dulled in the fog, but still had an edge. Since Annie's cottage is just next door, I knew, even as I came out of bed, that destruction stood at hand. Before other folks arrived, I led Annie inside my store, with the front door locked and only a night light showing. I walked her through darkness and shadow, somehow knowing the store must seem closed.

Annie sat stunned. She looked smaller than life. Blood from a cut flowed off her forehead, ran into gray hair, dripped onto her gown and smeared down her arms. She looked like she was dying, but was not. Head wounds always bleed heavy.

"I didn't find Sally," I told her.

"Visiting her daddy."

From the apartments, and from moored vessels, people poured into the fog. They fumbled their ways to the wrecked cottage. From inside the store I could hear shouts, exclamations, and frightened talk. When Pete showed up I unlocked the door. Stench layered in the fog, unpleasant but bearable.

"Lock it back up," Pete told me as he entered. "The misery's only just started." He walked to Annie and began treating her wound. In the near-darkness of the store he looked more like a shadow than a real person. "When that heals up," he said about Annie's head wound, "you'll find I've given you a twinkly little smile. Might help someday." To me, he said, "Hold them off for a good ten minutes. We'll meet you out back."

It was a difficult ten minutes. I held them off for five before I heard glass break. That being the case, I turned on lights and opened the door. Men poured in headed for the beer cases, some slouched, nearly ashamed; others talked rough to prove they had a right to commit wrong. As soon as I was able I slipped through the front doorway and out back.

"If you are a prayerful man," Pete said, "start praying that no one gets any news. Another child's been taken. We might have caught that one earlier."

We hung on to each other as Pete steered his way through fog like he had radar. Of course, Pete mostly lives in the fog. When we got to *Stinky Lou* the stench increased, and a tall, black man turned to Annie. "My dear," he said, "we escape south in a liberated momomoy. Join your daughter. Better do it now." His voice was gentle, the way one wishes fog would be gentle. "Go along now; there is man's work here."

And Annie, who could be as sassy as any woman who ever put foot to ground, reached to touch Rufus Middling's hand, sniffled, and hurried to waterside, where her voice joined with Sally's . . . something about visiting the Indians who raised Sally.

Rufus turned to us. "What you're smelling," he said, "lies over yon, and I'm in a hurry. And, while this is not the end of horrors, this will be the end of one. But I must not waste time." The musical voice that had charmed so many congregations seemed nearly ready to rise and sing. Yet all he did was lead us to the broken-boned professor. Professor lay moaning.

"Weren't you happy in hell?" It sounded like an honest question. Rufus stirred the body with his foot. He turned to us. "I used to love sinners. Still do, because I've been a sinner myself, but some creatures can't be loved." He looked down at the professor, and the professor issued groans and stench. "You came for me and you killed me," Rufus told Professor. "That I forgive. You tried to kill my child. That is not forgiven. How could he be so stupid as to try it twice?" He looked at Pete.

"I've been figuring on it," Pete said.

"And so this is my curse," Rufus Middling said. "For as long as time lasts there will be no Professor, no heart or soul or memory. But for all time there will be the professor's pain, and the professor's stench, that those who live may someday figure a way to live without them." He turned and left us, and he left a broken-armed figure of pain blasted permanently into the mud of the riverbank. When a black arm raised and threw a flaming torch aboard *Stinky Lou,* I knew their escape would be a success. I thought of all the oil soaked into those oak decks through the years. The old tug would send them safely away because now all attention must be paid to keep fire from spreading to the fleet.

"Not an answer," Pete said, and he was not talking about fire. "I reckon he thought he left an answer." Pete backed away from Professor. "Smells like rotten muskrat. Let's get the hell out, because there's gonna be company."

Fire mounted almost immediately and men came running. By the time they had fire hoses and axes aboard, the tug was a sheet of flame. Flame rose in the fog, steamed high above the river, fell back as rain. Flame illuminated the other craft, and it thinned the fog, but not so much that Pete and I could not get away unnoticed.

We sat on the stoop of my plundered store. At my hand was a package of crappie hooks, dropped and deemed too useless to pick up. A child's doll dangled grotesque among a display of toys. Here and there beer bottles stood half empty. Take it all for all my neighbors had stolen, but they mostly tried not to leave a mess. I paid attention to panting coming from the distance.

When the manifestation showed, it might have been anything; witchery, no doubt, but something greater. It rose before us robed in enough silken mist for a parachute. Oval eyes, but they didn't stare so much as recall ancient and other evenings of force and fire.

"I understand," Pete said. "Why bring only destruction?"

A thought spread, not a voice. "Destruction was already here. Since you abided it, I've left it for you, and I brought a chance at light. See to it." The thought was rounded and precise.

From behind a piece of tipped shelving came a woman's muffled sobs. These changed to desperate and pained battle, and the thin cry of a child . . . See what you are made of . . . the thought, not the words, filled the air. For one ugly moment I watched a dying collie, choking and dragging itself. I set it aside, as Pete and I hurried forward.

Millard Dee Grubbs had never, in all his years, looked like a man eaten by nothing but hate. Now he sat wedged between broken shelving and the floor. Behind him, now truly yelling, was a toddler, and before him a badly injured woman. She groaned and fought. I thought her brave but stupid. This particular woman had caused most of the hard talk about Sally. She had even listened to Millard Dee.

"Kidnap," Pete said. "I have to aid this man." He pulled a cigarette lighter from his pocket, together with a small scalpel. Then he turned the mother on her side. She spat white foam, sure sign of torn lung. "Your child is okay," he told her. To me he said, "Keep her in that position. We can't have the lungs filling up." Then he turned to Millard Dee.

"I have no time for you," Pete said. "Yet I can't set you free. Now this is gonna hurt a little." Swiftly, before I could understand what was happening, he sterilized the scalpel and sliced Millard Dee's tongue. "You won't sound much different," he told Millard. "It'll be dark where it's always been dark." To me, he said, "Go get us some help."

The skeleton of *Stinky Lou* was still aflame but under control. When I yelled for aid, I got it. Men who had surely raided my store rushed back to my store. They seemed confused, like they had never seen a place torn up, and especially this friendly place.

The woman lived. The child was unharmed, but frightened. Millard Dee was being attended to by Pete. There was no singing of hymns to warrior gods. Quite a stir, and in the middle of that stir I realized the Hand was nowhere to be seen.

"'The moving finger having writ moves on.'" I would have expected something Biblical from Millard Dee, but it was Pete who spoke. "'Taint Bible. Writ by a sharp Arab."

We awoke a confused community with more than enough shame to go around. The fleet moved slowly, if at all. Millard Dee left town looking for help and ended up in a mental ward. Nobody thought of arresting Pete. He'd just move to the hills, and he's the only doctor we've got.

"What was it?" I asked Pete while the community held a cleanup on my store. Insurance would handle the rest.

"Ourselves," he told me. "The evils of good men's past. It's what you turn away from that can't be turned away. It writes itself on the fog, just in case we forget. Call it regret. Call it history."

"And it comes from where?"

"Evil men pay no attention. With Millard Dee, should have slit that tongue twenty-five years ago. Two people might still be alive. Of course, I couldn't know that at the time. I've got the rest of my life for that regret."

"Taking law into your own hands?"

"That's what happened here twenty-five years ago and again last night." Pete sighed. "Don't know what happens to the spirit of Rufus Middling, but at least Annie and Sally got away.

"The poet I told you about. He was a great scientist as well. He had the soul to write about the greatness of people, and love. But because he was great, and fearless, he could also write about that part of the human that is pure horror."

—*for Val and Ants*

Jack Cady won *The Atlantic Monthly* "First" award in 1965 for his story, "The Burning." He continued writing and authored nearly a dozen novels, one book of critical analysis of American literature, and more than fifty short stories. Over the course of his literary career, he won the Iowa Prize for Short Fiction, the National Literary Anthology Award, the Washington State Governor's Award, the Nebula Award, the Bram Stoker Award, and the World Fantasy Award.

Prior to a lengthy career in education, Jack worked as a tree high climber, a Coast Guard seaman, an auctioneer, and a long-distance truck driver. He held teaching positions at the University of Washington, Clarion College, Knox College, the University of Alaska at Sitka, and Pacific Lutheran University. He spent many years living in Port Townsend, Washington.

USA Today bestselling author Kristine Kathryn Rusch writes in almost every genre. Generally, she uses her real name (Rusch) for most of her writing. Her novels have made bestseller lists around the world, and she has won more than twenty-five awards for her fiction, including the Hugo, Le Prix Imaginales, the *Asimov's* Readers Choice award, and the *Ellery Queen Mystery Magazine* Readers Choice Award. She edited *The Magazine of Fantasy and Science Fiction* from 1991 until 1997.

Extended Copyright Info